ERIN
HUNTER

HARPER
AN IMPRINT OF HARPERCOLLINS*PUBLISHERS*

Special thanks to Kate Cary

 For information address HarperCollins Children's Books, a division of HarperCollins Publishers, 195 Broadway, New York, NY 10007.
www.harpercollinschildrens.com

Library of Congress Cataloging-in-Publication Data
Hunter, Erin.
River of lost bears / Erin Hunter.—First edition.
pages cm— (Seekers, return to the wild ; bk. 3)
Summary: As the four bears head toward warmer territories, polar bears Kallik and Yakone wonder if they've made a mistake leaving their natural home, while Toklo, desperate to leave the struggles of their journey behind, thinks about leaving the group and starting a new life on his own.
ISBN 978-0-06-199642-9 (pbk.)
1. Adventure stories. 2. Fantasy fiction. [1. Bears—Juvenile fiction. 2. Fate and fatalism—Juvenile fiction. 3. Voyages and travels—Juvenile fiction. 4. Bears—Fiction. 5. Fate and fatalism—Fiction. 6. Voyages and travels—Fiction. 7. Adventures and adventurers--Fiction. 8. Fantasy.]
I. Title.
PZ7.H916625 Riv 2013 2012418645
[Fic]—dc23 CIP
AC

Typography by Hilary Zarycky
15 16 17 OPM 10 9 8 7 6 5 4 3 2
❖
First paperback edition, 2014

SEEKERS

Book One: The Quest Begins

Book Two: Great Bear Lake

Book Three: Smoke Mountain

Book Four: The Last Wilderness

Book Five: Fire in the Sky

Book Six: Spirits in the Stars

RETURN TO THE WILD

Book One: Island of Shadows

Book Two: The Melting Sea

Book Three: River of Lost Bears

Book Four: Forest of Wolves

MANGA

Toklo's Story

Kallik's Adventure

Seal Rock
Walrus Rock
Place of the Caribou Flat-faces
Place of Everlasting Ice
LAST GREAT WILDERNESS
BLACKWATER MOUNTAINS
Place of Fishing Flat-faces
Snowgoose Island
Ice Break River
Caribou Valley
Bear Rock
Great Bear Lake
SMOKE MOUNTAINS
Paw Print Island
Big River
The Claw Path
SKY RIDGE
Place Metal
TOKLO'S BIRTHDEN
Bear Snout Mountain
Three Lakes
LUSA'S BEAR BOWL
Great Salmon River

The Bears' Journey: Bear View

Lusa
Kallik and Yakone
Toklo

Island
Rock
BAFFIN ISLAND
The Melting Sea
BURN-SKY GATHERING PLACE

0
800 mi
0
1200 km
Arctic Sea
QUEEN
ELIZABETH
ISLANDS
Arctic
Village
Beaufort Sea
BROOKS RANGE
ARCTIC NATIONAL
WILDLIFE REFUGE
Parry Channel
BANKS
ISLAND
Kaktovik
Atigun
Pass
Alaska
VICTORIA
ISLAND
Fairbanks
Superstition
Island
Anchorage
Yukon River
MACKENZIE MOUNTAINS
Mackenzie River
Great
Bear
Lake
Arctic
Gulf of
Alaska
Whitehorse
Yellowknife
Great
Slave
Lake
Juneau
ROCKY MOUNTAINS
Prince
Rupert
CANADA
Pacific
Ocean
REVELSTOKE
NATIONAL
PARK
Edmonton
Calgary
VANCOUVER
ZOO
Vancouver
Regina
Canadian Pacific Railway
Seattle
Bismarck
Portland
Columbia
River
Helena
UNITED

The Bears' Journey: Human View
GREENLAND
ESMERE
LAND
BAFFIN ISLAND
Godthab
Iqaluit
Atlantic
Ocean
Hudson Bay
St. John's
urchill
WAPUSK
NATIONAL
PARK
Lake
Winnipeg
Quebec
Trans-Canada
Highway
Montreal
nipeg
Ottawa
Boston
Toronto
TATES
St. Paul
Minneapolis
New York

CHAPTER ONE

Lusa

Lusa dreamed that a breeze was whispering through the treetops. She pressed her paws into the soft, warm earth and stretched, rejoicing to be back in the forest. Sunshine sliced through the branches and pooled on her black pelt. Birds chattered overhead, sending leaves showering down. They danced in a shaft of light, and Lusa lifted her forepaws and swiped at them playfully.

"Lusa?"

Toklo was calling her.

"Lusa!"

"Go away." Lusa buried deeper into her nest. "I want to dream some more." She didn't want to wake to the freezing wastelands of the Melting Sea. She hated the thought of crawling out onto rough ice that scraped her pads. She didn't want to fight her way through biting wind that froze her ears and pierced her pelt. *Not another day chewing bitter seal blubber!* "Leave me alone," she mumbled, trying to slide back into her warm forest dream.

"Wake up, sleepyhead."

A paw prodded her ribs.

Lusa blinked open her eyes.

Toklo was standing over her. She could see his broad, brown-furred face through the branches. His eyes were gleaming. "We need to get moving."

Lusa sighed. "I'm coming." How could she leave her friends waiting in the cold while she slept warm in her nest? She hauled herself to her paws and screwed up her eyes, ready for the glare of endless ice.

Branches scraped her back.

Why am I sleeping under a bush?

Earth shifted beneath her paws. Lusa looked around. Trees crowded on every side, slender, dark-brown trunks stretching as far as she could see.

Trees!

She'd forgotten that they'd reached the forest at last! Relief flooded her, and she shook her head to clear it. Of course! It had been a quarter moon since they'd left the shores of the Melting Sea and headed inland. But they'd been on the ice so long, the memories of biting cold and savage sunshine refused to fade.

"I'll meet you by the river." Toklo was already lumbering away through the trees.

Lusa lifted her muzzle and breathed in the scent of pine. She knew she didn't truly want to forget her time in the snow. It had been their destination for so long, after all. Guided by the mysterious brown bear Ujurak, Lusa, Toklo, and Kallik had trekked for moons to reach the Place of Endless Ice, where the sea never melted. After Ujurak had left them, the three bears had been joined by another white bear, Yakone, for the long journey home. They had reached Kallik's birthplace first, the Melting Sea, where they'd fought alongside Kallik's brother, Taqqiq, to drive away the gang of mean bears who'd been bullying Shila, another white bear, and her brothers. Taqqiq had decided to stay behind with Shila—his new family. But Yakone had come with them, loyally joining Kallik as she insisted on traveling farther, until they found homes for Toklo and Lusa, too. Lusa pictured the white bear's shaggy pelt as he shambled along beside Kallik. Perhaps having another white bear to travel with had made it easier for Kallik to leave her brother behind.

Lusa shivered. Why did Taqqiq *want* to stay on ice? It was so cold. It had taken her days to warm up after the long swim from the ice to the shore. Her heart had quickened each day as the scent of bark and pine needles grew stronger, and when they'd finally reached the forest, she'd broken into a run, overjoyed to feel its precious earth beneath her paws once more.

A drop of water splashed onto Lusa's nose. She shook it away and looked up. Through the branches of the towering pines, she saw flecks of blue. Snow still weighed down the topmost branches, but it was melting. A steady thaw was finally pushing away the harsh days of cold-earth. Prickly needles crunched beneath her paws as she padded between the trees. Meltwater dripped from every branch. At the edge of the forest, Lusa pushed through thick bushes, blinking against the brightness as she burst into the light. A river crashed past, wide as the sky and white with foam.

"Toklo!"

Her friend was standing at the edge, staring into the water. It splashed his muzzle, but he didn't move.

"Toklo!" Lusa called again, but Toklo seemed lost in thought.

Lusa padded across the rocks, weaving between stubborn piles of snow, and stopped beside him. "Are you looking for the river spirits?" she whispered. Brown bears believed that their spirits shifted into the nearest running water when they died, to swim with the salmon out to sea.

Toklo nodded. "It's good to feel them near me again."

Lusa scanned the shore. "Where are Kallik and Yakone?" She wondered what the two white bears thought of the dark-green trees and white frothing water. Did they regret leaving the ice, the place where they belonged, and coming with her and Toklo on their journey home?

"They went hunting." Toklo twitched his ears upstream.

Lusa followed his gaze, still a little nervous of the wide, churning water. They'd followed this river since leaving the Melting Sea, sheltering in the deep woods at night, fishing the shallows by day. "Will Big River lead us to where you were born?" she asked.

There was silence for a while. Then Toklo said quietly, "I hope so. I mean, I walked by a river that smelled like this when I was with my mother." His voice faded, and Lusa winced, knowing how sad he had been as a cub. Then Toklo shook his fur and straightened up. "There is something inside me that pulls me toward the setting sun," he declared. "The noise this river makes, the scent of the trees, everything tells me this path will take me where I need to go."

"But we could stay right here, couldn't we?" Lusa ventured. "It has everything we need, and we're still close to the Melting Sea. Kallik and Yakone would be close to their kin, and we could live in these trees." The forest stretching away beyond the river filled her with excitement. She hadn't tried climbing a tree yet, but even though the trunks were wider than her reach, their bark looked gnarled enough to hook her claws into. She was sure she could make it as far as the lower branches. "Wouldn't it be great to stay in one place instead of traveling all the time?"

Toklo stared at her blankly. "But I'm not home yet."

A sudden splash sounded upstream, and a moment later Kallik appeared, dripping, at the top of a tall boulder, with a fish glittering in her jaws. Yakone scrambled up onto the rock beside her, his wet pelt slicked flat.

"Look!" Kallik tossed the fish down. It landed at Toklo's paws. "I finally caught one!" Kallik had been trying to catch river fish since they'd left the Melting Sea. She'd learned moons ago, but she was out of practice; she'd missed every one until now. "I remembered your lessons, Toklo."

Toklo sniffed the fish. "It's a good catch, Kallik."

"It's a dumb way to hunt." Yakone crossly shook the water from his fur. "How can anyone snatch a fish out of water when it's moving so fast?"

"There's really nothing to it," Toklo told him. "If you *know* what you're doing, it's easy." His tone was a little condescending, and Lusa remembered Toklo's frustration when he'd first had to learn the patience a bear needed for ice fishing. He was happier being a teacher than a student!

Wind ruffled the ferns at the edge of the trees. Yakone turned and bared his teeth. "What's that?"

"It's just a breeze," Lusa soothed. Yakone had been jumpy since they'd left the ice. She guessed he was unnerved by the strange, crowded world of trees and bushes and rushing water. He ducked out of the forest whenever he could to stare at the sky, as though he was checking that it was still above them.

Kallik skidded down the boulder and stopped beside the fish. Claws scraped behind her as Yakone followed, half scrambling, half falling.

"I can't dig my claws in here," he grumbled as he landed beside Kallik. "And they sink pawdeep in the soft forest muck."

Kallik touched his muzzle softly with hers. "I know you miss the ice."

Yakone snorted. "Who wouldn't?" He sniffed the fish. "Are we going to eat this, or what?"

Toklo tore the fish into four pieces.

"You can have mine." Lusa pushed her portion away.

Toklo narrowed his eyes. "You need to eat, Lusa," he growled softly.

"I'm fine," she reassured him. "I can find food in the forest later." Her mouth watered as she imagined scratching up pawfuls of juicy grubs and beetles from among the tree roots.

She'd almost forgotten how rich the forest was, with ant-filled crevices in the tree bark and soft soil where she could dig for sweet roots. But cold-earth still lingered. Fruits and berries hadn't flowered yet, and there was no sign of any soft green shoots in the undergrowth she could nibble on. Ants and grubs weren't always enough. So she was glad the river gave them fish. She'd eat anything rather than be hungry again. They seemed to have been hungry so many times before.

Toklo gulped down his share of fish and licked his lips. "Come on." He pointed his nose upstream. "The day is half over. We should keep moving."

As he ambled away, Lusa felt a stab of disappointment. Why *couldn't* he make his home here? She followed him with a sigh, glancing back at Kallik and Yakone as they crossed the rocks after her, their white pelts pressed together. They had each other. Toklo was ready to cross half the world to find his own kind. When he did, Kallik and Yakone would head back to the ice. *What will I do then?* She pushed the thought away. She didn't have to decide now.

They followed the river until the rocks rose steeply, too jagged to climb easily.

"Let's go around them," Lusa suggested. Without waiting for an answer, she charged into the forest. Pushing through a dense patch of bunchberry, she looked back, relieved to see the others following. The white pelts of Kallik and Yakone stood out like snow in the shadows. They glanced nervously at every tree they passed, as though they thought it was about to fall down on them.

"I think Kallik and Yakone are scared of the trees," she whispered to Toklo, who was close on her heels.

"Then they should have stayed on the ice," Toklo grunted.

Lusa stopped and stared at him. "But they chose to come with us!"

"We came because our journey is not over till you've reached your home."

Toklo whirled around in surprise as Kallik's voice sounded behind him. The white bears had caught up.

Toklo shrugged. "It was your decision." Then he added hurriedly, "But I'm glad you did. I . . . I would have missed you."

Lusa heard honesty in his growl, and knew that he admired Kallik for leaving her home to travel with them. And Yakone, too, for sacrificing the life he had known to be with Kallik. *Toklo really does appreciate it!* She willed the white bears to understand. *We're stronger together than apart.* Lusa's fur pricked as she wondered what the journey would be like if Kallik and Yakone hadn't come with them.

Yakone pushed past them and trudged away through the trees. "I thought we were trying to make the most of the daylight."

Lusa galloped after him, tearing through a bramble, relishing the prickles as they scraped her fur. As she raced past Yakone, the forest floor began to slope, plunging down into shadow. She could hear roaring ahead. "I think there's another river this way!" she called. She couldn't believe that she'd once thought the Bear Bowl, where she had been born, was big.

How had she ever been so bee-brained?

"Wait!" Kallik's terrified roar split the air.

Lusa tried to stop, but the ground fell away under each pawstep. Unbalanced, she tumbled down the slope, scrabbling to find a grip on the slippery needles.

"Lusa!" Yakone plunged after her.

Lusa flailed her paws. Why did the white bears sound so frightened?

An acrid smell hit her nose. Light flashed ahead. The roaring grew louder. *That's not water!* Terror thrummed in Lusa's ears as she fell. *That's a firebeast!*

CHAPTER TWO

Lusa

The firebeast roared past a moment before Lusa tumbled out onto the BlackPath. Blinking open her eyes, she stood frozen, watching it thunder away. She coughed, choking on its stench.

"Lusa!" Yakone plunged out of the trees and skidded to a halt, spraying Lusa with grit from the rutted BlackPath. Another firebeast was raging toward them. He grabbed her scruff and dragged her to the far side and threw her across the verge. The firebeast hurtled past.

"I thought you were used to the no-claw world!" Yakone glared at her, eyes blazing.

"I—I didn't expect firebeasts here," Lusa stammered. "Surely we're too far away from flat-faces?"

"No-claws are *everywhere*," Yakone growled. "I thought you'd learned that on the ice."

"Lusa!" Toklo called from the other side of the BlackPath. "Are you all right?" He and Kallik stood together at the edge of the trees, watching anxiously.

"I'm okay." The roar of another firebeast drowned her

bark. She jerked around and saw huge firebeast eyes flashing toward them.

Toklo and Kallik ducked into the forest. Yakone pressed Lusa back into the grass as the ground trembled beneath their paws. With a bellow, the firebeast thundered past. Lusa flattened herself on her belly as stones showered her pelt and wind roared in her ears.

Arcturus, save us!

The firebeasts were flowing past like logs on a river. She pressed her paws over her ears and tried to hold her breath. The noise and stench were sickening. After the long days on the ice, she'd forgotten the bitter tang of the BlackPath. She wanted to run and hide among the trees, but Toklo and Kallik were still stranded on the other side.

At last there was a moment of heavy silence, as if the forest itself was gasping for breath. Lusa felt Yakone's muzzle on her flank. Gently, he nudged her to her paws.

"Just stand still. We'll be okay," he murmured. Gratefully, Lusa leaned against him and stared across the BlackPath.

In the distance, more firebeasts were approaching. In a heartbeat, the first one was thundering by, followed by another, snorting smoke. Toklo's gaze was fixed on the firebeasts. His muzzle twitched as he watched each one pass, eyes round with concentration.

"How will they get across?" Lusa whispered.

"Toklo's working out the spaces between them." Yakone was watching the brown bear intently. "He needs to choose the exact right time to cross."

Toklo leaned toward Kallik and whispered something into her ear. Kallik nodded and focused on the BlackPath.

Another firebeast roared past.

"Now!" Toklo gave the order and Kallik bounded forward, crossing in the firebeast's wake while another bore down on her.

She reached the other side just in time. The firebeast tore past as she scrambled to a halt beside Yakone. "Thank the spirits!" Her breath was fast, and Lusa could feel heat pulsing from her. "I've never seen so many firebeasts!"

"You made it!" Lusa pressed against Kallik.

"Great spirits, protect Toklo." Kallik's gaze turned to the brown bear on the far side of the BlackPath.

He was still watching the firebeasts. They came faster and faster, a whole herd of them, stampeding from unseen terrors. Toklo flinched as each one tore past, but he kept his ground.

Lusa held her breath. *Please let him be okay.*

Suddenly, Toklo shot forward. Lusa gasped as he raced between the tail of one firebeast and the nose of another. His paws slithered on the grit.

Toklo!

Eyes wild with terror, he unsheathed his claws to get a better grip and hurled himself forward. He landed heavily on the edge of the BlackPath and rolled onto the stone-strewn grass.

Lusa crouched down beside him. "Are you okay?"

Toklo stood and shook the dirt from his pelt. He was trembling. "That was close."

"Too close." Lusa pressed her flank against his.

"But we're safe." Toklo nuzzled her gently, then pushed her away.

Yakone was already heading across a wide stretch of snow-flattened brambles toward pines. "Let's get away from here."

"The sooner the better." Toklo charged past him and took the lead.

Kallik gave Lusa a nudge and bounded after them.

"Wait." Lusa stared at the firebeasts. Some of them had long, flat backs, each carrying a heap of closely stacked trees. The branches and roots had been lopped off, and Lusa could see the insides of each trunk, starkly exposed to the sky. They trailed clouds of wood dust that drifted on the churned-up air. "They're taking the trees away," Lusa whispered.

"Come on, Lusa!" Kallik called. "We need to get out of sight."

Lusa charged past Kallik and Yakone and caught up with Toklo. As she fell in beside him, she sniffed the wood dust on her fur. It smelled tangy and fresh. She scanned the distant hills, looking for gaps in the endless sea of green. "Why would the flat-faces take the forest away?" Perhaps they were building a new one somewhere else. But wouldn't the trees need their roots and their branches to grow again?

Toklo nudged her. "Let's keep moving before those fire-beasts start wondering what white bears are doing in their woods."

"It's not *their* woods."

"Just keep moving." Toklo quickened his pace as bramble gave way to pine.

Lusa followed him into the forest, glancing back to make sure Kallik and Yakone were keeping up. Their pelts glowed eerily under the dense branches.

"Did we look that strange when we were out on the ice?" Lusa wondered.

Toklo grunted. "We probably looked like furry seals."

Behind them, Yakone paused to shake a twig from his claws. He gazed around at the leaf-strewn forest floor. "Does all this stuff melt when burn-sky comes?"

Lusa coughed with amusement. "No. It just rots down, making the earth smell even better."

Ahead, something sparkled between the trees. Lusa pricked her ears and heard the rushing of water. "What's that?" She didn't want to stumble across another BlackPath.

Toklo licked his lips, tasting the air. "It smells like Big River," he guessed.

Lusa slowed. "Will we have to cross the BlackPath again to reach it?"

"I don't think so," Toklo told her. "I can't smell fire-beasts here."

Lusa sniffed. Toklo was right; there was no smell here besides earth, trees, and meltwater. As they broke from the trees, she ducked her head, flinching from the light until her eyes adjusted to the glare. White clouds piled like snow on the far horizon, and the wide frothing river sliced open the forest. Toklo quickened his pace, crossing a swathe of bracken that opened onto a rocky shore. Lusa charged after him.

Water lapped the stones, slow and shallow near the river's

edge. Toklo waded in and leaned down to drink. Lusa followed him, suddenly realizing how thirsty she was. The water was so cold it made her shiver when she swallowed, but it tasted as fresh as a forest breeze. It swirled around her paws. "Are we going to fish?" She looked up, her muzzle aching from the chill.

Toklo glanced back at Kallik and Yakone. "I'll fish for us all," he called.

Yakone stiffened. "Do you think I can't hunt here?"

"You can't yet," Toklo pointed out, though he sounded gentler than before. "But that's okay. I'm happy fishing like a brown bear again." His eyes sparkled. "Let me hunt for us. You can rest." He nodded toward a stretch of flat rock beside the shore. "The stone will be warm from the sunshine."

"Warm!" Yakone snorted. "I'm sick of being warm."

Kallik nudged the white bear. "Stop being such a grumpy old seal."

Toklo snorted with amusement. "I was a grumpy old seal on the ice," he reminded Kallik. "It's hard feeling like a useless cub again, that's all."

"I'm hardly useless," Yakone grumbled.

Toklo waded away into deeper water as Kallik and Yakone settled onto the flat rocks and Lusa padded through the shallows, the stones shifting beneath her paws. She suddenly spotted a cluster of smooth silver fish, each a little longer than her foot. They were moving like shadows in the water around her paws. Excited, she lifted her forepaws and splashed them down onto the nearest fish.

Curling her claws, she felt for soft flesh. Something hard jabbed her pad.

A stone!

She hooked out a long, flat rock and stared at it, disappointed. Where had the fish gone? Had she really moved so slowly?

A huge splash behind her made her drop the stone. Toklo had jumped into the rapids. Water raced up against his wide back and splashed over his shoulders as he ducked his head beneath the waves. He loomed up again with a huge trout between his jaws and strode dripping to the shore. He laid the trout proudly onto the smooth rock beside Yakone and Kallik.

Lusa watched Yakone's gaze flick along Toklo's sodden pelt.

"It's a messy way of catching fish," the white bear huffed.

Toklo tossed his head. "But it works."

Yakone poked the trout. "It's more luck than planning," he grunted. "You don't need any of the skill and patience it takes for ice fishing."

"When you've finished grumbling, you can eat it." Toklo shook himself, showering Yakone and Kallik with silver droplets, and then headed back to the river. "I'm going to catch another one."

Lusa felt a rush of happiness. Now that Toklo was back in the forest, fishing swift, swollen rivers instead of the dead waters of the frozen sea, nothing seemed to bother him. Not even bad-tempered white bears. She waded farther upstream, her eyes fixed on the fish flitting tantalizingly around her paws. She spotted one as it darted into the shallow water pooled between two rocks. With a hiss of excitement, she followed it and pounced, spearing it with her claws before it had a chance to escape.

"Look!" She held it up for Kallik to see. "Black bears can fish, too!"

Kallik was eating. She looked up and swallowed. "Well done, Lusa!"

Lusa trotted back to join the white bears and dropped her fish beside the half-eaten trout. She wrinkled her nose, unimpressed by the sour tang her catch had left on her tongue. How she missed the sweetness of fruit!

Toklo emerged from the river with another fish in his jaws, just as he'd promised. He dropped it on the rock beside Kallik and settled down to eat.

"Look." Lusa nudged her fish toward him. "I caught it myself."

"Very good!" Toklo rumbled.

Yakone sat back on his haunches and began gnawing at a forepaw. "How do you get the dirt from between your claws?"

Toklo lifted a drenched paw. "The river's washed mine clean."

Kallik nudged Yakone's shoulder with her muzzle. "The sooner you learn to hunt in the river, the cleaner your paws will be," she teased.

Yakone snorted and padded down to the river's edge. With a growl, he jumped in and stood in the shallows while the water raced around his paws. "You know why the water here is in such a hurry, don't you?" His eyes flashed, suddenly mischievous.

Lusa took the bait. "No, why?"

"Because it wants to get to the Melting Sea, where it can be *proper* water."

Toklo tore a strip from his fish. "Don't tell me you prefer it salty!"

Yakone lapped from the river. "This stuff's got no taste."

"Don't be mean about the forest!" Lusa scowled at Yakone. "At least you can drink river water without being sick."

"Ow!" Kallik's yelp made Lusa jump.

"What's the matter?"

Kallik was twisting desperately, trying to reach something in her flank.

Lusa stiffened. Had something bitten Kallik? She glanced along the crevice running between the rocks beside her. Were there snakes here?

Toklo nosed Kallik's muzzle out of the way, then plucked a pinecone from her fur.

"I sat on it," Kallik complained, and lapped at her sore flank.

Lusa snorted with laughter. "Just be glad it wasn't a teasel."

Kallik blinked at her. "A teasel?"

"Like a pinecone but much pricklier," Toklo explained.

"Great." Yakone padded heavily from the water. "More forest treasures to discover."

Lusa gazed at him earnestly. "You'll get used to it," she promised. "And then you'll see what a wonderful place the forest is."

As she spoke, a deep growl rang from the trees. Lusa's pelt bristled with fear. "What was that?"

Toklo was already beside her, teeth bared. "I'm not sure," he said, letting the fur stand up along his spine, "but it sounds fierce."

CHAPTER THREE

Toklo

Toklo flexed his claws. He had started to recognize the scent flooding from the forest. "Get behind Kallik, Lusa." He pushed in front of the two white bears. "I'll deal with this."

Lusa hesitated, staring wide-eyed into the trees.

"Now!" Toklo's growl hardened, and Lusa scrambled backward, fur on end. Toklo was cursing his own stupidity. *I should have realized this was some bear's territory.* How had he missed the scent? *I'm such a fur-brain! Splashing about in the river like this was my home.*

The bramble bushes swished ahead. Toklo stiffened as a black bear swaggered from the trees. He was full-grown, half as big again as Lusa, and though still a head smaller than Toklo, his body was lean and tough looking. His muzzle was scarred, his ears torn. His muscles were solid beneath his bristling pelt. This was a fighter.

The black bear stared at them, eyes hard as flint. "What are you doing here?"

Toklo stared back. "We're just passing through." If it came

to a fight, he'd win easily, just because he was so much heavier than the black bear.

"And helping yourself to my fish," the black bear snarled. He took a step forward, clearly not intimidated by Toklo's size.

Toklo thought fast. Perhaps this bear was more dangerous than he looked. Perhaps he had friends nearby. Whatever, this wasn't a battle worth fighting. "Sorry about the fish," he said. Toklo heard a growl rumble in Yakone's throat, suggesting the white bear would rather fight than apologize, and he shot him a warning glance. *We don't need to prove we can beat a black bear!* "We've been away from the forest for a while," Toklo went on. "We're not used to smelling out territory yet."

The black bear peered past him at Kallik and Yakone, muzzle wrinkling in disgust. "*They* shouldn't be here."

Kallik strode forward and stood shoulder to shoulder with Toklo. "Who says so?"

Toklo's fur lifted along his spine. Kallik's tone carried a threat. He glanced anxiously at Lusa. Her eyes were round with alarm. *Back off, Kallik,* Toklo thought.

The black bear's fur bristled. His lip curled. "I say so," he snarled. "And so do the other bears who've seen *white* bears traveling where they shouldn't travel."

Lusa darted forward. "Have there been other white bears in the forest?"

"Too many," the black bear snapped. "There's been talk about white bears coming inland. They should stay on the Melting Sea where they belong."

Lusa blinked at him. "But these bears are helping us—"

Toklo cut her off. "Look, we're just passing. We don't want your territory, and we won't take any more of your fish."

The black bear narrowed his eyes. "Then I'll let you go this time," he rasped. "But I don't want to see you again."

"Thanks," Toklo said quickly. Indignant heat flashed beneath his pelt. Didn't this bear realize they'd beaten enemies three times his size?

Kallik must've felt the same. She stiffened beside him. "What do you mean, 'thanks'?" she whispered.

"Let's just go," he hissed back. "If he wants to think he's letting us off lightly, that's up to him."

"Why are you whispering?" the black bear snapped.

Toklo turned around to meet his gaze. "I was just explaining that we're going to leave."

"Yeah." The black bear snorted. "White bears are pretty dumb."

Toklo's claws itched. He pressed them harder against the rock to stop himself from swiping the bear across his muzzle. "We're going, okay?" He turned and padded upstream.

He could feel the black bear's angry gaze on his back as he led Kallik, Yakone, and Lusa over the rocks. "Let's stay close to the river." He glanced at Kallik, catching her eye to make sure she understood. Their lives had been hard enough on this journey. It would just be easier to stay out of the black bear's territory.

Kallik nodded, but Yakone was still growling under his breath. "We should have chased him away," the white bear muttered. "We outnumbered him three to one."

"Four to one," Lusa corrected him.

Toklo blinked at Lusa. "Would you have fought a black bear?"

Lusa huffed. "I'd fight any bear who was a bully!"

"I know you would." Toklo thought of Taqqiq's thieving friends. Lusa had faced them as bravely as a brown bear. "But you heard what that black bear said. The bears here don't like white bears on their land. If we'd fought him, word would have spread. Then we'd have to fight every bear between here and—"

"And where?" Yakone challenged. "Do you even know where we're going?"

Lusa scrambled ahead. "He'll know when we get there."

"If we follow the river toward the setting sun, I'll find my home in the mountains." Toklo felt certainty like a stone in his chest. The river scent had woken an old longing that tugged at his heart, a longing for the place that he had once called *home*.

Yakone caught up with him. "Are you sure we should be traveling with you?" he grunted. "If what that bear said was true—if the bears here hate white bears in their forest—maybe we should leave you and Lusa to travel alone."

Toklo's chest tightened. What if Yakone persuaded Kallik to go back to the Melting Sea? They'd promised to stay with him and Lusa till they got home!

Kallik's growl sounded behind them. "We travel where we like, Yakone. No bear's going to scare us away. Not now, when we've come this far together."

"But if we're just going to attract trouble because we stand out here—"

Lusa stopped and turned on Yakone. "That bully would have driven you off whatever color your fur was."

"It *was* his territory." Kallik nudged Yakone gently. "Would you have picked a fight with a bear on his own territory on Star Island?"

"I guess not." Yakone glanced toward the forest. His nostrils twitched as though he was checking for scents.

Toklo picked up the pace, leading Lusa out of earshot of Kallik and Yakone. "I'm not letting Yakone split us up."

"He's just nervous." Lusa glanced back at the white bear. "Don't you remember our first days on the ice? Everything seemed so strange."

"I guess." Toklo peered over his shoulder. Yakone and Kallik were picking their way across the boulders, navigating the fissures and cracks, as clumsy as newborn cubs. Whenever they crossed a patch of melting snow, their pawsteps grew firmer.

"Admit it," Lusa puffed. "You wished you were back in the forest with every frozen step. Just like me."

"But we didn't go back, did we?" Toklo pointed out. "We stayed till we'd done what we said we'd do."

"So will they," Lusa promised.

Toklo huffed. "I hope so."

The sun was reaching higher. Lusa paused to nuzzle for roots among the sedge from time to time, then caught up with Toklo and chewed noisily as she trotted along beside him.

"Toklo!"

Kallik's call made him turn. He was surprised to see

how far behind the white bears had fallen. "What's up?" He stopped.

She stared at him wearily. "I'm used to the coldness of the ice."

"It's not even warm yet." Toklo could feel the breeze in his fur. It still had the freshness of cold-earth.

"It might not be warm for you," Yakone puffed. "But we're melting as fast as the snow."

"Why don't you go for a swim?" Lusa suggested. "The river's freezing."

"Good idea." Toklo glanced toward the trees. Had they cleared the black bear's territory yet? "And in the meantime I'll find somewhere cool for you, sheltered from the sun."

Yakone and Kallik waded into the river and let the rushing torrent sweep over their backs while Toklo and Lusa scouted the shore.

"There's a cove down here!" Lusa called from a boulder a few bearlengths ahead. She scrambled down out of sight.

Toklo clambered up the rock and peered over the edge. Below, a pebbly beach lined the shore. "Lusa?" There was no sign of the black bear. Quickly, Toklo clambered down to the beach. "Lusa!"

"I'm in here!" Her voice echoed from beneath the boulder.

Toklo peered into a smooth, shallow cave.

Lusa stood in the shadows, water puddling around her paws. Floods had hollowed out the rock. She lifted her muzzle. "It's nice and cool in here."

The wind whisked in from the river, lifting Toklo's fur. "Good find, Lusa!"

"I'll get Kallik and Yakone!" Lusa flicked her muzzle toward the two white bears. They'd waded farther out and were diving in the fast-running water.

As Lusa bounced happily past him, Toklo sniffed the cave, checking for bear scent. *Nothing.* Just the cool smell of water and moss. Of course! Why would a black bear hang around here when he had a whole forest?

"They're fishing!" Lusa appeared at the mouth of the cave, shaking water from her short, black fur. "Kallik's teaching Yakone how to catch like a brown bear."

"Good." Toklo padded into the sunshine and stopped beside Lusa. The fresh scents of the forest tugged at him. "Why don't you fish, too? I want to check and make sure we're out of that black bear's territory."

"We must be by now," Lusa huffed. "We've been walking for ages."

"We don't know how big his territory is," Toklo pointed out.

"Be careful." Lusa headed into the river and waded downstream.

"You too," Toklo called. "Stay in the shallows. The currents farther out are too strong for you."

Lusa glared over her shoulder. "Just because I'm small doesn't mean I'm stupid." She pointed her nose at the thundering river. "Only an idiot would go fishing in the rapids!"

"Sorry." Toklo knew that Lusa had proved herself as brave and smart as any bear while they were on the ice. But she was so small, it was hard not to feel protective.

He climbed the rocks from the shore and plunged through

the sedge bordering the forest. The cool scents of tree sap and pine needles drew him into the shadow of the trees. Green hummocks, thick with moss, sat between the slender trunks. Toklo padded forward, nostrils wide, and sniffed the roots of a spruce. No bear markings here. Sunlight dappled the forest floor, and he sprang from hummock to hummock, icy water squelching between his claws. The forest sloped upward, and the hummocks gave way to smooth forest floor. Budding ferns unfurled among tree roots, and Toklo relished the swish of them against his paws. Birds twittered from every branch, and high above the treetops, he caught a glimpse of an eagle, circling. After the long journey across the ice, it felt good to be plunging through the forest alone. For the first time in moons, he felt at ease.

Suddenly, a vicious snarl ripped through the peace.

Toklo froze, sniffing for scent. Had the black bear spotted him?

A frightened yelp answered the snarl. "Stop, Hakan! Leave me alone!" It was the cry of a she-bear. Toklo raced toward the sounds, crashing into a shallow clearing.

Toklo recognized the black bear from earlier. He was growling at a smaller bear as she cowered against a tree. She was a black bear, too, not much bigger than Lusa.

"No, Hakan!"

Her eyes widened with horror as Hakan stretched up on his hind legs and swiped at her.

Toklo snarled. "Leave her alone!"

Hakan snapped his head around. "You again?" He turned

on Toklo. "I thought I'd told you to get lost. This is none of your business!"

"It's always my business when I see a bear picking an unfair fight," Toklo growled.

The she-bear wriggled out from behind Hakan. "It's okay! Really."

"Yeah," Hakan sneered. "Get out of here. I'm sick of chasing you off."

Toklo smelled blood and saw a patch of red welling on the she-bear's ear. "I'm not going anywhere until I know she'll be safe."

"I'm safe now." The she-bear shook out her fur.

Toklo stared at her bleeding ear. "It doesn't look like it."

She swiped a paw over her wound, smearing the scarlet beads. "Look, I'm fine. Okay?"

"Of course you're fine." Hakan jerked his nose toward the trees. "Now, get out of here, Chenoa. And next time you want to leave the territory just because you feel like it, let me know first, so I can come and get you out of trouble."

"Fine!" Chenoa stomped away through the trees.

The black bear watched Chenoa disappear, then swung around to face Toklo. "Don't mess with things you don't know about. If my sister doesn't stay inside my territory, I can't keep her safe."

She's your kin*!* Toklo's thoughts flashed back to the day his mother, mad with grief, had driven him away. Oka's cruelty still shocked him, and he never imagined there might be other bears who would behave like that toward their family. Anger pulsed beneath his pelt. He suddenly felt fiercely protective of Chenoa. "You didn't look like you were keeping her very safe just now."

Hakan flexed his shoulders. "She should listen to me. She's *young*, and I know what's best for her. I've raised her since our mother was crushed by a firebeast—" He broke off, his eyes suddenly glittering with grief. "Get out of here. This is my territory! If I see you here again, I'll rip your fur off!" He lashed out furiously at Toklo.

Toklo sidestepped, and Hakan's paws thumped bare earth.

"Okay, I'm going!" Toklo turned away. He didn't want to fight. Hakan was smaller than him. Besides, he understood the pain of losing a mother. Toklo paused. *But what about Chenoa?* She'd lost her mother, too. How could Hakan be so unkind to her? Anger tightened his chest and he glanced over his shoulder, wondering whether to remind this bear what a ripped ear felt like. He crushed the urge and walked away, muttering, "You're not worth the fight."

"Not worth the fight?" came a bellow behind him.

Pain burst through Toklo's body as claws raked his rump. Shocked, he dropped and rolled. Hakan lunged at him again. Scrambling to his paws, Toklo escaped just in time, but Hakan still came for him.

Toklo reared onto his hind legs, claws stretched out. *How does this bear think he can win?*

Hakan rose to meet him. "I'll show you who's not worth the fight!" Eyes blazing, the black bear swiped at Toklo.

Toklo knocked away a blow, then another, but a third

caught his cheek. Pain seared through his face, and blood welled around his eyes. He staggered backward and dropped onto all fours.

Hakan glared at him. "Had enough?"

Fury pulsed through Toklo. "Back off before I hurt you."

Hakan roared and swung at Toklo. His paw thumped Toklo's ear. Toklo stepped away, thinking fast. He needed to end this fight, but he didn't want to hurt Hakan too badly, not if his sister really did need him for protection. Ducking, he nipped at Hakan's hind legs.

"You fight like a wolverine!" Hakan swung a forepaw at him.

Toklo struck the black bear's chest before the jab reached him. Hakan staggered backward, gasping. Toklo lunged after him and swiped again. He landed a blow on Hakan's shoulder. He held back his full strength, but it was enough to knock Hakan sideways.

Shock sparked in the black bear's gaze. He staggered as he fought to keep his balance. Had he finally realized he'd taken on a bear twice his size?

"Get out of here," Toklo snarled. "Before I really shred you." Pain flashed in the wound on his cheek.

"Don't think you've won." Hakan puffed out his chest. "Next time I won't give up so easily." Growling under his breath, he limped away between the trees.

Toklo shifted his paws uneasily. Even though the black bear had started the fight, he didn't like that he'd come close to hurting a bear smaller than he was just for the sake of proving his strength. He pushed his way through a clump of ragweed and padded onto a soft stretch of moss.

"Hello."

A whisper from the ragweed made him jump.

"Who is it?"

The younger black bear crept out and stopped in front of him. Toklo remembered Hakan had called her Chenoa. "Thanks for sticking up for me," she said. Her gaze clouded as it flicked over Toklo. "Are you hurt? Did Hakan do this?"

Toklo lifted his head. "It's just a few scratches."

Her eyes were as round as Lusa's. "You fought for me?"

"It wasn't for you." Toklo wished she'd go away and stop staring at him. His fight with Hakan had been dumb. His pelt bristled hotly. "Has your brother always been such a sore-paw?"

"I guess so." Chenoa tilted her head to one side. "He's been worse since I killed our mother."

"*You* killed your mother?" Toklo choked on the words. "But Hakan said a firebeast killed her."

"It did." Chenoa's eyes glittered with pain. "But it was my fault." She paused to take a trembling breath. "I was on a BlackPath and I tripped." She dropped her gaze. "My mother came back to help me, and that's when the firebeast hit her." Her voice thickened as if grief choked her. "Hakan was watching from the trees. He said it was my fault. He says only *I'd* be stupid enough to trip on a BlackPath."

Toklo wanted to say something to make her feel better, but the young bear was lost in her misery.

"He doesn't need to keep blaming me!" she hissed. "I *know* it was my fault. I *know* I'm clumsy and stupid, and if I wasn't such a wrong-paw, our mother would still be alive." Her eyes flashed with anger as she lifted her head and glared at Toklo.

What can I say? Toklo gazed back at her. Chenoa must have been just a cub when it happened. It wasn't her fault. "My brother died," he blurted. Perhaps if she knew that bad things happened to everyone, she wouldn't feel so bad. "Tobi was my littermate. He was always sick. I tried to play with him. I tried to teach him to hunt, but he was never strong enough. I was angry that he slowed us down. And then he died and after that, my mother didn't want me anymore." He paused, suddenly breathless.

Chenoa gazed at him, wide-eyed. "She didn't want you? *Why?*"

Toklo swallowed. He didn't want to think about it. "Because . . ." He groped for words. "I guess she was scared I was going to die, too." He stiffened, surprised how much had tumbled out to this unknown bear.

Chenoa blinked. "That must have been terrible."

"It was."

"I guess I still have Hakan."

"I'm not sure that's such a good thing."

"He means well," Chenoa insisted. "But he doesn't realize that I'm not a cub anymore."

Toklo looked her up and down. She wasn't exactly a full-grown bear, either.

She went on, lifting her muzzle. "I can't stay here forever. I need a territory of my own, or I'll never be able to look after myself." She eyed Toklo, suddenly curious. "Where's your territory, by the way? I don't recognize your scent."

Toklo glanced over his shoulder. The others would be missing him. "We've been traveling."

"We?"

"Me and Lusa, Kallik, and Yakone. And Ujurak." He stopped, the pain in his cheek suddenly numb as his mind swirled. He missed Ujurak. The young bear had left them moons ago, but his spirit was still traveling with them. He had been a special bear, like no other. When he'd been alive, he had changed into other creatures, shifting his shape to become whales or birds—whatever he wanted. And now he still visited in dreams and visions.

Toklo tugged his thoughts back to Chenoa. She was watching him with round eyes. "We've been to the Endless Ice, and now we're traveling home. Well, Lusa and I are going home. Kallik and Yakone are traveling with us till we get there."

Chenoa gazed at him steadily. "Where is your home?"

"In the mountains. I was born there."

Chenoa sat down. "You've really been to the Endless Ice?" Her words were hardly more than a breath. "Everyone's heard of it, but I never believed it existed." She stared away through the trees. "I'd like to travel, far away from here. Perhaps if I wasn't around, Hakan wouldn't be so angry all the time."

Toklo wasn't convinced. "Really?"

"I remind him of our mother." Chenoa shrugged.

Toklo stared at the young bear. She looked more like a cub

than a mother. "I've got to get back to my friends." His pelt prickled. This wasn't his problem. He wanted to get home. "We need to move on."

Chenoa jumped to her paws. "I could show you the way."

"No, thanks." Toklo turned away. "We're following the river." He began clambering away over the mossy hummocks. "Don't let Hakan push you around," he called over his shoulder. "It's a big territory. Stay out of his way."

He broke into a run, bounding between the trees, his scratches stinging once more. The air tasted damp with dew, and the shadows were growing longer. Toklo bushed his fur out against the evening chill as he hurried from the trees. They'd have to move fast. He wanted to be clear of Hakan's territory before nightfall. There wasn't time for any distractions.

He crossed the sedge, climbed the rocks edging the pebbly beach, and paused. Below, Lusa was scampering around Kallik, the stones clattering beneath her paws. Toklo glanced over his shoulder. Had Chenoa followed him? He searched the shadows of the forest. Nothing moved among the trees.

Good.

He didn't have time to worry about other bears. Shaking out his fur, he jumped down onto the beach.

CHAPTER FOUR

Kallik

"Where have you been?" Kallik hurried to meet Toklo as he landed on the pebbles. The scent of blood hit her nose. "What happened?" His cheek was scratched, and clumps stuck out of his fur. Kallik's pelt prickled with worry. "Did something *attack* you?" She glanced toward the forest. Were there more bears there?

"It was that black bear," Toklo huffed.

Kallik blinked in surprise. The bear had acted tough when they'd met him earlier, but he must be crazy to attack a brown bear.

Lusa bounded over. "Are you okay, Toklo?"

Kallik shifted her paws. "He had a run-in with that black bear."

"I had no choice." Toklo's pelt was still ruffled. "He started it because I told him to stop bullying his sister. He nearly ripped her ear off."

Lusa's eyes widened. "He attacked his sister?"

Yakone was dozing in the shade of the cave. He opened an

eye. "What's going on?" His nose twitched. "Who's bleeding?"

"Toklo." Kallik sniffed Toklo's stained ear. "He had a fight with that black bear."

Yakone sat up. "So you *did* chase him off after all. I thought you—"

"He started it," Toklo interrupted him.

Lusa paced in front of the cave. "Toklo was defending another bear."

"His sister," Toklo explained. "Hakan was angry with her for trying to leave his territory."

Kallik bristled. "Surely she can go where she likes?"

Toklo frowned. "Chenoa's only one suncircle old. Hakan thinks she has to do what he says."

Lusa dragged her claws through the pebbles. "I knew he was a bully the first time we saw him."

Toklo turned away and gazed at the sky. "The sun's sinking," he growled. "We should get moving."

Kallik watched Toklo's pelt twitch. Was he uncertain about leaving? "We can stay if you're worried about Chenoa," she offered.

Toklo's pelt twitched harder. "If Chenoa wants to leave, she can leave by herself. She doesn't need us."

Kallik shifted on the pebbles uncertainly. It wasn't like Toklo to ignore a bear in trouble. "Why don't you go splash in the river before we leave? The water will cool your wounds."

"I'm fine." Toklo looked away.

"It'll just take a minute," she urged. "You can wash Hakan's stench off."

Growling under his breath, Toklo stalked into the river.

Lusa looked at Kallik. "Why's he so grumpy?" She watched Toklo as he stood stiffly in the water, waves washing his back.

"I'm not sure." Kallik felt a wave of sympathy for the young brown bear. The call of home must be getting stronger now that he was surrounded by woodland scents. Was he torn between moving on and staying to help Chenoa? "Come on, slow-paw." She dipped her head to Lusa. "Let's get moving."

Yakone hauled himself to his paws as the sun slowly sank behind the distant treetops. Shadows slid across the shore. Kallik relished the chill. She padded across the beach and leaped onto the rocks. They were smooth, but her pads still stung. She was used to the numbing coldness of ice; without it, every scratch and blister stung like fire.

Lusa scrambled up the rocks after her. "Aren't we waiting for Toklo?"

"He'll catch up when he's ready." Kallik glanced back. Toklo was on the beach, shaking water from his pelt.

Yakone fell in beside her, gazing at the tree line as they passed. "I can't wait till we get back to the ice."

Kallik nudged him affectionately with her shoulder as they walked. "I'm looking forward to our first burn-sky together."

"We can hunt for each other," Yakone murmured. "And watch the sun climb over our heads."

"Be careful where you walk," Kallik cautioned. The stones were smooth, but there were still plenty of cracks and crevices to catch careless paws.

Yakone ignored her. He was busy planning their future.

"When snow-sky comes, we can share an ice-den and stay warm." His paws slid suddenly from under him and thumped against a rock.

Kallik saw pain cloud his gaze.

"Spirits help me!" Yakone sounded more angry than hurt. "How did you survive your journey to the Endless Ice? Terrain like this is enough to break a bear's claws."

Lusa dodged ahead of them. "You'll get used to it."

"So you keep saying." Yakone rubbed grit from his pads. "I guess if you and Toklo can get used to ice, then I can get used to rocks."

Lusa scampered around him. "You might even get used to having warm paws!"

"Warm paws?" Kallik chuffed, amused by Lusa's enthusiasm. "Never!"

The shore between forest and river grew narrower. Kallik let Yakone take the lead as the bears slipped into single file and began to thread their way around the jutting tree roots.

Kallik glanced over her shoulder. Toklo had almost caught up to them. As he fell in behind her, she heard him sniffing the air. "What are you looking for?" she asked.

"I don't want to stumble into another bear's territory," he growled.

As Yakone picked up the pace, Kallik glanced into the forest. Shadows pressed between the trees. How could bears live in such darkness? She suddenly longed for the wide stretches of the Endless Ice.

Pink clouds streaked the sky and deepened to purple as

the sun disappeared. Before long they were walking through nightfall. Kallik's unease grew with every pawstep. At least there was more room beside the water as the trees drew back from the shore, and the river widened and calmed. Toklo hardly spoke, his attention fixed on the forest. Yakone was stomping along, growling each time he stumbled or his paws slid on loose rocks.

Only Lusa moved with ease, but even she was quiet.

Kallik squinted, trying to see the way ahead. The shore was hidden in shadow, and stones jabbed her pads. "We should rest," she suggested.

"Yes, please," Yakone puffed.

Kallik's shoulders loosened. Weariness flooded her.

"I'll find shelter." Toklo disappeared into the trees.

"I'm not sleeping in the forest!" Yakone called after him. "I can hardly breathe in there."

Toklo stuck his head out. "We can't sleep on stones."

Kallik felt tension spark between the two bears. They were both tired and sore, Toklo from his fight, Yakone from days of paw-slips on the rough terrain.

"What about here?" called Lusa.

Kallik felt a rush of relief as Lusa scrambled across the rocks and stopped beside a straggling juniper bush that spilled out from the tree line.

Gingerly the black bear climbed onto the low, springy branches. "It's soft!" she called.

Yakone lumbered over and scrambled in beside her. "It's spiky, but not bad."

Toklo huffed wearily. "I guess we can sleep in the open." He circled beside Lusa, then settled on the juniper.

Kallik nosed her way in beside Yakone. The twigs pricked her pads, but when she lay down, she found the mesh of tiny branches was dense and comfortable beneath her. She rested her head on her paws and closed her eyes.

"How's a bear meant to sleep with the river roaring like a herd of hungry caribou?" Yakone muttered.

Kallik kept her eyes shut. "You'll get used to it."

"It'd be quieter if we'd found a den in the forest," Toklo muttered.

"With trees creaking and cracking like they're about to snap?" Yakone snorted.

"The ice used to creak, too, remember?" Lusa replied.

Kallik grunted. Tiredness was making everyone bad-tempered. "Let's go to sleep. We're all tired." Her bones ached. Of course it was strange for Yakone, but she wished he'd stop drawing attention to how alien this environment felt to him. She tried to recall how *she'd* felt when she'd first left the ice, but the journey to Great Bear Lake had seemed such a desperate fight for survival, she could hardly remember the sound of trees and water.

Trees and water.

Trees and fish.

Her thoughts became jumbled as she drifted into sleep.

CHAPTER FIVE

Kallik

Kallik was dreaming. She felt rock, smooth beneath her paws, and saw forest sprouting beyond a craggy slope. A river tumbled past. She had been here before.

"I've caught it!"

She jerked around as Ujurak scooped a salmon from a river, hooking it into the air with a curled paw while the shallow water flowed around his legs. The salmon flapped madly. Ujurak's muzzle opened in surprise as his catch leaped from his paw back into the river.

Lusa, watching from the shore, rolled on her back, huffing with laughter. "Why don't you change into a salmon and chase it?" she teased.

Toklo was sunning himself on a flat rock beside the stream. "Then what? Persuade it to jump out of the river to be eaten?"

Ujurak sat down in the water with a splash. "I thought I had it this time."

Toklo raised his head and blinked at the young brown bear. "Prey doesn't give up till it's dead."

Kallik saw Ujurak's shoulders slump as he gazed at the water flowing away downstream. "Never mind, Ujurak." She felt a wave of sympathy. "I'll catch something for you." She wondered if his heart was ever truly in hunting. He'd changed into so many animals that he must understand the terror his prey felt when under attack. How could he hunt knowing that?

Ujurak rubbed his snout with his paw. "I'm not in the mood for salmon anymore."

Lusa sat up. "I can teach you which berries are sweetest."

Ujurak's eyes shone. "Yes, please." He bounded from the river and shook out his pelt.

"Watch out!" Toklo hid his muzzle as water showered over him.

But Ujurak was already chasing after Lusa. In a moment they'd disappeared into the woods. For a few heartbeats, Kallik could hear them crashing through the bracken, then the sound was swallowed by the roar of the river, close to her ear. . . .

Kallik woke up and gazed blearily around her. Yakone's pelt pressed next to her. Toklo and Lusa were sleeping, curled tight beside each other on the juniper branches.

Ujurak, where are you? A sharp pang of loss jabbed at her heart.

Kallik sat up. Grief tugged at her belly. The river shone in the half-light. The distant horizon glowed red. Sunup was not far off. Kallik quietly picked her way between her companions. She padded onto the shore, pebbles crunching beneath her paws. Yakone moved in his sleep, murmuring, then fell still.

Kallik gazed into the sky, searching out the stars that

shaped Ujurak and his mother. But the dawn sky was too pale, and she could only make out the faintest pine-needle pricks where Ursa and Ujurak should be. "Ujurak?" she whispered. "Are you there?" Her heart ached with longing.

Sighing, she lumbered down the shore. She waded into the shallows and let the water pull at her fur. Gazing into the smoothly flowing stream, the reflection of the stars caught her eye. They shone brighter in the water, shimmering on its surface. Suddenly fur brushed her pelt. Kallik froze, her heart leaping like a salmon inside her chest.

"I am still with you, Kallik."

Ujurak!

His voice whispered in her ear. "Don't miss me too much."

Kallik breathed deeply, hoping to smell the familiar scent of her old friend.

"Hey, Kallik!" Yakone landed with a splash beside her.

Water sprayed her flank and face.

"Yakone!"

"Did I surprise you?" He blinked at her, water dripping from his ears.

"I was talking to—" Kallik broke off. "It doesn't matter."

Yakone rolled in the shallows, making waves in the fast-flowing stream.

"You seem more cheerful today," Kallik commented.

"I guess I'm getting used to not being able to see the horizon." Yakone stared into the endless green. Far ahead of them, the river curved away into the woods. "Don't the trees ever end?"

Kallik understood the wonder in his voice. She felt like she could walk forever and never reach the horizon, lost in a sea of pine. She pushed the thought away. "Let's catch something to eat."

Toklo and Lusa were stirring on the juniper patch. Lusa rummaged intently through the fur on her flank, looking for fleas, while Toklo stretched up and smelled the air.

Yakone waded into deeper water. He looked more at home in the river than he had yesterday. He dove beneath the waves, then surfaced with a splash. "Nearly got a trout!" Taking a gulp of air, he disappeared again.

Kallik waded upstream, keeping to the shallows and watching the water funneling between her paws. She glimpsed the dark shape of a fish gliding toward her. Standing still, she waited, remembering what Toklo had taught her. *Don't aim where the fish is. Aim where it will be.* With a lunge she leaped and slapped her forepaws down into the water. Triumphant, she felt flesh squash beneath them. Digging her claws in, she hooked a trout from the river, grabbing it between her jaws before it could struggle free.

It flapped wildly as she waded ashore. She made a quick, killing bite and carried it over to Toklo and Lusa.

Lusa wrinkled her nose. "Nice catch, Kallik! But I'm going to dig for roots." Shaking out her fur, she headed into the forest.

Kallik noticed Toklo's ears prick as he watched Lusa stomp away. He looked worried. She dropped her fish. "She'll be okay."

Toklo was still watching the little brown bear. "I don't want her bumping into Hakan."

Kallik tasted the air. "I thought we'd left his territory."

"We have," Toklo told her. "But I don't trust a black bear who's dumb enough to attack a brown bear."

Stones clattered as Yakone bounded from the shallows, a fish in his mouth. He laid it beside Kallik's. "I might get used to river fishing!"

Kallik fell in beside Toklo as they headed along the shore. They'd reached the curve in the river, but Toklo was still glancing into the forest every few paces. "Even a dumb bear won't have tracked us this far, surely?"

"I guess not." Toklo shrugged, fur ruffling behind his ears.

"Then what are you looking for?" *Why is he looking so flustered?* "Other bears?"

"I guess."

"Any sign?"

"No." Toklo hurried to catch up with Lusa.

"What's up with Toklo?" Yakone padded beside Kallik. "He seems distracted."

"I think he's nervous about running into other bears after his clash with Hakan," Kallik replied.

"But we've traveled for a day and not even smelled another bear," Yakone pointed out. He slowed as Lusa and Toklo halted where the river changed direction.

Kallik and Yakone reached them. "Are we stopping to hunt?" Kallik asked.

"Toklo says if we keep following the river, it'll take longer to get home," Lusa explained.

Yakone tilted his head. "Are you sure?"

Toklo nodded. "The cold wind blows us home." He looked back along the river, the breeze rippling his fur. "If we head straight through the forest instead of following the river around, we'll get there quicker."

Kallik heard excitement in his voice.

Yakone's eyes darkened. "Won't we get lost if we leave the river?"

"It'll meet our path again," Toklo told him.

Kallik felt queasy at the thought of plunging into the dark woods. What if they never found their way out? "How do you know?"

"The water smells of home," Toklo told her. "It's mountain water—I can remember its taste. It comes from where we're headed. We'll cross it again."

Yakone leaned closer to Kallik. "How will we stay cool without the river?"

"It'll be shady in the forest," Lusa promised.

Kallik gazed across the wide stretch of water, her belly tightening at the thought of leaving it. She looked at Toklo. "You decide," she told him. She trusted the tug of home. She could feel the ice pulling in the pit of her belly. Surely, Toklo felt the same wrench. "It's your journey home, Toklo. You should choose the path."

Toklo glanced uncertainly from river to forest. "I wish Ujurak was here," he murmured. "He was good at guiding us."

"He was good at everything," Lusa whispered.

"He's still with us in spirit," Kallik reminded them. "I dreamed of him last night." She didn't mention the soft voice she'd heard on the wind after she'd woken from her dream and padded into the shallows. She wanted to keep it as her own quiet memory.

"Which way would he choose?" Lusa wondered.

Kallik lifted her muzzle. "He'd tell Toklo to follow his instinct."

Toklo straightened. "Then we head through the forest." Without waiting, he headed upshore and pushed his way through the sedge.

Kallik hesitated as Yakone and Lusa followed him into the woods. Gazing at the river, she took a final drink and hurried after them.

The pines closed over her head like storm clouds. The sound of the river faded. Lusa was right, it was shady here, but the trees kept out the wind and Kallik felt suffocated by the stillness. Toklo and Lusa pushed ahead, threading easily between the shrubs. Yakone grunted as he tripped over a root. Kallik kept her eyes on her paws.

"Ow!" A bramble caught her pelt and ripped at her fur. She struggled, but more thorns hooked into her flank, and they held her fast. She jerked her muzzle around and nipped at one of the branches. Pain stabbed her jaws as prickles dug in. The bramble trembled as though it was about to tumble over her.

Panic rising, Kallik turned to Yakone. But his pelt was disappearing among the trees. Toklo and Lusa were already swallowed by shadow. For a moment she imagined being stuck here forever, the trees crowding around her, the sky gone.

"Yakone!"

Yakone jerked around. "Kallik?"

Toklo stopped and turned.

Lusa hurried back. "You're caught! Hold on." Stretching out her muzzle, she began to pick Kallik free of the sharp thorns.

Kallik huffed crossly. "How do you make forest walking look so easy?" she growled. "If I watch for bushes, I trip over roots, and if I watch for roots, I get shredded by bushes."

"Have you forgotten?" Lusa tipped her head. "Just pick up your paws."

Of course! Kallik remembered how she'd done it before.

Yakone lowered his head. "What do you mean, *pick up your paws?*"

"Like this." Lusa finished unpicking Kallik and high-stepped in a circle, raising each paw a muzzlelength off the ground as she walked. "You're used to half sliding over ice, like this." She pushed her paws across the forest floor.

Yakone tipped his head. "It'll be a hard habit to break when I've been doing it my whole life."

Toklo joined them. "Would you rather stub your claws? Or walk into trees?"

Lusa's eyes widened. "Don't walk into trees! The spirits won't like it!"

Yakone stared at her. "Why not?"

"That's where they live!" Lusa exclaimed.

Kallik nodded solemnly. "When black bears die, their spirits go into trees."

"Look!" Lusa pointed her snout to a knot in a fir tree. "Can't you see its face? There are its eyes." She reached up the trunk and stretched out a paw. "And here is its muzzle." Dropping on all fours, she dipped her head respectfully to the fir.

Yakone's ears twitched. "If you say so."

Kallik nudged him. "It's what Lusa believes."

Toklo shifted restlessly. "Come on, let's get moving." He turned and headed between the trees.

Lusa stared at Yakone. "You will be careful, won't you?"

"I'll be careful," Yakone promised.

As Lusa hurried to catch up with Toklo, Yakone snorted. "Spirits in trees! What will she think of next?"

Kallik bristled. "Respect Lusa's beliefs! You believe white bear spirits are trapped beneath the ice before they are freed into the stars."

"But you can see them moving," Yakone pointed out. "Lusa was just staring at a gnarly bit of bark."

"To her, it's a spirit." Kallik pushed on, lifting her paws high as Lusa had shown her.

"What's more believable? Spirits that move or spirits that are stuck in old knotholes?"

Kallik shot him a fierce look.

Yakone dipped his head. "I give in," he rumbled fondly. "If Lusa says there are black bear spirits in the trees, then there are black bear spirits in the trees."

Kallik spotted a thorny tendril swaying across their path. "Look out!" She blocked Yakone before he walked into it.

He rolled his eyes. "Perhaps there *are* spirits in the trees and they're trying to rip my fur off."

"Don't say you weren't warned," Kallik teased.

Ahead, Toklo had stopped and stretched onto his hindpaws. He was tasting the air. Kallik let the forest scents bathe her tongue. She smelled the musk of woodland prey.

"It's a deer," Toklo hissed. "Let's catch it." He dropped onto his forepaws as Kallik and Yakone hurried to catch up. "We could hunt like we hunted caribou."

Kallik's fur rippled. She had to admit that hunting on land could be more exciting than waiting beside ice holes.

Yakone shifted beside her. "Caribou?"

"We circle the prey like wolves," she explained.

He nodded, catching on. "Then move in for the kill." He looked thoughtful. "Toklo and Lusa are better at running through the forest," he mused. "Kallik and I could wait there." He nodded to a gap in a long stretch of brambles. "You could drive it toward us, and we'll attack as it races through."

"Good plan." Toklo signaled to Lusa with his muzzle. "Come on."

As they stalked away, Kallik felt a rush of pride. "How did you think of that?" she asked Yakone.

His eyes twinkled. "I guess prey is prey. Getting it to run the way you want is the same on ice and land." He headed for the brambles and crouched on one side of the gap.

Kallik ducked down on the other. Bushes swished in the distance, and hooves thrummed the earth. "It's coming." She bunched her muscles, ready to spring as the ground trembled beneath her. She flattened herself harder against the earth, aware of how white their pelts looked in the gloom of the forest. What if the deer spotted them?

The brambles crackled beside her. Deer musk washed her nose. Its pelt blurred before her eyes as it leaped through the gap. She lunged for it, cursing as a root caught her hindpaw. With a cough, she collapsed onto her belly. Yakone dashed away. He charged after the fleeing deer, swerving with ease around a clump of tall knapweed. Kallik watched, wide-eyed. He ran as though he'd hunted in forests all his life. With a roar, he leaped, stretching out his forepaws to grab the deer and bring it down.

As Kallik scrambled to her paws, Toklo and Lusa charged through the gap in the brambles.

"Great catch!" Toklo skidded to a halt where Yakone was standing proudly over the dead deer.

Lusa circled Yakone and his catch. "You're a natural!"

Yakone's eyes shone. "I guess instinct took over."

Toklo nudged him. "You're turning into a brown bear."

Yakone glanced over his shoulder at his grubby pelt. "I'm even changing color," he remarked.

Kallik touched her nose to his cheek. Perhaps they would get used to the forest after all.

By the time they'd finished eating, the sun had dipped below the horizon.

"It's too dark to go on." Kallik licked blood from her muzzle.

Lusa's eyelids drooped. "I'm sleepy."

"We can rest here and start up again at dawn." Toklo glanced at his companions across the deer carcass. "Okay?"

"Fine with me." Yakone stretched and got to his paws. He

wandered back toward the swathe of brambles where they'd waited for the deer.

Kallik heaved herself up, drowsy from the meal, and followed Yakone. Lusa stumbled after her sleepily. Behind them, Toklo was hardly more than a shadow in the darkness. Kallik heard earth spattering the ground. *He must be kicking dirt over the remains of the deer, hoping to disguise the scent.* They didn't want to attract other predators when they were sleeping.

Yakone lay down beside the bramble. Lusa curled into a ball close by, tucking her nose under her paw. Kallik yawned and settled onto the soft earth. She rested her muzzle on Yakone's back. As his breath grew shallow with sleep, she gazed into the shadows. The ice was never this dark. Even on the cloudiest night, it still glowed, as though it remembered moonlight.

Toklo lumbered from the shadows, reeking of leaf-sap. "I scattered muskroot, to hide the smell of blood." He sat down beside Kallik.

She closed her eyes. "How long till we reach the river again?" she asked with a yawn.

"I don't know." The pine needles rustled as Toklo settled down to sleep. "Maybe tomorrow?"

"Good." Kallik imagined Ujurak overhead, shining beside his mother. "Sleep well," she murmured.

A strange scent woke her. The warm tang of another animal. She lifted her head and blinked in the darkness. Heart quickening, she tried to adjust to the gloom, but the forest shadows made it impossible to see. She felt Toklo stir beside her.

"Did you hear something?" he whispered.

"I *smelled* something." Kallik licked her lips, gathering scent. There was definitely a warm, breathing body close by. "Is it Hakan?"

Toklo's nose snuffled. "No."

"Chenoa?"

"No."

The scent was getting stronger. Kallik's ear twitched as she heard pawsteps. Slowly, silently, she got to her paws. She tried to see her companions in the gloom, but she could only make out the white shape of Yakone's pelt.

Toklo stood up. "It must be something after the carcass."

"Another bear?" As Kallik spoke, pawsteps scurried in the shadows.

Behind us! Jerking around, she tried desperately to see through the gloom. Fur brushed the earth. Tainted breath turned the air sour.

"Toklo?" Shapes were moving around them, fast.

She yelped as teeth pressed through her fur and sank into her flesh. With a roar she reared, swiping at the creature that had bitten her. Her claws hit fur. *Too rough for a bear. Wolf?* But the creature was small. And vicious. Another leaped at her, burying its teeth in her flank. She staggered and lost her balance.

"Wolverines!" Toklo roared, and the ground shook as he stumbled under the attack.

"What's happening?" Lusa's panicked yelp sounded from the darkness.

Yakone's pelt flashed past Kallik. "We're being attacked!"

Kallik flailed as she fell, trying to shake off the wolverines. They were tearing at her pelt. She struggled to get up, but her hindpaws slipped into the bramble, where countless thorns snagged her fur. She rolled, trying to knock her attackers away, but they swarmed over her. She glimpsed Yakone beyond the brambles. Toklo bellowed several bear-lengths away. The wolverines had separated them. Kallik tore her hind leg free with a grunt. She pushed up, desperate to get on her paws, but a wolverine clambered over her shoulder and sank its teeth in her throat.

Shock sliced through her as she collapsed to the ground. She kicked out, finding only brambles with her paws. The wolverine snarled at her throat, ripping harder at her flesh. Rage surged through Kallik. With a mighty heave, she tore free of the wolverine and hauled herself to her paws. Turning, she swiped with claws spread, catching her attacker with a blow that sent it flying.

She glimpsed fur darting through the darkness. Something moved at the corner of her eye, and she slammed her paws down. A wolverine collapsed under her blow. With a yelp, it struggled free and raced away howling into the shadows. Turning, Kallik spotted another slippery pelt and lunged at it, snapping with her jaws. She felt fur between her teeth and hauled the wolverine high into the air before tossing it away.

"Kallik?" Toklo's voice sounded nearby.

"I'm okay!" she called back. "Yakone?"

An angry roar rang through the trees. "Run, you coward!" Yakone sounded triumphant.

Another wolverine raced away into the woods. Kallik turned, scanning the ground. "Have we chased them away?"

Toklo's eyes glittered beside her. "I think so."

Yakone bounded toward them. "What *were* they?"

"Wolverines," Toklo growled. "They don't usually attack in packs."

Kallik's heart lurched. "Where's Lusa?"

"Lusa!" Toklo called into the darkness.

Fear flared in Kallik's chest. "Can you see her, Toklo?"

"No."

Oh spirits, give us light! Kallik stared into the night-black forest. "Lusa, where are you?"

CHAPTER SIX

Lusa

Lusa pelted through the forest. Pawsteps thrummed after her. She glanced back through the shadows, horrified to see eyes glinting a bearlength behind. *Three pairs of yellow eyes!* Three wolverines!

She'd woken to find herself under attack and bolted out of pure terror. *Why did I run? Why didn't I stay with the others?* Panic roared in her ears. If she doubled back, could she make it to the others before they caught her? *No.* The wolverines would cut her off if she turned.

Lusa scanned the trees, straining to see through the darkness. A pine tree towered ahead. If she could make it up the stretch of trunk to the branches, she'd be safe! She sprang into the air and clung to the bark with her front claws. Scrabbling upward, she hauled herself onto the lowest branch and glanced down.

The wolverines were swarming up after her.

They can climb! Spirits, save me!

Lusa pulled herself higher. Balanced on her hindpaws on

a branch, she reached above her head and swung onto the next. A wolverine snapped at her rump. Yelping, she scrambled higher. The wolverines clamored below her, teeth bared. Their greedy eyes shone in the darkness. They weren't going to give up easily.

Lusa clung on tight. Her claws ached. She reached for a higher pawhold, but her legs slipped beneath her, weak from running. She flopped onto the branch. *Send me strength before the wolverines reach me!* She peered through the shadows, wondering if she could make it to the next tree, but its tips hardly grazed the closest branch. She'd never make the jump.

"Toklo! Kallik!" she howled into the trees.

An owl screeched overhead, but there was no reply from her friends. How far had she run? She searched the trunk for the face of a bear spirit. There was nothing but bark. She was completely alone, apart from the animals trying to drag her out of the tree.

Hot breath grazed her hind legs as the wolverines stretched hungrily up. Lusa kicked out, and her paw hit something. Glancing down, she saw one of the wolverines tumble off the trunk, and she heard the thump as it hit the forest floor. A second later a sharp bite scorched her rump as teeth clamped deep into her flesh. She felt the agonizing weight of a wolverine hanging from her. Shrieking, she fought to kick it off, but it clung like a burr.

Pain seared through her, red-hot and unbearable. Roaring, she struggled, too terrified to look down. Then she felt her flesh tear. With a tortured yelp, she glanced at her rump.

The wolverine had gone! Something had torn it away, taking a chunk of her with it. Half-blind with agony, Lusa struggled to see what had happened. A dark shape moved below her. Lusa heard the snarl of a bear.

Toklo?

No, she couldn't smell his scent.

Another bear!

Lusa froze. Was it attacking her, too?

Bark ripped beneath fierce claws as the bear hauled itself higher. Another wolverine yelped and disappeared. A thick-furred paw swung beneath Lusa, and the last wolverine fell, squealing, to the ground.

Lusa closed her eyes and hung on to her branch. Would the bear keep climbing until it was high enough to reach her?

"It's okay," a voice barked below her. "They're gone. It's safe to come down."

Lusa clung on harder. "Who are you?"

"Chenoa."

Relief flooded Lusa. Hakan's sister! Toklo had met her before.

"Are you Lusa?"

"How did you know?" Lusa slowly eased herself downward.

"I just guessed." The black bear backed away from the tree as Lusa slid onto the forest floor.

Lusa's wounded rump stung furiously. "Thank you," she whispered, her voice shaking.

Chenoa sniffed her. "Are you okay?"

"I think so." Lusa swallowed against the pain. "You came

just in time." She stared at Chenoa. "You were so *brave*!"

"Lusa!" Kallik's panicked call sounded through the trees. A moment later the white bear crashed through a swathe of bracken. "There you are!" She raced over and pressed her muzzle against Lusa's cheek. "What happened?"

"They chased me up a tree." Lusa pressed against Kallik, relieved to feel the warmth of her thick, white fur.

Toklo pushed through the undergrowth, Yakone on his heels. "Is she okay?"

Lusa couldn't stop trembling. "They were dragging me down when Chenoa saved me."

"Chenoa?" Toklo stared at the young she-bear. "What are you doing here? We're a day's walk from Hakan's territory."

"I followed you." Chenoa met Toklo's gaze. "Didn't you know you were in wolverine country?"

Toklo shifted his paws. "I was too busy smelling for bears."

Yakone snorted. "How come you didn't smell Chenoa?" he grumbled.

Chenoa gazed at him, her eyes widening with surprise. "I've heard of white bears, but I've never *seen* one." She stretched her muzzle toward Kallik. "Now I've seen two." Her eyes shone in the darkness.

Toklo interrupted. "Can we talk in the morning once we've had some sleep?" He began to head back toward the brambles.

"You can't sleep here!" Chenoa dashed into his path. "The wolverines will keep coming back. They see you as a threat to their own prey."

Toklo halted. "Where should we sleep, then?"

"The river's not far," Chenoa told him. "That's outside their territory."

Kallik tipped her head. "How do you know?"

Chenoa shrugged. "My mother used to bring Hakan and me here when we couldn't find enough food in our own territory. She told us wolverines were mean." She glanced at Lusa. "But I've never seen them attack *bears*."

Yakone growled. "They must have fish for brains."

Lusa's paws trembled. Her rump felt like fire. "Will we really be safe by the river?"

Chenoa nodded. "I can show you the way." She padded through the trees.

Yakone lumbered after her. "Thank the spirits we're all safe."

"*And* Chenoa!" Kallik fell in beside him.

Lusa limped after, not wanting to be last. She glanced over her shoulder, relieved to see Toklo close behind.

Chenoa led them past their sleeping place by the brambles and on through the forest. Lusa winced with every step. Her pelt felt cold where blood soaked the fur. She could feel it getting sticky and matted as she moved but kept going, desperate to be safely out of wolverine territory. "That's the river!" She heard its roar with a rush of relief.

"I didn't realize we were so close." Kallik picked up the pace.

Lusa struggled to keep up. Breathless, she followed Kallik and the others as they broke from the trees into moonlight. Wind lifted her fur, stinging like fury where it touched her wolverine bites. The river tumbled and surged, spraying the rocks lining the shore.

Chenoa nodded toward a stretch of smooth stone. "Can

you sleep there? It's hard, but it's safe."

Yakone sat down. "Let's just hope nothing comes out of the river and attacks us."

"Like what?" Toklo rumbled. "Bear-eating fish?"

"I can sit guard if you want," Chenoa offered.

"No," Kallik told her firmly. "They're just joking. It's been a tough night. You rest. You must be as tired as we are." She moved closer to Lusa. "I'm sure we'll be safe here."

"I hope so." Lusa leaned against her, weak with pain.

Kallik stiffened. "Are you okay?"

"Just a few bites," Lusa murmured. "They'll feel better in the morning." The moon lit dark stains on Kallik's white fur. "Did they hurt you?"

"I'm fine," Kallik promised. She leaned closer. "Are you sure you're okay?"

Lusa nodded. "I just want to sleep."

"Keep an eye on her, Kallik." Toklo padded across the stones and settled at the far edge.

Kallik nudged Lusa toward Yakone and settled down beside her.

Squashed between the two white bears, Lusa let herself relax. As their bodies softened into sleep, she closed her eyes. At once, snapping teeth flashed in her mind. She buried her muzzle into Kallik's fur and tried to imagine catching fish in the shallows.

One fish. Two fish. Three fish . . .

As she counted, her thoughts slowed until at last her muscles loosened and she slid into a fitful slumber.

* * *

The sky was heavy with cloud when Lusa woke. It was hard to tell where the sun was, but from the warmth in the air, she guessed it was late. Kallik was stretching beside her while Yakone stood in the shallows, yawning as water washed around his paws.

Lusa sat up. She winced as pain sliced through her rump.

"Thanks again, Chenoa." Toklo was standing at the water's edge with the young black she-bear. The fur along his spine twitched. He looked uncomfortable. "But I think you should stop following us."

Lusa pricked her ears.

Chenoa shuffled her paws. "I just wanted to see the bears you were traveling with."

"And now you've seen them." Toklo glanced into the forest. "You should go home. Hakan will be worried."

"You told me to stay away from him."

Toklo dipped a paw in the water. "I meant find your own territory, not follow us."

Chenoa flattened her ears. She looked scared.

How bad is that bear? As Lusa gazed at Chenoa, she felt breath on her rump. She flinched, hot with pain. "You're really hurt!" Kallik stared at the bloody stone where Lusa had been lying.

"Stand up and let me look," Kallik ordered.

Wincing, Lusa struggled to her paws. Sleep hadn't soothed the pain. It had just made her hind legs stiff.

"Those are nasty bites!" Kallik sniffed Lusa's wounds. "Why didn't you say anything?"

"I didn't want to—" Lusa gasped as her hind legs buckled.

The sky flashed above her as she collapsed with a thump onto her side.

Yakone bounded out of the river. "What's wrong with Lusa?"

"Wolverines bites." Kallik thrust her muzzle toward Lusa's. "You're going to be okay, Lusa," she promised. "We'll take care of you."

Lusa swallowed. "I'm sorry," she whimpered. She was going to slow them down.

Toklo hurried over. "Lusa?"

"She's hurt." Yakone sniffed at her wounds, eyes dark with worry.

Lusa tried to struggle to her paws. "I'll be okay."

Kallik nosed her gently down. "You need to rest." She began lapping Lusa's pelt with soothing strokes of her tongue.

Lusa lay limp, suddenly weary with pain.

Toklo peered at her bloody, matted fur. "What would Ujurak have done to make it better?"

Chenoa squeezed between Toklo and Kallik. "Who is Ujurak? You mentioned him before."

"He used to travel with us," Kallik answered softly. "He was a brown bear. He knew a lot about plants that make wounds better."

"Where is he now?" Chenoa asked.

Lusa glanced at Kallik. Who was going to explain?

Yakone stuck his muzzle closer. "You can't make wounds better. They have to heal by themselves."

Kallik shook her head. "Some plants make wounds heal

more quickly." She frowned. "I just wish I could remember what they were."

Chenoa's eyes brightened. "I know an herb my mother used to stop scratches from going bad." She bounded away over the rocks, heading downstream. "It's this way," she called. "I'll get some. It grows in the shallows, between rocks."

"We should go with her," Yakone suggested. "Those wolverines might still be around."

Lusa lifted her head. "Don't let them hurt her!"

"We won't," Kallik soothed. "Yakone and I will go with Chenoa."

Toklo shook his head. "Let's stick together. It's safer."

"But Lusa can't walk," Kallik pointed out.

Lusa pushed up with her forelegs. "I can try." Her paws shook. Pain flashed from her haunches.

Toklo ducked and shoved his snout beneath her. "Help her onto my shoulders," he told Kallik.

With a nudge, Kallik heaved Lusa up onto Toklo's back. Lusa gasped, her wounds stinging like fire, then flopped with relief as her paws straddled Toklo's wide pelt.

Toklo twisted his muzzle to see her. "Comfortable?"

His fur felt thick and warm beneath her. "Yes," she sighed.

"You're heavier than the last time I did this," Toklo huffed with amusement.

Lusa remembered the days on the ice when she'd been too sleepy to walk. "That's because I'm *older*," she sniffed.

Chenoa was disappearing around a bend in the river.

"Come on." Walking slowly, Toklo headed after the young

she-bear. Lusa gripped on with her forepaws as he rocked beneath her.

By the time they caught up with Chenoa, she was pawing leaves from a plant growing thickly at the water's edge.

Kallik sniffed the pile she'd made. "This is the plant that Ujurak used!"

Lusa watched from Toklo's shoulders. "Will it stop the stinging?"

"Let's see." Kallik motioned to Toklo to lean down. As he did, Lusa began to slide. Her heart lurched, but Kallik caught her scruff gently between her teeth and eased her onto the soft grass lining the shore.

Lusa lay panting, as tired as if she'd walked the shoreline herself. Chenoa chewed a mouthful of her leaves and licked the pulp lightly over Lusa's wounds.

Kallik leaned closer. "Make sure you cover all of it."

Lusa screwed up her eyes when it stung like a swarm of bees. Then, suddenly, the pain in her rump started to ease. She let out a slow, deep breath.

"Better?" Chenoa looked at her with concern.

Lusa nodded. "Thank you."

Chenoa shrugged. "I'm glad I could help."

Lusa looked guiltily at her friends. She was keeping them here when they should be traveling. But the grass beneath her felt so soft, and the river rumbled past like an old friend.

Kallik's belly rumbled. "Is anyone else hungry?"

"I am," Yakone confessed.

"I know a good fishing spot," Chenoa told her. "Do you

want me to show you? You can come, too, Toklo."

"Is it far?" Toklo scanned the tree line. "We should stay close to Lusa."

"I'll stay with her."

Lusa jerked around in surprise as Yakone settled beside her.

He touched his nose to her shoulder. "You go to sleep. I'll stay with you while Kallik fishes."

Lusa blinked at him gratefully, then watched Chenoa, Kallik, and Toklo as they headed along the shore. When their pelts had blurred into the distance, she turned her gaze to the water sliding past. Eyelids heavy, wounds throbbing, she escaped into sleep.

CHAPTER SEVEN

Toklo

Toklo glanced back along the shore. In the distance he could see the small, dark shape of Lusa, curled on the rocks beside Yakone. Why hadn't he noticed she was so badly hurt? The fur rippled along his spine. *Thank the spirits for Chenoa's healing leaves.*

Water sprayed his pelt as Kallik splashed into the shallows. "Are you coming?" The white bear waded toward deeper water.

Toklo hesitated. Lusa seemed a long way away. What if the wolverines attacked again? Their boldness had shaken him. First Hakan, then wolverines! *Aren't the animals around here scared of anything?* His thoughts darted forward. What would happen when he got home? Would he ever manage to stake out his own territory? He pushed the thought away as butterflies fluttered in his belly. *It'll be fine.*

Chenoa fidgeted beside him. "Don't you want to fish?"

He flicked his snout toward Lusa. "I don't like leaving her."

Kallik followed his gaze downstream as water flowed around her belly. "Yakone will protect Lusa."

"Of course he will," Chenoa agreed. "And we could hunt in the woods."

Toklo stared at her. "What about fishing? You said this was a good spot."

Chenoa headed for the trees. "There's something I want to show you."

Kallik lifted her dripping muzzle. "Is that wise?"

"The forest doesn't belong to the wolverines." Toklo puffed out his chest. He'd chased them off once. He could do it again. "Do you want to hunt in the woods, Kallik?"

Kallik reared up and plunged her paws into the water. She hooked out a fish and snapped it between her jaws. Her voice too muffled to hear, she shook her head. Toklo guessed that she wanted to stay here.

Sedge rustled as Chenoa bounded into the woods.

"We'll see you later, then." Toklo followed. The rich scent of peat filled his nose.

"Hurry up!" Chenoa was already racing between the trees, her small paws light on the springy moss as she wove around hummocks and ducked low branches.

Toklo broke into a run, skidding clumsily on the uneven ground as he tried to follow her path. A branch jutting low from a fir caught his cheek. He stumbled against a tussock and twisted his paw. "Ow!"

Chenoa spun around. "What happened?"

"This ground is too uneven!" Toklo crossly shook the pain from his paw.

"Should I go slower?" Chenoa padded to his side.

Toklo huffed. "What are you rushing for, anyway?"

"I told you! There's something I want to show you."

"I thought we were hunting." Toklo wanted to give his throbbing paw a rest. "We'll scare every bit of prey in the forest if we run."

"It's not my fault if you thump along like a white bear." Chenoa sniffed his paw. "Is it okay?"

"Yeah." The pain was easing. Toklo put weight on it, relieved to find it wasn't injured. He twitched as rose-colored feathers flashed beyond Chenoa. "Prey!" Silently, he stalked past her.

A dove was strutting along the top of a long anthill, pecking at the tiny insects. Toklo could already taste it. His mouth began to water. He crept closer, thankful for the soft moss muffling his pawsteps. Less than a bearlength away, he paused, hunkering down, ready to pounce.

"No!"

Chenoa's bark shocked him. Her paw jabbed Toklo's flank, hard as stone. He staggered, fighting to keep his balance, then tripped on a stone and hit the moss with a peaty splash.

"What was that for?" Toklo yelped as he sprawled on the wet forest floor. Anger flared in his belly. "What in the stars are you doing?"

Feathers fluttered as the dove escaped into the branches. Toklo jumped up and glared at Chenoa. "I was about to catch it!" he growled.

"You can't kill a dove!" she exclaimed.

"Are you crazy?"

"No!"

"Why? Are they poisonous here?"

"No!" Chenoa's eyes were round. "My mother told me my name means 'dove'!"

"Chenoa?" Toklo stared at her, incredulous. "So you can't kill them?"

"It feels wrong." Chenoa gazed up into the tree where the dove had settled.

Toklo sighed. What was the point of arguing?

"There's plenty of other prey," Chenoa reasoned.

Toklo stomped away. "Let's find some, then." He glanced over his shoulder. "What does *Hakan* mean? Just so I don't waste my time stalking his namesake."

"Snake." Chenoa padded after him. "You weren't planning on hunting snakes, were you?"

Toklo scowled at her. "No. Were *you*?" Had she just brought him into the woods to show him he didn't belong here? Why was she hanging around, anyway? *We're just passing through.*

Chenoa looked at him. "Do you want to hunt or do you want to argue?" She turned and pushed past a clump of bracken. "We can do both if you want."

Growling under his breath, Toklo followed. Chenoa glanced over her shoulder, eyes sparkling, and broke into a run.

Toklo raced after her. *What's the rush?* The soggy moss sucked at his paws. It was like running through quicksand. Chenoa zigzagged between tussocks, skimming the ground. Toklo began to pant, hot beneath his pelt.

The ground sloped upward and grew drier.

"Nearly there," Chenoa called. A few moments later, she skidded to a halt.

Toklo stopped beside her, on the brink of a clearing where long grass swished in the breeze. Overhead, torn clouds opened onto blue sky.

"Birds love to nest here." Chenoa nodded toward the ragwort and knotweed clumped around the clearing.

"You seem to know this territory well," Toklo commented. "Do you come here a lot?"

"It's where I come to get away from Hakan when he's being a real sore-paw. It's no-bear's-land." She lifted her muzzle toward a ridge beyond the trees. "Way over there is Alach's territory. Back there"—she tipped her snout—"is Hakan's."

Toklo wondered if there'd be empty stretches of forest like this when he reached the mountains. "Why don't you make this land yours?" he asked.

Chenoa snorted. "Do you really think Hakan would let me?"

Toklo felt a flash of impatience. "Then find somewhere else. I wouldn't let some bear tell me where I could live."

"He's not *some* bear, though," Chenoa growled. "He's my brother."

"He's not much of a brother."

"What do *you* know?"

"I've seen him try to rip your ear off, remember?"

"It's not that simple, okay?" Chenoa turned and stalked away. She sat down and leaned against a tree. "Go hunt."

"Don't you want to help?"

"Why?" She glared at him. "So you can tell me what to do some more?"

Toklo pushed into the long grass and snuffled among the roots of a wide swathe of knapweed. Didn't Chenoa realize that she didn't have to stay with Hakan? He shoved the thought away. Why was he worrying about her? *I've got my journey; it's up to Chenoa to make her own.*

Something rustled ahead of him. He stiffened, excited, and tasted the air. *Grouse.* The musky smell was familiar from hunting before they reached the Endless Ice. As the knapweed shivered, Toklo pounced. Plunging his forepaws among the leaves, he flailed until he felt feathers, then grabbed on. The grouse squawked and struggled, but his grip was tight. He thrust his muzzle through the grass, caught the grouse by the neck and, with a snarl, snapped it cleanly.

Exhilarated, he carried his catch to Chenoa. She didn't look up, so he quietly laid it at her paws. "You have first bite."

She glanced at him, then grabbed the grouse and ripped it in two. "Thanks." She flung one part onto the ground in front of him.

The scent of blood made Toklo's belly rumble. Was Chenoa going to spoil his meal by grumbling through it? "I'm sorry, okay? It's none of my business."

"Yeah." Chenoa took a mouthful of grouse and chewed on it sulkily.

"I know it's hard to leave your family behind." Toklo took a bite. The flavor sang on his tongue.

"So why'd you leave yours?" Chenoa asked.

Toklo stared at the grouse. "Every bear needs to find his own territory."

"But I thought you said you were going home." The sharpness had left her growl.

"That doesn't mean I've staked out a territory yet."

"You said your home was in the mountains." Chenoa swallowed. "But the mountains are huge. How will you know which part is home?"

"I remember the SilverPaths." Memories of Tobi and Oka made his chest feel heavy. "We used to scavenge for grain there when I was a cub. And there was a wide river where we fished." He took another bite of grouse.

"Like Big River?"

Toklo swallowed. "Not that big. It's where I taught myself to fish." His heart twisted as he remembered watching a mother teach her cub how to catch salmon in the fast-flowing stream. "I nearly drowned in it once. Some big bears held me under the water." His heart lurched; the memory was old, but the fear still felt fresh.

Chenoa leaned forward. "What happened? Where was your mother?"

Toklo stared at her, his mouth dry as he remembered how Oka had ignored his cries for help. "It doesn't matter," he murmured. "I survived."

Chenoa watched him curiously for a moment, then went back to her share of the grouse. She finished it in a few bites, spitting out the feathers, and climbed to her paws. "Come on."

Toklo licked blood from his nose. "Where?"

"I was going to show you something, remember?"

Toklo swallowed his last morsel and stood up. Chenoa was already trotting away through the trees. She headed upslope, keeping a brisk pace, and Toklo followed. The land rose steeply, the pines pressing ever denser. The higher they climbed, the darker the forest got. It felt as though they were climbing into storm clouds.

"Is it much farther?" Toklo was worried about leaving the others for so long.

Chenoa scrambled up through a rocky gully. "No."

At the top, the world opened around them.

"What do you think?" She led Toklo out onto the bare hilltop. It was black with the charred stumps of trees.

Toklo wrinkled his nose at the tang of smoke and ash. "What is this place?"

"I call it the Fire Ridge." Chenoa looked around. "The fire happened just before cold-earth. We saw it from the river. It was like the whole hill had caught light. Hakan wanted to swim the river to get away from it, but I was too small." She scuffed her paw through the ash. "So we waited by the shore and watched it swallow the forest. We thought it would eat everything, but the flat-faces brought clattering birds to drop water on the flames. They made huge clouds, like the earth was snow-day breathing."

The breeze, strong up here, stirred the ash and blew it into Toklo's fur. He sneezed as it went up his nose. "Is this what you wanted me to see?" He glanced around the desolate hilltop.

"Look beyond the stumps." Chenoa stared into the distance.

Toklo followed her gaze. The land dipped and rose, wave upon wave of deep green forest. Far below, the river curved one way and then the other, weaving a silvery path between the hills. Toklo cocked his head as he noticed bare swathes here and there on the hillsides, like flesh where fur had been ripped away.

"What's that?" He flicked his snout to the nearest wound.

Chenoa squinted. "That's where flat-faces steal the trees."

"So many?" Toklo wondered how such clawless creatures could do so much damage.

Chenoa pointed her short black muzzle toward the distant mountains. "Is that where you're going?"

Toklo could just make out a hazy, purple range of mountains beyond the forest. "Yes." Forgetting the wounds on the hillside, he felt his heart tug toward the distant peaks.

Chenoa blinked. "That's a *long* way! How do you know which way to go?"

"I trust my instinct." The river would lead him.

"This is the farthest I've ever been." Chenoa's gaze lingered on the far horizon.

Toklo shrugged. "But this is your home."

"I don't want to stay here."

Toklo hardly heard her. He was trying to guess how many days it would take to reach the purple mountains. What would happen when he got there? Was he strong enough to fight for his own territory yet? Yakone and Kallik would go back to the ice. Lusa would find her own home. He'd be alone. His thoughts swam, his belly hollow despite his meal. Was he really ready for this?

A muzzle nudged his flank. "Let's go see how Lusa is."

Toklo dragged his gaze from the horizon. Chenoa was already heading down the slope. Charred wood crunched beneath Toklo's paws as he followed. He was relieved when they reached the forest and breathed air sharp with the tang of sap.

As he breathed it in, a new scent touched his nose.

Meat. Not prey, but flat-face food.

He licked his lips and veered away from Chenoa, making his own trail down the slope.

"Where are you going?" Chenoa called across the brambles.

"Can't you smell food?"

"That's not bear food." Chenoa chased after him. "Don't go there!"

"Food is food." Toklo quickened his pace, belly growling. "And this food smells great." Toklo ignored the sour scent of firebeasts that hung in the air as he headed for the rich smell of fire-scorched meat. He was remembering Lusa's raiding trips when she'd bring back burned prey. It had been as tasty as real food.

The woods grew lighter as the trees thinned out. A BlackPath cut a canyon between the trees. Toklo paused and peered along it. It was empty.

Chenoa stopped beside him. "Let's get back to the others," she urged.

Toklo jumped out of the trees and walked along the grass at the edge of the BlackPath. "Think how happy Lusa will be when we take her back something tasty."

"You're thinking of your own belly, not Lusa's," Chenoa growled, following.

"That's not true." The scent of charred meat drew him on. His mouth watered. "Lusa needs cheering up."

The scent was stronger than ever, meat and fire mingling. Toklo slowed as the BlackPath curved through the trees. He glimpsed something white fluttering between the trunks. Curious, he crept forward, until he could see a pelt-den in a clearing beside the BlackPath. He'd seen pelt-dens before. Flat-faces used them to shelter in. Growling with frustration, Toklo halted.

"There's only one reason flat-faces make pelt-dens in the woods," Chenoa spoke up, nodding toward the den. "They're hunters. Which means they'll have firesticks. Which means we should get out of here."

"Wait." Toklo spotted a fire outside the den. A lump of meat dangled over the flames. They hissed and sparked as juice dripped from the meat. "I can grab it before anyone sees me." He bounded across the BlackPath.

"No!" Chenoa grabbed at his flank.

Toklo turned on her. "Let go!"

The black bear's eyes were white-rimmed with fear, every hair on her pelt bristling. "Don't go. Please!"

"I won't be long." Toklo headed for the fire. A single swipe and he'd be back in the forest with a delicious treat for Lusa.

"Toklo! No!" Chenoa roared at the top of her voice.

Toklo froze. *You fish-brain!* Now the flat-faces would know they were here!

Yelps sounded from the white den, and two flat-faces burst out. Toklo recognized the firesticks they were carrying at once. Spinning so fast his pads burned, he raced back toward Chenoa. "Run!"

The firesticks cracked behind them, splitting the air. Bark sprayed from the tree trunks as Toklo hurled himself into the shelter of the forest. The ground blurred beneath his paws as he pelted up the slope. Brambles ripped his fur. Branches whipped his muzzle. He flattened his ears, relieved to hear Chenoa's pawsteps echoing his. Glancing back, he saw her a few pawsteps behind and kept running as the firesticks crackled.

They burst out of the trees into the scorched clearing.

"We're safe!" Chenoa panted as the firesticks fell silent.

Toklo slowed to a halt. "What in all the spirits made you roar like that?" He glared furiously at Chenoa.

"They could have hurt us!" Chenoa stared back. "Have you never seen a firestick before?"

"Of course I have! But there wouldn't have been any firesticks if you hadn't made all that noise!" Toklo was trembling, not sure if he was angry or scared.

"Do you think flat-faces are fish-brains?" Chenoa hissed. "Do you *really* think you could have snatched the food from their fire without them noticing?"

Toklo loomed over her. "Yes!"

"Then *you're* a fish-brain!"

"At least I'm not a *coward*!"

Chenoa reared up, reaching her muzzle toward Toklo's.

"Don't you ever call me a coward!" she spat. "I saved your pelt back there!"

"I didn't need saving!" Toklo snarled.

Chenoa dropped onto all fours, her eyes clouding. "You can't always be right, Toklo," she murmured. "No one is."

An image of Tobi flashed in Toklo's mind. His brother lay feeble and dying while he nudged him impatiently.

"Come on, Tobi. Stop being lazy. Come and play with me!"

As the image vanished, a new one appeared: Ujurak dancing into a stone-black sky, scattering trails of stars. Then Nanulak's eyes burned through the darkness, wild and angry.

"You betrayed me!"

Toklo backed away, his fury draining as memories flooded his mind. "No," he breathed. "I'm not always right."

As he spoke, he thought he saw a small brown shape stir in the bracken. A familiar scent wreathed around him. *Ujurak?* Toklo whipped around, scanning the forest.

"What is it?" Chenoa caught his eye. "Are you okay? Have you seen something?"

"No." Toklo steadied his breath, his heart slowing. "I thought I did. But there's nothing there."

Chenoa stared at him for a moment, then pushed away through the bracken. "Let's get back to the river."

Toklo followed, sadness tugging at his heart. *I'm not always right.* He watched Chenoa's black pelt as it moved through the sea of brown fronds like a fish. Her shoulders were hunched defensively like the time when Hakan had ripped her ear and sent her packing. With a pang of guilt, Toklo realized that he must have seemed exactly like Hakan when he'd loomed over her just now.

He hurried to catch up to her. "I'm sorry I lost my temper."

Chenoa didn't look at him. "I'm sorry I made the flat-faces come out of their den. I was scared for you."

"I can take care of myself," Toklo promised.

Chenoa paused and met his gaze. "Everyone needs help sometimes, Toklo."

Toklo jerked away and headed for the river. Keeping a bearlength ahead of Chenoa, he watched his pawsteps as the slope eased toward the shore.

As he passed a crop of boulders jutting up from the forest floor, Chenoa hissed behind him. "Stop!"

He turned. "What?"

Her nose was twitching. "Get behind those rocks!" She nudged him hard in the ribs. "And stay still!"

Toklo bristled. "Why?"

"Hakan's coming!"

"Hakan?" Toklo glimpsed black fur between the trees. "What? Where?"

"Just *hide*!"

Growling, Toklo ducked behind the rocks. Perhaps Chenoa was right. He didn't want to fight Hakan, but he didn't want to back down to the bad-tempered black bear, either. It was better to avoid him.

"What are you doing *here*?" Hakan barked at Chenoa. "I've wasted a day's hunting trailing you!"

"I go where I want," Chenoa snapped.

Hakan ignored her. "I can smell those other bears," he growled. "You've been following them, haven't you? You've got no sense of loyalty! Following a bunch of outsiders."

Toklo's pelt pricked with rage.

He heard Chenoa's voice harden. "Why don't you go back to your territory, Hakan? This is none of your business."

"And leave you here with them? What kind of brother do you think I am? I'm staying here till I know you're safe."

"Of *course* you are," Chenoa snarled scornfully. Then she yelped in shock and pain.

Chenoa! Toklo dug his claws into the earth to stop himself from leaping out. Cautiously, he straightened and peered over the rocks. Chenoa was crouched on the ground, clutching her snout.

Hakan reared over her. "I hope you haven't been helping them steal prey, because if you have, you'll feel more than my paw on your hide!" Growling, he stomped into the forest.

Toklo darted from his hiding place. Chenoa was hauling herself to her paws. He sniffed her muzzle. There was no sign of blood, but he could feel heat pulsing where Hakan had hit her. "Are you okay?"

"I will be," Chenoa snuffled.

Fur bristling on his shoulders, Toklo paced in front of her. "You shouldn't have to put up with the way he treats you!"

Chenoa licked her nose. "When our mother died, it broke his heart."

"What about *your* heart?" Toklo growled. "You lost her, too."

Chenoa flashed him a look. "I made her *die*, remember?"

Without waiting for an answer, she headed for the river.

Toklo swallowed an angry retort. Why was she so willing to take the blame? Couldn't she see that Hakan was just a bully? *Heartbroken?* Hakan was about as heartbroken as a weasel swallowing a chick!

Toklo stalked after Chenoa, a growl rumbling in his throat. He wanted to find Hakan and teach him not to be a bully. *But wouldn't that make me a bully just like him, using my weight to get what I want?* Prickling with frustration, he scrambled over a tussock. *I just want to go home!* The mountains were tugging at him even more strongly now that he'd seen them. There wasn't time to worry about Chenoa and Hakan. She wasn't helpless. Toklo had seen her stand up to Hakan. She was going to have to sort this out herself.

CHAPTER EIGHT

Lusa

"Look!" Lusa lifted the piece of squawroot between her paws to show Toklo and Chenoa as she spotted them padding from the trees. "Yakone dug it up." She took another bite of the tasty flesh, relishing its musky flavor.

Beside her, Yakone lifted his head from the trout he'd been stripping. A small pile of fish lay beside him. Kallik, who'd caught them, was dozing on the rock, letting her pelt dry in the setting sun.

Lusa frowned. Toklo and Chenoa hadn't looked up. She sat up, wincing as her wounded rump brushed the rock. "What's wrong?" She stared at Chenoa's swollen muzzle. Had they been fighting?

"Nothing." Chenoa stopped beside Lusa. "How are your wounds? Do you need more hornwort?"

"You sound just like Ujurak!" Lusa dropped her squawroot.

Chenoa tipped her head to one side. "You still haven't told me where he is."

Lusa looked at Kallik, unsure what to say.

Kallik lifted her head and blinked sleepily at Lusa. "Is everything okay?"

"Where's Ujurak?" Chenoa asked again.

Toklo padded away and sat on a rock. "He's dead," he growled.

Kallik looked around sharply. "No, he's not. Ujurak had to leave us."

Chenoa looked confused. "So is he dead or isn't he?"

Lusa pictured the huge starry bear who'd come down to fetch Ujurak. That was like dying, wasn't it? But not like *prey* dying. He was still with them. Right? She searched Toklo's face as he scowled into the river.

Kallik nudged a trout toward Chenoa. "Are you hungry?"

Toklo watched the water. "We ate."

Chenoa sniffed the fish. "Did you catch all this?"

"Yes," Kallik huffed proudly.

"I didn't think you'd actually *catch* one!" Chenoa exclaimed. "I didn't know white bears could river-fish."

Kallik's eyes glowed. "You'd be surprised at what we can do."

Chenoa called to Toklo, "Did you ice-fish when you were on the Endless Ice?"

"Yes." Toklo didn't look up. *"So?"*

Chenoa ignored him. "What's it like on the ice?" she asked Kallik. "Don't you hate being cold all the time?"

Lusa heaved herself to her paws and limped toward Toklo. He looked stiff and unhappy. She stopped beside him and nuzzled close, sheltering in his fur from the brisk wind. "Chenoa's a friendly bear, isn't she?"

"When she's not picking fights." Toklo felt rigid as a tree against her.

"Did you fight?" Lusa asked.

Toklo sighed. "Not really."

"Where did she take you?" Lusa was determined to find out why Toklo was so upset.

"A burned hilltop."

"Burned?"

"A forest fire had killed all the trees," Toklo explained. "Chenoa wanted me to see beyond the forest."

"Did you?"

Toklo nodded. "I saw mountains."

Lusa's belly fluttered. He'd be home soon. Shouldn't he be happy? "Are they close?"

Toklo's shoulders drooped. "No."

"We've traveled far before," Lusa reminded him. "It won't be long before we get there, I promise." She snuggled closer. "You've always managed to do what you set out to do, Toklo. You'll get home. And we'll be with you all the way."

Toklo grunted softly and curled around her. Feeling safe and warm, Lusa watched him close his eyes. The river washed past, and she stared into the growing darkness. What would happen when they did reach Toklo's home? Kallik and Yakone would return to the ice.

What will happen to me?

Wondering whether she'd ever find a home of her own, Lusa rested against Toklo and slipped into sleep.

* * *

Lusa dreamed she sat in a patch of soft grass. Around her the forest bloomed, lush and green. Sweet berries clustered above her head. As she reached up and hooked the branch closer with her claws, a growl sounded from beyond the trees.

Lusa stiffened. She let go of the berries and scrambled to her paws. The forest faded. Fear dropped like a stone in her belly as the growl sounded again.

This wasn't part of the dream. *I need to wake up!*

Lusa blinked open her eyes. The edge of the forest glowed in dawn light. A roar shattered the air. She jumped as Toklo leaped to his paws.

Hakan was charging from the trees, heading toward Kallik, Yakone, and Chenoa.

"Look out!" Lusa jumped up. Pain seared from her wound.

Kallik and Yakone were struggling to their paws. Chenoa was already rearing up as her brother raced toward them.

"Stay here, Lusa." Toklo bounded away and stopped shoulder to shoulder with the white bears.

Hakan skidded to a halt a bearlength in front of them. "Why are you all still here?"

Lusa stared. Was Hakan crazy? Picking a fight with three bears twice his size, when they weren't even on his territory?

Chenoa padded forward. "Go away, Hakan!" Her fur bristled along her spine.

Hakan puffed out his chest. "I found feathers and blood in the forest. You've been hunting there."

Toklo stepped forward. "It's not your territory."

Hakan curled his lip at Chenoa. "You've been hunting with them, haven't you? How dare you betray me? I have been nothing but loyal to you, yet you give prey to my enemies!"

Lusa saw Yakone show his long, white teeth. Hakan was going to get hurt if he didn't back down. She limped forward. "We're not your enemies!" Wincing at the pain in her rump, she nosed her way between Toklo and Kallik.

Hakan ignored her. "Come home with me, Chenoa." There was menace in his growl.

Yakone's claws scraped rock as he flexed them.

"Leave her alone, Hakan," Lusa pleaded.

Kallik leaned forward. "Chenoa, come with us. You don't have to go with him."

"Yes, she does," Hakan snapped. "She owes me that much."

"Chenoa doesn't owe you anything!" Kallik met Hakan's gaze.

"She killed our mother!"

Lusa blinked. What did he mean? She felt Toklo bristle beside her. "Do you know what he's talking about?" she whispered.

Toklo didn't answer. Instead he snarled at Hakan. "You can't blame her for your mother's death!"

Hakan's eyes glittered. "If it wasn't for Chenoa, she'd still be alive!"

Lusa pushed past Toklo and stopped a muzzlelength away from Hakan. He was stocky and scarred, and his hot, sour breath bathed her nose. Weak with pain, she fought to stop trembling. "You must miss your mother, Hakan." She turned to Chenoa. "You too."

Chenoa dipped her head.

"I miss *my* mother," Lusa went on. "I know she's still alive, but I'll probably never see her again." The words pierced her heart. "But I don't let it stop me from going on with my life and doing what I want to do. If I did, I wouldn't be here." She glanced back at her traveling friends. "Nor would they."

Kallik caught her eye, her gaze softening.

"We've all lost someone, Hakan." Lusa turned back to the black bear.

Hakan's snout dipped. "I don't want to lose anyone else." He glanced at Chenoa.

"She'll always be your sister," Lusa reassured him. "But you can't keep her near you just to make yourself feel better. She has her own life. You have to let her go if that's what she wants."

Lusa held Hakan's gaze for a moment, hope fluttering in her belly. *Please let her go without a fight.*

Brown fur flashed on the edge of Lusa's vision. She jerked around. Toklo was backing away. "Come on," he growled. "This is none of our business."

Lusa stared after him. *"What?"*

Toklo paused. "Hakan's right. Chenoa's his sister. She doesn't know us. She should stay with him."

Chenoa's eyes widened. "But I thought—"

Toklo cut her off. "Thanks for the help, Chenoa, but it's time we moved on."

"Toklo!" Kallik sounded shocked. "Lusa's injured, remember?"

"I'll carry her if I have to." Toklo dipped his head to Hakan. "Your sister's been a great help, but we're leaving now. I promise you won't see us again."

Lusa saw Yakone and Kallik exchange glances. They were as confused as she was.

Toklo nudged Lusa with his muzzle. "Come on."

She staggered as he jostled her away down the shore. "But we can't just—"

"It's for the best." Toklo halted. "Do you want me to carry you?"

Lusa shot him a furious look. "No, thank you!" She didn't care how much it hurt to walk. She glanced back at Kallik.

The white bear was leading Yakone after them. Chenoa watched them go, her eyes clouded with confusion.

"Toklo!" Lusa called out, but Toklo was stomping away along the shore.

"Come on, Lusa," Kallik whispered gently as she passed.

"But it's not fair," Lusa objected.

"There's nothing we can do." Kallik headed away after Toklo, Yakone at her side.

Swallowing her anger, Lusa followed. Her wounds stung like fire, but she kept walking. There was no way she was asking for help. Especially from Toklo! What was up with him? Perhaps he just wanted to get home, back to brown bears. Lusa could understand that. It'd been great having another black bear around. She hadn't been the only small bear anymore. And Kallik clearly enjoyed having Yakone with her. Was Toklo just jealous that he was the odd one out? Was that why he'd abandoned Chenoa?

But did it really matter anymore who was a brown bear or a black bear or a white bear? *We're like family, aren't we?*

Her pelt pricked with unease. *But Toklo's going home; Kallik and Yakone will return to the ice. We're not bound like kin at all.*

Stones rolled beneath her paws and she stumbled, choking back a squeak of pain. Her vision darkened, Kallik and Yakone melting together as though she was seeing them through water. She felt a nose nudge her flank. *Yakone.* He was easing her up onto his shoulder with Kallik's help.

Weak with relief, Lusa hung there, rolling with the movement as he padded on beside Kallik. The thick fishy scent of him filled her nose, and she let the forest blur in front of her eyes. She buried her nose deeper into his pelt. *We are like family!*

But what had happened to Toklo? Why had he abandoned Chenoa? Yesterday he had been so fired up, ready to defend her. Why had he stopped caring? Anger surged through Lusa. *Chenoa saved my life!* Didn't that count for anything?

The stony shore gave way to dry, crackly sedge stalks. Yakone waded through them, Kallik at his side. The heavy clouds shielded the sun, and a brisk breeze chilled the air.

"Are you glad to be back by the river?" Kallik asked Yakone.

"I like anywhere I can see the sky," Yakone answered. "Besides, it's too easy to get lost in the woods."

"Not when we were with Ujurak," Kallik murmured wistfully. "He always knew the route. There were signs only he could see."

Lusa felt Yakone's pelt twitch beneath her. "Like what?"

"The way plants grew in a certain direction," Kallik explained. "Or stones that seemed to block the wrong path."

"Plants and stones?" Yakone huffed. "I prefer a nice,

wide-flowing river. It's a lot easier to spot."

Lusa closed her eyes. Their voices gradually blurred into a single murmur as she drifted into sleep.

Movement woke her. Yakone was sliding her into a bed of bracken. Lusa lifted her head and gazed around. The river here ran smooth and flat, lapping at a long stretch of pebbly shore. Toklo was sniffing at the bushes edging the tree line, rearing onto his hind legs now and then to peer into the woods. "Are we stopping?" Lusa murmured.

"Yakone's tired," Kallik told her gently.

Lusa felt hot with embarrassment. The clouds showed late, fading light. Yakone must have been carrying her for ages. "Sorry!"

"You don't have to apologize. You can't walk yet." Turning, Yakone headed for the river. "I'm going to cool down."

"How are your wounds?" Kallik sniffed at her rump.

"They hurt," Lusa admitted. "But the plant juice has helped." The scorching pain had definitely eased. She sniffed her bracken bedding. "Did you make this for me?"

"Yes." Kallik patted at a stray strand of brittle fern. "I want you to rest comfortably."

Lusa lay back, enjoying the springy softness. "Thanks, Kallik. And tell Yakone I appreciate him carrying me."

"He knows." Kallik lumbered away after Yakone, who was already splashing in the water downstream.

"I'm sorry, Lusa."

Toklo's voice surprised her. She jerked her muzzle around.

Toklo was standing behind her, his eyes dark.

"What for?" Did he regret leaving Chenoa?

"I should have saved you from the wolverines."

Lusa blinked. *How?* "It was dark, and I was too far away."

Toklo frowned. "It's up to me to keep you safe. I let you down. I should have made sure you slept closer to me."

Lusa bristled. "You're not responsible for me. I can look after myself!"

Toklo tipped his head. "So you keep saying."

Anger surged beneath her pelt. "Why do you keep acting like you have to be in charge of everything? It isn't all about you, all the time!"

"I never said it was!" Toklo defended himself. "I just want you to be safe!"

"What about Chenoa?" Lusa demanded hotly. "She needed rescuing, but you walked away. It's *her* you let down, not me." She rolled over and closed her eyes tight. *You did let me down, Toklo. I thought you were kind, but you're not.*

Behind her, Toklo sighed heavily.

Please change your mind about Chenoa. Lusa held her breath, praying Toklo would relent and go back for the young she-bear. Pebbles swished as he padded away.

Disappointment jabbed Lusa's belly. She lay still, listening to Kallik and Yakone calling to each other as they hunted in the river.

"The fish are slow here!"

"They're swimming into my paws!"

"Come on, Toklo! Join us!"

Lusa lay limply. She'd slept all day, but tiredness dragged at her bones. Too weary to be angry, she let sleep draw her in again. She dreamed she was beside a river. A rowan tree stretched delicate branches above her head. Sunshine dappled through the leaves onto her back, and beneath her paws the earth felt soft.

Where am I? Lusa scanned the river, which was no more than a rippling brook. It didn't look like any place she'd been before.

Paws scuffed the earth beside her.

Lusa turned, gasping in surprise. *Ujurak!*

The brown bear hadn't changed since she'd last seen him. He was hardly bigger than she was. Cub fluff still softened his face. Yet his pelt was glossy, as though it had never been touched by wind or rain. His gaze met hers steadily, and Lusa realized she was wrong.

Ujurak *had* changed. She saw wisdom in his round, dark eyes. She looked closer. *Is that starlight shining in them?*

"It's good to see you, Lusa!" Ujurak pressed his muzzle happily against her cheek.

"Where are we?" Lusa asked. "Why are you here? Is this your new home? Or is it my dream? Where are the others?"

"Lusa?" Ujurak interrupted her gently. "I have something to show you."

Lusa frowned. "What?"

But Ujurak was already padding away, climbing the slope up from the brook, his paws hardly brushing the grass, leaving no pawprints as he wove between the slender trees. Lusa scampered after him, relieved to feel that her wounds hadn't followed her into her dream. She broke into a gallop as Ujurak reached the top of the slope, and caught up with him as he stopped. Ahead, the trees opened into a clearing. Lusa's eyes widened.

A full-grown brown bear was piling stones at the center of the clearing, wedging sticks between them to hold them in place, while a cub sat and watched her.

"It's Toklo!" Lusa recognized the cub's face, even though he was much younger than the bear she knew now. He had the same serious expression, his shoulders hunched with worry. Lusa turned to Ujurak. "That big bear's Oka, isn't it? His mother?"

Ujurak nodded. "She's burying Tobi."

Lusa's heart twisted with grief. "Poor Oka!" Memories flashed in her mind of the Bear Bowl, where Oka had been brought at the end of her life, grieving for her lost cubs. Lusa could see the same grief now, knotted into Oka's shoulders as she piled stone upon stone.

Lusa started forward, but Ujurak blocked her path. "No," he murmured. "We are only here to watch."

As he spoke, Toklo-cub got to his paws and padded over to his mother. Eyes round, he nudged her with his small, wet nose.

Oka whirled around with a snarl. "Get away!" With a mighty paw, she knocked him away.

Toklo staggered backward, his eyes wide with shock. "Mother?" He padded toward her again, head low, his gaze anxious.

"Get *away!*" Oka didn't even turn this time, but kicked out with a hindpaw and knocked Toklo flying. He fell, sprawling, in the dirt.

Lusa yelped. "Why's she doing that?"

Ujurak answered softly, "She doesn't believe she can keep Toklo safe anymore."

"That's not true!" Mothers always kept their cubs safe.

"She lost Tobi even though she did everything she could to help him. She's scared she'll lose Toklo, too. She'd rather chase him away than go through the pain of another loss."

"But isn't chasing him away the same as losing him?" Lusa didn't understand.

"No," Ujurak told her. "She'll be able to imagine that he's still alive. She can't do that with Tobi."

Sadness swept through Lusa's dreamworld. She could feel grief like a breeze rippling through the grass and making the leaves shiver. "Oka told me she'd driven Toklo away, when she was in the Bear Bowl. But I didn't realize how awful that must have been." She gazed back at Toklo as he circled the clearing, keeping a wary distance from Oka, his eyes clouded with sadness and confusion. "Poor Toklo!"

"And poor Oka," Ujurak added. "She's in so much pain. And she feels helpless to stop it from happening again."

Lusa couldn't drag her gaze from Toklo. "Is that why he's so protective of me and Kallik? Because he's scared of losing us like he lost Tobi and Oka?"

"He blamed himself for Tobi's death. It *had* to be his fault, otherwise Oka's anger made no sense." Ujurak pressed against her. "But that was just the start. Toklo has lost so many bears since. With each loss, he's blamed himself more. He feels responsible for everyone."

Lusa blinked. "Including Chenoa!" She understood now. "If Chenoa joins us, she'll be his responsibility. And he's terrified of losing another bear." She turned and stared at Ujurak. "Is that why you brought me here? So I'd understand?"

Ujurak was starting to fade, the trees showing through his hazy pelt. "Yes." He turned and began to pad away.

"Wait!" Lusa tried to spring after him, but the dream dragged her back. "Please!" She wanted to tear free and race after him, but her paws wouldn't move. "Come back!" Heart aching, she watched as Ujurak merged with the grass and the trees and became part of the forest.

She blinked open her eyes and found herself awake in her nest of bracken, beside Big River.

CHAPTER NINE

Toklo

Toklo dozed. He could half hear Kallik and Yakone splashing while Lusa fidgeted in her nest. He was trying to hide from the dull ache he'd had in his belly since leaving Chenoa.

Toklo! She called to him in his dreams. *Help me, Toklo!*

"I don't have time." Toklo growled, half-awake. "I have to get home!" He rolled over, tucking his nose under his paw and squeezing his eyes tight shut.

A paw jabbed his ribs.

"Go away." Toklo screwed his eyes tighter shut.

"Toklo." It was Lusa.

"I can't help you."

"Yes, you can." Lusa's paw prodded him again. "We have to talk."

"I don't want to talk, I want to sleep."

"Toklo!"

Grumpily, Toklo sat up. *"What?"* Purple clouds streaked the sky. The day was drawing in. Upstream, Kallik and Yakone lay in the shallows, letting the cool water stream around them.

Lusa gazed at them. "Don't they ever get cold?"

"Is that why you woke me?" Toklo glared at her. "To ask if white bears get cold?"

"No." The breeze lifted Lusa's pelt. Toklo realized that it carried the chill of the Melting Sea even here. "I just wish they liked being warm," Lusa said. "Then I wouldn't feel guilty, wishing for sunshine."

Toklo pictured walking beneath the wide blue sky beside Oka and Tobi with the sun hot on his back. "When Tobi and I were cubs, I thought that there was only sunshine and water in the whole world."

Lusa gazed calmly into his eyes. "You must miss Tobi."

She woke me up to ask about Tobi? Toklo's paws pricked with irritation. "So?"

"But you don't like talking about him."

"He's dead. There's not much to talk about."

"So you're not going to think about him ever again?" Lusa sounded angry.

"No." Why did she suddenly care about Tobi?

"Are you never going to think of Chenoa, either?"

"Chenoa?" Had a bee flown into Lusa's ear? "What are you talking about?"

"I know why you left her," Lusa declared. "You were scared she'd end up traveling with us, and you don't want to be responsible for another bear."

"I just want to get home, that's all."

"Then why not let her travel with us? Her legs are as long as mine. She wouldn't hold us up."

Toklo opened his mouth, but no words came out.

Lusa went on. "You feel responsible for Tobi's death, don't you? When Oka drove you away, you thought it was because you'd let him die." She shook her head fiercely. "That's not true. It wasn't your fault he died. It wasn't your fault Ujurak left. And the wolverines attacked me because I ran away, not because you didn't stop them."

How do you know I feel like that? Toklo stared in astonishment as more words flooded from the black bear.

"You're not responsible for us, Toklo. You may be bigger and stronger than me. You may be more used to the forest than Kallik or Yakone. But it doesn't mean you have to protect us from everything. We've traveled as far as you, Kallik and I. We've seen the same things and survived the same dangers. Our fate is our own. Our lives are not in your paws." She sat back on her haunches and stared at him. "Do you understand?"

Toklo felt unease tightening his belly. "But I have to look after you."

"No! You don't!" Lusa pressed her muzzle against his cheek. "We travel with you because you're good and kind and loyal. Not because we need you to look after us. We look after one another. You're not responsible for everyone. And if Chenoa traveled with us, you wouldn't be responsible for her, either."

Toklo felt suddenly light, his breath coming deeper and easier than it had for a long while. He understood why Lusa had woken him. "You want me to go back for Chenoa."

She nodded.

"Can we trust her?" Toklo gazed along the shoreline.

"Remember Nanulak? I trusted him, but he lied from the start."

Lusa shrugged. "That was Nanulak, not Chenoa. Chenoa hasn't asked us for anything. But you've seen how Hakan bullies her. And you *know* that if he keeps blaming her for their mother's death, she'll never stop grieving."

Something seemed to loosen in Toklo's chest.

Lusa pressed on. "She needs our help, Toklo."

"But I'm going home." Toklo dipped his head. "What's going to happen to Chenoa when I get there?"

"She'll still have me." Lusa stared at him. "She can help me find *my* home."

Toklo blinked. He hadn't thought about what would happen to Lusa when he reached the mountains. He stiffened. Lusa alone? But not if Chenoa was with them . . . His belly tightened. "I'll go back for her."

"I'm coming, too." Lusa paced in front of him.

"No." Toklo was firm. "You're injured. Besides, Chenoa already trusts me. She'll believe me when I tell her she can't waste her life trying to make Hakan happy."

Along the shore, Kallik and Yakone got to their paws and shook water from their pelts. The droplets traced an arc through the air, turning sunshine into rainbows.

Toklo frowned. "What if she doesn't want to come with us?"

"Then at least you've given her the choice."

"You're right." *Chenoa's not like Nanulak.* She'd fought wolverines. She'd saved Lusa's life. Letting her travel with them was a way to thank her. Toklo stared downriver, his gaze wandering back the way they'd come. How could he think of leaving her with Hakan? Chenoa deserved a better life. He began to stride along the shore, against the flow of the waves.

"Toklo?" Kallik scrambled across the rocks and skidded to a halt beside Lusa.

Yakone lingered behind, his pelt dripping. "Are you going somewhere?"

Toklo paused. "I'm going to find Chenoa."

Kallik gasped. "You're going to ask her to travel with us!"

"Yes." Toklo glanced at Lusa. "It's the right thing to do."

"Will she be able to keep up?" Yakone warned. "We're used to walking all day. She's not."

Lusa huffed. "If she was ready to take on a bunch of wolverines, then she'll be ready for anything."

Toklo headed downstream, leaving his friends behind. He heard them whispering to one another.

"What made him change his mind?"

"Should he go alone?"

"He'll be fine," Lusa answered Kallik and Yakone. Their voices melted into the river as Toklo leaped from boulder to boulder along the rocky shoreline. He knew he was doing the right thing. Energy surged through his paws. He quickened his pace. The light was fading, the shallows turning black beneath the darkening clouds. He tasted the air for scents, hoping Chenoa and Hakan hadn't already left for their territory. Their black bear scent still hung fresh on the air. They were traveling along the shore.

Toklo broke into a run, scrambling over the rocks. As he

rounded the foot of a hill, he spotted a shape balanced on a boulder, far out in the white water.

Chenoa.

She was watching the river foam around her paws. Taut as a bobcat, she leaned over the frothing water. Any moment now, she'd lunge forward and grab for a fish. Toklo waited, not wanting to disturb her mid-hunt.

Suddenly, paws slammed into his back. Flying forward, he gasped at the weight of the blow. Black fur flashed behind him.

Hakan!

Toklo scrabbled to regain his footing, but it was too late. His forelegs slid into the water, and he tumbled after. His cheek hit the pebbly riverbed. He floundered, trying to find his paws. Grabbing at rocks, he broke the surface and turned.

Hakan reared up at him from the bank. "I told you not to come back!" With a roar, the black bear lunged forward. He hit Toklo like a rock slide, sending him staggering back. With a gasp, Toklo sank once more beneath the water. Paws pressed him down, grinding his spine into the pebbles.

Panic fired through Toklo. He struggled, trying to free himself from Hakan's grip, but the paws pressed harder. Bubbles streamed around his snout. He could see the dark green of the forest swirling beyond the surface. His chest began to scream. Toklo closed his eyes.

Suddenly he felt Hakan's hind legs beside his. Hope flashed. With a mighty kick, he thrust his hindpaws against Hakan's. The claws in his pelt pressed harder for a moment, then slid away.

Toklo exploded to the surface and took a huge gulp of air. Water sprayed his muzzle. He lunged for the bank, scrabbling for dry land. No one was going to drown him! But Hakan grabbed him and dragged him back.

Fury surging, Toklo ripped free of the black bear's claws. With a roar, he struck Hakan's snout. Blood spurted, and Hakan howled. The black bear hit back, pounding Toklo's head with a flurry of well-aimed blows that unbalanced him. As Toklo fell backward, Hakan hooked his pelt with his short, sharp claws. Toklo gasped in pain, choking as he slid underwater. He tried to struggle free, but pebbles rolled beneath his paws and he couldn't get a grip. The current tugged his fur and dragged both bears, writhing like eels, downstream.

Toklo stretched for the surface and gulped air. They were heading for rock-strewn rapids, and the noise of the river as it bubbled and foamed filled Toklo's ears. He glimpsed a boulder a moment before it struck his flank. The current tumbled them on. Hakan pulled him back down, but Toklo had time to see another boulder rushing toward them. He twisted just in time, letting Hakan slam into it. The black bear let go. Toklo plunged his hindpaws into the riverbed and reared up. As he hit air, Hakan swept past. Toklo sank his claws deep into Hakan's pelt. He dragged him up and flung him back against the boulder. He held him there, snarling. "You fight like a coward."

Hakan's eyes clouded.

"Get off my brother! You'll kill him!"

Toklo gasped as claws dug into his back and tugged him away. "Chenoa?" He whipped around, spraying water.

Chenoa stood up to her belly in the rapids. "Stop it! Both of you!"

Toklo stared at her. "But Lusa sent me back for you!"

Chenoa tipped her head in surprise. "She did?"

Hakan shook the clouds from his eyes and lunged toward Toklo. Chenoa flung herself between them. "No!" she howled above the roaring of the river. "Enough! I can't live with you anymore, Hakan! Go back to your territory. Find a mate! Raise cubs! My home's not with you. It's somewhere else."

Hakan stared at her, flanks heaving, his breath coming in gasps. Toklo tensed, ready to protect Chenoa if he lashed out.

"I didn't ask our mother to save me," Chenoa hissed. "That was a choice she made because she loved me. She chose her own destiny. Let me choose mine. If you truly love me, you'll let me go without a fight."

Hakan blinked. "You're really going to leave me?"

Chenoa didn't flinch. "I'll come back one day and meet your mate and your cubs. I'll never stop loving you. And if I have cubs, I'll tell them all about you."

Toklo felt a rush of pride as Chenoa defiantly lifted her muzzle.

Hakan's gaze hardened. "Go, then!" He splashed to the shore and bounded up onto the rocks. "At least our mother isn't here to see this. She'd never forgive you for leaving me. It would be like killing her all over again!"

CHAPTER TEN

Toklo

Chenoa stood, frozen in the flowing water, and watched as her brother stalked into the woods.

Toklo leaned closer to her. "He'll understand eventually." He nudged her toward the shore and waited as she heaved herself onto the bank. Toklo leaped up after her and shook the water from his pelt, wincing with pain. Hakan hadn't hurt him badly, but he could still feel where the black bear's claws had ripped his fur.

Chenoa gazed into the woods, her eyes sharp with grief.

"There's nothing more you can do," Toklo told her softly. "Perhaps you'll come back one day and tell him it was the right decision."

Chenoa looked at him, eyes round. "Is it the right decision?"

"Of course!" She couldn't waste her life being bullied by Hakan. "You have to live for yourself, not for Hakan."

Chenoa sighed. "I hoped it'd be different."

Toklo shook his head. "Sometimes doing the right thing feels worse than doing the wrong thing." With a prick of grief, he remembered Ujurak leaving them in the cave of stars. "Come on." Steering her along the shore, he guided her upstream. "Lusa will be thrilled to see you again." The sun was sinking down toward the horizon. The trees stretched long shadows over the shore.

Chenoa glanced backward as they followed the curve of the river. Toklo guessed she was hoping Hakan would appear to say a kinder farewell. *She's got more faith in him than he deserves.* He looked back, too, relieved that there was no sign of the bad-tempered bear.

Chenoa dragged her paws, but Toklo didn't hurry her. Leaving Hakan was probably the biggest decision she'd ever made. But when her steps slowed more, worry pricked at his pelt. She couldn't change her mind now. Hakan would never stop bullying her.

"Let's fish," Toklo suggested. It might cheer her up. He waded into the river. The shallows here raced over smooth rock. "Come on."

Chenoa lingered on the shore.

"You must be hungry," Toklo prompted. "You never got a chance to finish your fishing."

"I guess." Chenoa splashed into the water and stopped beside him. "This *is* a good spot."

Fish flashed past, swept over the smooth rock by the current. Toklo plunged his paws onto one, growling as he missed. The water moved faster than he expected. Chenoa snorted, amused, then made her own lunge. She hooked out a fish and tossed it to the shore.

Toklo watched it flap on the rocks. "You're quick!" He was impressed.

"I'm used to fishing this river."

"I guess I'm out of practice." Toklo shrugged. "I've spent too much time sitting beside ice holes and waiting for the fish to come to me."

Chenoa stared at him. "I can't imagine you on the ice. Kallik and Yakone grew up there, but it must have been horrible for you and Lusa."

"It is good to be back in the forest," Toklo conceded.

"I'll bet!" Chenoa swung her head, taking in the wide sweep of trees and river. "The ice must be weird without forests or hills. Isn't it spooky, all that whiteness?"

Toklo let his thoughts drift back to the Melting Sea. "When you get used to the white, you see other colors there." He huffed. "You have to look pretty hard, though."

The fish had stopped flapping on the shore.

"Let's take our catch back to the others," Chenoa suggested. "I can't wait to see Lusa!"

Toklo bounded toward the bank. "Yeah." He appreciated the way Chenoa was eager to share her catch with Kallik, Yakone, and Lusa. He was glad Lusa had persuaded him to go back. Chenoa was going to make a good traveling companion.

Night had fallen by the time they reached the others. Toklo spotted Lusa first, a black smudge pacing on the moonlit shore, and then Yakone, standing in the river. Kallik was sleeping in a nest of twigs and leaves.

"Chenoa!" Lusa limped toward them, her eyes flashing in the starlight. "You came!"

Chenoa rushed forward and touched Lusa's muzzle with her own. "Thanks for letting me."

Yakone called from the river, "Chenoa's here!"

"Chenoa!" Kallik scrambled to her paws, shaking leaves from her pelt. Chenoa galloped to greet her.

Lusa nestled against Toklo. "Thank you," she murmured.

He nudged her playfully. "You can rescue the next bear yourself," he teased.

They padded after Chenoa. "Did you see Hakan?" Lusa asked.

Toklo rolled his eyes. "He saw me first."

Lusa stiffened. "Did you fight?" Her gaze swept Toklo's pelt.

"Yeah." Toklo shrugged. He lowered his voice as they reached Chenoa and the others. "But it was okay. Chenoa was the brave one. She stood up to him, perhaps for the first time."

Kallik was gazing at the sky. "Shall we travel, while the moon's bright?"

Toklo scanned the horizon. Clouds bubbled ominously. He tasted rain in the air. It would be a good idea to push on before it hit them. "Are you okay to walk?" he asked Lusa.

She stretched her hind legs, wincing a little. "Walking might help," she told him. "I'm getting stiff from resting."

Yakone led the way. Toklo stayed close to Chenoa, while Kallik and Lusa brought up the rear.

"It's almost like traveling over ice," Yakone commented as he padded along the moonlit stone.

"Except you can't fall through it," Toklo grunted.

Chenoa stared at him with round eyes. "You didn't!"

"I did." Toklo shivered at the memory of the shocking coldness.

"Ujurak rescued him," Lusa called from behind.

Chenoa swallowed. "Ujurak must have been a brave bear!"

Her voice faded as memory swallowed Toklo. He was back in the freezing ocean, lungs bursting and panic roaring in his ears as he scrabbled at the jagged ice above his head. And then Ujurak had appeared, not as a bear, but as an orca. He'd been so huge; Toklo thought his heart would explode from fear. Powerful and swift, the Ujurak-orca had swept Toklo from beneath the ice and lifted him safely onto the surface.

Chenoa's voice broke into his memories. "How did he save you?"

Toklo shook away the fear flashing through his pelt. "He just jumped in and hauled me out."

Rain darkened the forest ahead. Before long it was beating against Toklo's muzzle. He called to Yakone through the rising wind. "Let's stop here."

Yakone nodded and turned his paws toward the trees. "I prefer snow," he grunted, his ears flat against his head. He led Kallik, Lusa, and Chenoa through a swathe of brambles at the forest's edge until they were sheltering under the pines. "It sits on your fur; it doesn't try to get inside your pelt."

Toklo shook water from his snout. Above, rain thrummed the trees, but only a few drops made it through the thick branches. He headed deeper into the shadows until, among the clustering trunks, he found a shallow scoop in the earth, soft with a thick coat of pine needles. "Over here."

Kallik caught up with him and padded down into the dip. "Nice find, Toklo." She settled down, and Yakone nestled beside her.

Chenoa curled up near the edge, wriggling to get comfortable. She scrabbled at the needles, hollowing her own nest. There was something awkward in her movements, as though she felt out of place. Toklo hesitated, wondering if he should curl up next to her.

Lusa beat him to it. She scrambled down beside Chenoa. "You must miss your own den." She nestled beside the she-bear. "But you'll get used to sleeping in a new place every night."

"I hope so." Chenoa tucked her nose under her paws.

As her breath grew shallow with sleep, Toklo clambered down the slope and curled up beside Lusa. "Will she be okay?" he whispered.

"She's with friends now," Lusa murmured. "She'll be fine."

Soothed, Toklo closed his eyes and let sleep wash over him.

A twig cracked beside his ear. Alarmed, Toklo jerked up his head and growled.

"It's just me." Chenoa was gazing down on him, glowing in the pale dawn light. Rain was still pattering on the branches, and Chenoa's black pelt was dripping. "Did you think I was a wolverine?" Her eyes flashed teasingly.

Toklo scrambled to his paws. "No." Kallik, Yakone, and Lusa were still sleeping. "How long have you been up?"

Chenoa shrugged. "Before sunup. I couldn't sleep."

Toklo smelled fish. "Have you been hunting?"

Chenoa lifted her muzzle toward a pile gathered at the top of the hollow. "I thought I'd make myself useful."

"You don't have to hunt for us." Toklo climbed the slope and sniffed the fish. They were still wet from the river. His mouth watered.

Chenoa bent and nosed one toward him. "I was standing in the shallows, and they kept leaping into my paws," she joked. "It seemed rude to ignore them."

Toklo crouched and began eating. His belly rumbled happily. Chenoa sat beside him and gazed down into the hollow. Toklo watched her from the corner of his eyes. She seemed distracted. "Are you okay?" he mumbled through a mouthful of fish.

"I guess." She sighed. "I wonder how Hakan is."

"He'll be fine," Toklo promised. "And this won't always seem so strange. The traveling, I mean. We all found it hard at first."

Chenoa let out a slow breath. "Don't you miss having a home?"

"I'll have one soon," Toklo told her.

Yakone jerked his head up, nose twitching. "I smell fish."

Kallik scrambled to her paws in the hollow. "Have you been up long?" she called to Toklo.

"I just woke." Toklo tossed a fish down to the white bears. "Chenoa caught this."

"Thanks, Chenoa." Yakone caught a second fish as Toklo tossed it down.

Kallik nosed Lusa gently. "How are you today?"

She raised her head, yawning. "Hungry."

"That's a good sign." Kallik looked up at Toklo.

"It is." He flung Lusa a fish. "How's the pain?"

"Better than yesterday." Lusa took a bite from the fish. She screwed up her nose and grimaced. "I can't wait for berry season."

When they'd eaten, Toklo led the way out of the forest. As he broke from the trees, rain lashed his face. He glanced back at Yakone and Kallik. They were going to hate this weather. Lusa was limping. Had she lied about the pain in her rump?

Chenoa must have noticed, too. "I'll look out for more hornwort," she promised.

Lusa looked gratefully at her. "Thanks."

"Do you want to be carried?" Kallik offered.

Lusa shook her head. "I'll manage."

Toklo watched her anxiously as he padded onto the shore. Were her wounds healing? The mountains were tugging harder in his belly, but he didn't want Lusa to suffer. Should they rest until she was better? At least there was food and shelter here. What if Lusa collapsed when they reached the mountains? There were stretches of barren rock where prey and herbs were scarce.

With worry prickling in his fur, Toklo pushed on. He kept one eye on Lusa as she followed beside Chenoa. The rocks were wet with rain and slippery underpaw. They made slow progress upstream. Yakone didn't complain, but Toklo saw him sliding and stubbing his claws with winces of pain. Kallik padded carefully beside him, stopping every now and then to shake the rain from her eyes.

Toklo felt a wet pelt brush his. Chenoa had caught up with him. "How are you doing?" he asked.

"Wouldn't it be easier walking in the forest?" Water dripped from Chenoa's snout and eyelashes.

"Kallik and Yakone aren't used to the roots and brambles yet," Toklo told her. "They manage better here. They won't yank out a claw or twist a paw."

Chenoa glanced back at the two white bears slithering over a smooth, wet boulder. "Are you sure?"

Toklo glanced up at the gray clouds. "I'm sorry about the weather."

"Not your fault," Chenoa pointed out.

"We're just used to traveling whatever the conditions."

"What's the hurry?" Chenoa asked. "Are you hoping to be home before cold-earth?"

Toklo snorted. "I hope I'm home way before that."

"So what's the rush?"

"If we waited out every bad-weather day, we'd never have made it to the Endless Ice."

"Why did you go there in the first place?"

Toklo stopped and stared, not listening to Chenoa's question. Ahead, a flat stone bridge spanned the river. Its legs sank into the frothing water. Firebeasts roared across its back. "We're going to have to cross a BlackPath," he called over his shoulder. He saw Yakone's fur spike.

"Do we have to?" Lusa queried.

"The current's too strong to swim under it." Toklo eyed

the river churning angrily beneath the bridge. He padded forward, following the shore till the shadow of the raised BlackPath was a bearlength away. Then he veered into the cover of the trees. They thinned here, where the bridge jutted into the forest. The roar and stink of firebeasts filled the air. Toklo smelled fear and knew it wasn't just his own. No one spoke as they padded over the forest floor. Then light showed ahead, and the trees opened onto a bracken-covered stretch at the edge of the BlackPath.

"Wait." Toklo stared at the hard, dark surface. A firebeast sped past, sending up a shower of filthy water. He watched the gap that followed it, feeling for its length before the next firebeast.

"They're huge," Chenoa breathed beside him.

This BlackPath was as wide as a river. Toklo guessed that its firebeasts were bigger than any Chenoa had seen on the sheltered BlackPaths in the deep forest. Their faces flashed, wide and shiny. The ground shook beneath their spinning paws. Another thundered past, spraying Toklo's fur and washing his snout with choking fumes. Chenoa retched beside him. He glanced at her. Her eyes were streaming, her rain-soaked pelt slick against her body. She suddenly looked as small as a newborn cub.

Will she make it across?

Toklo lifted his muzzle. He'd get her across. "Kallik," he said, glancing past Yakone. The white bear was peering from the trees. "You keep an eye on Lusa."

Lusa jerked around, as though she were about to snarl at

him. Then she paused and nodded. "Just give us the signal, and I'll stay close to Kallik."

"Chenoa?" Toklo turned to the young she-bear. "Are you ready?" He could see a space behind the next firebeast. It looked like there'd be time for them all to cross together.

Chenoa didn't answer. Her wide gaze was fixed on the BlackPath.

"Just run when I give the order," Toklo told her.

The firebeast howled past.

"Now!" Toklo sprang forward, crashing through bracken, out onto the stone. His claws skidded on the hard, wet surface. The white fur of Kallik and Yakone flashed at the corner of his eyes, shadowed by Lusa's black pelt.

Chenoa? He glanced over his shoulder. *Where is she?*

"I can't!" Chenoa stood trembling at the edge of the Black-Path. "I can't do it!"

CHAPTER ELEVEN

Kallik

Kallik's paws thumped heavily over the rain-slicked BlackPath. Toklo, Lusa, and Yakone streaked along beside her. The other side was close. One leap and she'd be clear.

"Chenoa!"

Toklo's panicked cry made Kallik skid to a halt. Through the driving rain, she could see Chenoa still crouching on the other side. "Chenoa! Hurry up!"

A firebeast thundered over the horizon. Kallik caught Toklo's gaze. It was wild with panic. "I'll get her!" she called.

"No!" Toklo began to turn.

Kallik glimpsed Lusa stumbling beside Toklo. *She doesn't have the strength to cross on her own!* "Help Lusa," Kallik barked at Toklo. "I'll go get Chenoa!" She swung around, away from Toklo, Lusa, and Yakone.

"Kallik! No!"

She ignored Yakone's angry howl and raced back for Chenoa.

"Leave me!" Chenoa cringed, flat against the ground. "Don't come back!" Her glazed eyes were lost in terror. "You'll die!"

The glittering face of the firebeast raced closer. Kallik's paws burned as she pelted across its path. The stink of it choked her. "Get back!"

Chenoa was frozen at the edge of the BlackPath as the firebeast thundered closer. It would smash right through her if she stayed where she was. Pushing hard with her hind legs, Kallik leaped and slammed into Chenoa, sending them both tumbling into the bracken.

The firebeast passed like a hurricane, ripping the stalks nearest to them and tearing at the fur on Kallik's back. She sprawled on her side, trying to catch her breath. Suddenly she noticed Chenoa struggling beneath her. Rolling off, Kallik filled her lungs with dirty air. Chenoa lay limp beside her.

"Are you okay?" Kallik thrust her muzzle close to the black bear.

Chenoa whimpered. "I can't do it."

Kallik bared her teeth. "Yes, you can." She scrambled to her paws and scanned the BlackPath. Yakone, Toklo, and Lusa sheltered in the trees beyond, watching with round, anxious eyes. "We can't stay here. We need to move."

"I can't do it," Chenoa repeated stubbornly.

"If you live your whole life without crossing BlackPaths," Kallik growled, "it'll be half a life. Like a captured bear. No choice. Just the same small stretch of forest for as long as you live."

"I don't care."

Kallik shoved her muzzle under Chenoa's flank and heaved her to her paws. "I care," she spat. "We're crossing that BlackPath. The others need us."

Chenoa turned stiffly and gazed at Toklo, Yakone, and Lusa.

Toklo called across the gap, "Come on, Chenoa. You can do it!"

"They're waiting," Kallik pressed. She felt a glimmer of relief as Chenoa lifted a paw and began to pad to the edge of the black stone. "I'll make sure you get across," Kallik promised.

"And what about you?" The young she-bear's eyes clouded. "Will you make it?"

"Of course I will," Kallik huffed. "I've crossed more BlackPaths than you've eaten bunchberries."

A firebeast roared past. Kallik pressed against Chenoa, keeping her from whirling around and racing back into the trees. The young bear was as stiff as day-old prey.

"Look." Kallik pointed her snout to the next firebeast, then to the space beyond it. "We'll go after this one. There'll be plenty of time, but hurry."

Chenoa nodded her head slowly.

Kallik took a breath, to calm her own fear. She screwed up her eyes as the firebeast tore past. "Now!" Wind screaming in her ears, she nosed Chenoa onto the BlackPath.

Chenoa lunged forward.

"Keep going!" Kallik urged.

Chenoa plunged ahead, ears flat, head down as she raced for her life. Kallik charged after her, keeping a few steps behind, ready to shove Chenoa forward if she slowed even a pawstep. Blinded by rain, Kallik felt the ground soften beneath her paws. They'd reached the other side!

Chenoa stumbled into the forest. Lusa rushed to meet her,

pressing her muzzle into Chenoa's ruffled pelt.

"What in the spirits were you doing?" Yakone's angry bark took Kallik by surprise. "You seal-brain, you almost got flattened!"

"Someone had to help her," Kallik said.

Yakone's eyes blazed. "You risked your life!"

"She's one of us now!" Kallik bristled. "We take care of one another, or hadn't you noticed?"

She stomped into the woods. Toklo and Lusa were already pushing past a bramble bush up ahead, guiding Chenoa between them. Kallik followed them. Yakone trailed a few steps behind her, growling under his breath every time he had to climb over roots or veer around brambles. Kallik's pelt itched with irritation.

As the noise of the BlackPath faded, Chenoa lifted her muzzle and began to trot more calmly. She stopped when Lusa stumbled. "You need some help." Before the black bear could argue, Chenoa grabbed her scruff and started to shove her onto Toklo's back.

Lusa grabbed onto his thick pelt and clambered onto his shoulders. "Thanks."

Kallik smelled blood. A dark patch was staining Toklo's fur where Lusa lay. The race across the BlackPath must have opened her wounds.

"Are you going to ignore me all day?" Yakone muttered.

Kallik glanced over her shoulder. "If I have to."

"You should have let Toklo go back for her," Yakone growled.

"He was taking care of Lusa."

"What if you'd been killed?" Yakone snorted. "I'd be stuck here on my own." He glanced past Kallik at Toklo and Lusa.

Chenoa was padding at Toklo's shoulder, snuffling with amusement. "Can I have the next ride?" she teased.

Lusa lifted her head. "You could hop on behind me."

"Don't even try," Toklo puffed. "Lusa's heavy enough as it is!"

"Hey!" Lusa prodded him with a paw.

Yakone growled again. "So it's okay for black bears to stick together. But not white bears."

Kallik turned on him. "It's not like that and you know it!"

"Really?" Yakone halted. "Look how easily they move through this bear-trap." He kicked a trailing bramble with his paw. "We're like fish on ice here."

Kallik felt unease tug at her belly. "Do you wish you'd stayed on the Melting Sea?"

Yakone dropped his gaze. "You wanted to stay with your friends," he grunted. "And I promised to come with you."

"They're your friends, too," Kallik reminded him.

Yakone glanced at the other bears. "I know."

"They'll be the best friends you'll ever have, if you let them," she urged. Toklo and Lusa were far more than friends to her. They were her family now. She glanced sideways at Yakone. Would *he* ever feel that way about them? "Please let them be that for you, too, Yakone," she begged. What if she *had* been killed on the BlackPath? Yakone would need their friendship more than ever.

Ahead, Toklo paused and lifted his nose. "Can you hear that?" Lusa grabbed onto his fur with her forepaws to stop from slipping off.

"What is it?" Kallik hurried forward, ears pricked. The forest hummed with a noise that sounded like the buzzing of giant bees.

"Where's it coming from?" Yakone scanned the trees.

Toklo flicked his snout forward. "Over there."

"How can you tell?" Yakone cocked his head. Kallik understood his confusion. On the vast stretches of ice, it was easy to work out where noises came from. In the woods, sounds bounced from tree to tree until they sounded like they came from every direction at once.

"I don't like it," Chenoa muttered, a shiver running through her body.

"It sounds like firebeasts," Lusa said.

Toklo shook his head. "It's not growly enough."

"Firebeast *cubs*?" Lusa guessed.

Kallik touched her nose to Lusa's flank. "I don't think they have cubs."

Toklo shifted his paws; Lusa rocked on his shoulders. "Let's head for the shore," Toklo suggested.

Chenoa frowned. "Do you think we'll be safe there?"

"At least we can escape into the water if we have to." Kallik glanced anxiously at Yakone. Was this new danger going to make him more bad-tempered? Perhaps he should never have agreed to come. She shook the thought away. Yakone was brave and loyal. And he was her friend. Of course he had to come.

Toklo headed through the trees toward the river. Kallik could glimpse it already, flashing between the trunks. The land sloped downward under their paws, growing steeper and stonier. As they broke from the trees, it hardened to rock.

"Careful!" Toklo warned as he jarred to a halt. They were standing on the brink of a short, steep cliff.

Kallik peered over the edge. The river churned below, its shallows lapping a narrow, rocky shore. "How do we get down there?"

Chenoa hurried along the cliff top, sending grit showering over the edge. "There's a track here." She stopped and looked down. Jutting rocks made a steep path down to the shore. She headed down it, and Kallik flinched as more stones rattled down onto the beach.

"It's very narrow," Yakone muttered.

"You can climb an iceberg," Kallik reminded him. "Just stick your claws in and pray to the spirits."

"They're back at the Melting Sea," he grunted.

Kallik ignored him and marched past Toklo. Following Chenoa, she started down the narrow slope. It was little more than rocks clustered into a steep-sided pile. The cliff scraped one flank while spray whipped the other. Kallik focused on her paws, claws stretched as they slid on loose grit. Her heart lurched as she leaped across a gap, landing clumsily on the rock beyond.

"Come on, Kallik!" Chenoa had reached the beach and was calling from below. "You can do it!"

Taking a deep breath, Kallik scrabbled down the last three boulders and crunched onto the shore. A yelp made her turn. Lusa was clinging to Toklo's shoulders, wide-eyed, as the brown bear gingerly followed the path down.

"Careful!" Kallik called. "Watch your—"

She broke off with a gasp as the rock gave way and Toklo's hindpaw slid from under him. Stones showered Kallik's face. She shook them off and stared upward in horror.

Toklo was wobbling on three paws while he scrabbled for the edge with his flailing hindpaw. Lusa was barely hanging on, her legs dangling over Toklo's flank.

"Stay still!" Yakone roared from the top. Weaving his way down the slope, he caught up with Toklo and nipped the brown bear's stubby tail between his jaws. As Yakone held tight, Toklo lifted his hindpaw and placed it firmly back on the path. He leaned against the rock while Lusa scrambled back onto his shoulders.

Kallik's heart leaped in her chest. "By all the spirits!"

"We're okay!" Toklo called down. Slowly, he moved forward with Lusa clinging on. Yakone let go of his tail and followed close behind.

Kallik sighed with relief as the bears reached the bottom. "Lusa, are you all right?"

"I think so," she said in a small voice.

Kallik sniffed the black bear; fear-scent mingled with the smell of blood. Her wound was still seeping. "Chenoa." Kallik glanced over her shoulder. "Can you keep a lookout for more hornwort?"

Chenoa nodded, her eyes bright.

"Are you okay, Toklo?" Kallik touched her muzzle to his.

"I'm fine." Toklo pulled away. His eyes glittered. The slip on the path had scared him.

"You've been carrying Lusa for a while," Kallik pointed out. "Let me take her."

"I'll do it." Chenoa pushed between them. "I haven't carried her yet."

Lusa huffed, amused. "I'll forget how to walk if you all carry me."

"No way." Chenoa pushed close to Toklo, and Lusa hauled herself from one bear to the other. Kallik saw Chenoa's legs wobble for a moment, before she bravely trudged on as if Lusa were as light as a cub. "Once I find you some more hornwort, *you* can carry *me*."

Lusa poked her with a paw. "You just wait. One day I'll be big enough to carry Toklo!"

"I'd like to see that!" Chenoa set off upstream, snorting.

"Toklo?" Kallik searched his gaze. "Are you sure you're okay?"

"I nearly dropped her." He dipped his head, avoiding her gaze.

"But you didn't," Kallik soothed.

Yakone padded past them.

Toklo blinked. "Thanks for helping me."

Yakone shrugged. "You'd do the same for me." He followed Chenoa as she bounced from rock to rock along the narrow shore. Kallik hurried to catch up with him. There was just enough room to walk side by side, but where the rocks rose and fell, they had to take it in turns to jump the gaps.

They spoke little, concentrating on their paws. Kallik could still hear the angry buzzing from the forest, despite the river's roar. But it gradually faded behind them, and her shoulders relaxed.

The craggy shore gave way to smooth rocks, then a wide pebble beach. Toklo hurried past and caught up to Lusa and Chenoa.

"I miss the murmuring of the ice." Yakone's soft words surprised Kallik.

She nodded. "And the taste of salt in the air."

"At least it's stopped raining." Yakone looked up. Dark clouds streaked toward the horizon where the sun touched the treetops, setting the forest alight. Shadows crept across the shore.

Toklo turned and called across the beach. "We should stop for the night." He headed through a clump of knotweed into the forest. "Let's find somewhere to sleep before we hunt."

Yakone frowned as Toklo disappeared. "Not *another* night in the forest," he grunted. "Can't I sleep on the shore?"

"We have to sleep together," Kallik pointed out. "It's safer. And it'll be warmer for Lusa among the trees."

"I can't wait till we're back where we belong." Yakone padded heavily toward the trees, disappearing through the knotweed after Toklo.

"Look, look!" Lusa's voice rang from the woods. Kallik hurried to see. The black bear was limping around a fallen tree.

Chenoa was sniffing the hollow where the roots had been torn from the ground. "Soft, warm earth!" she exclaimed. She slithered into the dip and looked up at the wall of roots jutting above. "It's perfect to shelter us for the night."

Lusa tugged a thin root and began gnawing at it. "Still sweet!" she announced happily.

Toklo nodded. "You'll be able to see the river through the trees, Kallik."

Yakone sighed. "It's no ice-den, but it'll do."

Toklo headed for the shore. "Who wants to fish?"

"I'm happy here." Lusa didn't look up from the root she was happily chewing.

"Chenoa?" Toklo beckoned her with his muzzle. "The shallows look like good fishing. Do you want to join me?"

"Yes, please." Chenoa shook out her fur.

Kallik guessed she wasn't used to having a pelt full of dust from traveling. Her own fur itched with it. "Let's try fishing the deep currents, Yakone."

Yakone's gaze brightened. "I bet there are some fish worth catching there."

Kallik chortled. "We might find one as big as a seal." She headed for the shore, pebbles crunching underpaw as she reached the wide beach. Toklo and Chenoa were already splashing in the shallows. Kallik headed straight for deeper water, relieved to see Yakone bounding past her. A decent meal would cheer him up. And the water was freezing. He'd like that.

As the waves lapped her shoulders, Kallik dove beneath the surface, heading for the fast channels in the middle of the river. The tug of the water was exhilarating, like a mother pulling her cub in for its first swim. Kallik let it draw her downstream, watching bubbles swirl around her. Twirling, she spun through the water. Sky and river blurred as she tumbled.

The water swept through her fur, rinsing away the dirt and cooling her weary muscles. Bobbing to the surface, she floated on her back. The blue sky arced above her as an eddy swirled her around. Kallik kicked out with her powerful hind legs and dove under again. Swimming against the current, she pushed down to the riverbed. She was used to the black, bottomless sea, but here she could see rocks and pebbles streaming with weed, like a tiny landscape spread out beneath her. A fat sturgeon nibbled on a trailing plant, holding its place in the current with slow flicks of its tail. Kallik lunged and clamped her jaws around its belly. It was dead by the time she burst through the surface, and she carried it ashore, her neck aching with the weight of it.

Lusa stood on the beach. "Wow! That's huge!"

Toklo and Chenoa waded in the shallows. They hardly looked up as Kallik strode past and dropped the sturgeon at Lusa's paws.

"Guard it while I catch another." Kallik tossed her head, spattering Lusa with water.

"You love the river, don't you?" Lusa called as Kallik headed back to the water.

"It's not bad," she admitted.

Toklo ran his paw through the water as she passed. "The spirits of brown bears enter the river when they die," he was saying.

Chenoa stared into the shallows. "Really?"

Kallik slowed, pricking her ears.

"They are swept along with the fish that fed them and gave them life," Toklo explained to the wide-eyed black bear.

Kallik plunged into the depths once more, water blurring her sight. If she slept in the forest, she wouldn't see the stars. How would she see her mother glittering among the other stars, now that the ice had melted and set her spirit free? Had Nisa met Ujurak in the night sky?

A trout darted past, and she whipped around and grabbed it with her claws. Snapping it with her jaws, she held it fast till she'd caught another. Then she swam back to shore.

Yakone was still fishing far out as Kallik dropped her catch beside Lusa. She could see his white pelt cresting like a wave in the water.

"Lusa!" Toklo was trotting toward them, Chenoa at his side. The young she-bear held green stalks in her mouth.

"Hornwort!" Kallik recognized the shape of the leaves, and as they reached her, she detected the familiar scent.

Chenoa chewed the leaves to pulp and smoothed them into Lusa's wounds. Lusa winced, and Kallik peered at her rump anxiously.

"It's okay," Chenoa reassured her. "There's less swelling. It's healing well."

"What about the bleeding?" Kallik whispered. She didn't want to worry Lusa.

"Just a crack in the scab," Chenoa promised. "The hornwort will stop it from going bad."

Kallik sat down, and Lusa leaned against her. As they stared out across the river, Chenoa sniffed at the sturgeon.

"Take a bite," Kallik offered.

Toklo sat back on his haunches and scooped up a trout. "Can I eat this?"

Kallik chuffed. "Of course."

"Mmmm." Chenoa smacked her lips as she swallowed a mouthful of the sturgeon. "That's good." Her eyes sparkled. She looked so different from the young bear Hakan had bossed around.

Lusa was watching the black bear with her head on one side. "Wouldn't you rather eat berries or grubs than fish?" she queried.

Chenoa shrugged. "My mother always fed us fish, so I guess I'm used to it. Berries are great when they're around, but you can always find fish in the river."

Lusa shuddered. "You wouldn't say that if it was the only thing you could eat, *ever*."

"What do you mean?" Kallik teased. "You had some delicious fat seals to eat, as well!"

Lusa made a face, and Chenoa huffed with amusement. "I'm so glad I'm here," Chenoa said impulsively. "Thank you, all of you. I . . . I don't think I've ever felt more at home."

It was a moving burst of honesty, and Kallik dipped her head to the black bear. Friends could feel like home, as well as family. She knew exactly what Chenoa meant.

She looked up and saw Yakone padding from the river, a pike flapping in his jaws. He dropped it and leaned down to give it a killing bite. *I just hope Yakone feels the same. If not now, then someday.*

CHAPTER TWELVE

Lusa

Lusa woke with a start. She blinked open her eyes, surprised. Her wound wasn't throbbing. That hornwort really worked!

"You're awake at last." Chenoa was sitting back on her haunches beside her. She looked up from grooming her belly and stretched her muzzle toward Lusa. "You slept well."

Lusa glanced around the empty hollow. "Where is everyone?"

"Toklo took Yakone and Kallik hunting."

"Didn't you want to go?"

"I didn't want you to wake up alone."

Lusa sat up, careful not to scrape her wound on the pine needles. Moving didn't make it sting. She stood and stretched out one leg, then the other. "I'm better!"

"Let me check." Chenoa sniffed Lusa's rump. "You've got a nice tough scab and no swelling."

"Hornwort is great!"

"My mother taught me how to find it." Chenoa snorted cheerfully. "Hakan was always getting into scrapes. Always trying to climb too high. Our mother used to say he thought he was a squirrel, not a bear. Then he'd lose his grip and tumble through the branches. He used to hit every one on the way down. They broke his fall, but scratched him worse than brambles."

Lusa glanced at Chenoa, her heart twisting. How could she have happy memories of such a bully? Perhaps it was best that way. With luck, Chenoa would never see Hakan again. At least she could still think of him fondly. He was the only family she had left. *Apart from us, of course.*

Lusa pushed herself to her paws. "Let's go for a walk." She was feeling restless after too many days being carried.

Chenoa jumped up. "Where?"

Lusa glanced through the trees to the river, then back into the shadowy woods. The air was tangy with sap. Leaftime was near. "This way." She set off along a stale-smelling fox track. *The fox must be holed up with cubs somewhere.* Lusa opened her mouth warily as she moved, tasting for fresh scents. She didn't want to surprise a mother fox looking for food. It could be vicious if they scared it accidentally. Wolverine bites were bad enough.

Chenoa trotted after her as Lusa pushed past a clump of ragweed and headed toward sunlight. The pines thinned and gave way to birch and trembling aspen. The fox scent faded and quillwort sprang up, shimmering like grass across the forest floor. Lusa relished the warmth of the sun dappling her back. She searched the trees for a friendly spirit face. "Look." She halted.

Chenoa stumbled into her. "What?"

Lusa pointed to a lopsided knot halfway up an aspen trunk. "I bet he was grumpy when he was alive."

Chenoa followed her gaze, squinting. "Who was?"

"The spirit in that tree," Lusa whispered. "He's frowning even now." She shook out her pelt. "I wouldn't sleep under his branches. He'd drop leaves on me."

Chenoa made a face. "He does look a bit like a sore-paw."

"Hush! He'll hear us." Lusa hurried away.

Chenoa paused. "Look at that one!"

Lusa followed her gaze past the low branches of a birch. In the flaky bark, she saw a neat, round knot. "She must have been beautiful when she was alive."

"Ew!" Chenoa's gaze flicked to the next tree. "*She* wasn't!" A lumpy old knot stuck out from the bark.

"Be quiet!" Lusa hissed. "You're going to get us into trouble."

Chenoa waded through the quillwort. "Where are *your* family spirits?"

Lusa hurried after her. "My family is still alive." Her belly ached with a small twinge of longing. "At least, I think they are. They're back in the Bear Bowl."

Chenoa halted. "What's that?"

"It's where I lived before I escaped into the forest."

"Escaped?"

"The Bear Bowl is a special place where bears are looked after by flat-faces."

Chenoa blinked. "That sounds terrible!"

Lusa shook her head. "It was okay. They gave us food, and the Bear Bowl was pretty nice, and new flat-faces came every day."

"Why?"

Lusa tipped her head. "I don't know. They just stared at us. Sometimes they gave us fruit." She licked her lips, remembering.

"And you ate it?" Chenoa began pacing around Lusa, the fur pricking along her spine. "Did you trust them?"

"Why not?" Lusa started to feel defensive. "They never hurt us. They just looked at us."

"Flat-faces are strange," Chenoa decided.

"I guess," Lusa agreed. "But they gave us everything we needed. We were safe. There weren't BlackPaths or mean old bears like Hak—" She stopped when she saw Chenoa's eyes narrow. "There were a few grumpy bears, of course. But they never attacked anyone."

Chenoa searched Lusa's gaze. "Do you miss it?"

Lusa frowned. Her life there seemed so long ago. She'd traveled farther than she'd ever dreamed since then. "Sometimes. But I'm happier now."

"Do you ever wish you could go back?"

"Why would I? I'm a wild bear now, like you. Would you want to live in a Bear Bowl?"

"No!"

White petals fluttered at the corner of Lusa's eyes. When she turned, she saw it was a butterfly. Scampering after it, she swiped the air.

Chenoa chased after her. "I bet I can catch it." As the butterfly jerked upward, she jumped and clapped her paws together.

"You missed!" Lusa watched the white wings flicker away

through the branches. "Look, buds!" A green haze enfolded the tree. "There'll be blossoms soon."

Chenoa nudged Lusa. "And berries!" She bounded up a rise in the leafy forest floor. At the top, the leaves on a bush shivered as Chenoa stopped beside it. "Muskroot!" She sniffed at the leaves. "This'll have berries."

Lusa hurried to look. White flowers peeped out among the leaves. "Will they be eating-berries?"

"Oh, yes. They're delicious."

Lusa heard the rippling of a stream and saw water sparkling between the trees. She scrambled down the far side of the rise. A fallen tree blocked her way, but she scrabbled onto it.

"Careful!" Chenoa warned, catching up. "You don't want to open your wounds again."

Lusa had forgotten the wolverine bites. She stopped on top of the log. "I'm okay," she promised, but she slithered carefully down the other side.

Chenoa hopped over it easily and raced past Lusa. She splashed into the stream and let the bright water wash her paws. "Come on. It feels great!"

Lusa was already sliding down the bank. The water was cool, and the streambed was soft and sandy. Lusa stood and let her claws sink in as she leaned down to lap the cool water. After the heavy pull of the river, the gentle stream felt soothing.

Chenoa stared into the water, then frowned.

"What's wrong?" Lusa shook water from her snout.

Chenoa shrugged. "Nothing but minnows." She sighed. "Not worth catching."

Lusa hopped onto the bank, suddenly realizing she was hungry. "Let's find the others. They might have caught something."

They found Toklo, Kallik, and Yakone dozing, round-bellied, in the shade beside the hollow. The smell of fresh-killed prey swirled around them. Yakone's muzzle was stained with blood.

Toklo half opened an eye. "We were wondering where you were."

Lusa nudged him with a paw. "Were you?"

"I knew you'd be safe with Chenoa." He burped lazily and waved a paw toward the hollow. "We saved you a wood duck."

Lusa's mouth watered when she saw the juicy bird. She didn't eat a lot of meat when she had other choices, but this was one of her favorites. "Thanks." She crouched beside it and tore off a piece for Chenoa.

"I love duck." Chenoa scooped it up and chewed happily.

Lusa took a bite. It felt good to have a black bear to travel with. Now, when she thought of reaching the mountains, she didn't get the same fluttery feeling in her belly. *Toklo will be happy to be home, Kallik and Yakone can go back to the ice, and I'll have Chenoa.* She watched her new friend munching. *She'll stay with me, won't she?* Lusa swallowed, vowing to be the best friend Chenoa ever had. *Then she'll never want to leave.*

Yakone sat up. "Are we traveling today?" He looked up through the branches. The sun was already sliding down toward the horizon.

Kallik rolled onto her back. "Perhaps we should have a day's rest to give Lusa a chance to heal."

"I'm feeling a lot better," Lusa told her.

Kallik's eyes slowly shut. "I'm glad." A moment later, she was snoring, her full belly moving gently with each breath.

Toklo yawned. "I guess we're staying here another night."

Lusa's paws itched. It was comfortable here, but she felt she'd held them up long enough. Shouldn't they be moving on? She finished her piece of duck and glanced up at Chenoa.

The she-bear was rubbing feathers from her muzzle. "What's up?"

Lusa looked around at her sleeping companions. "I've had enough rest," she whispered.

"Let's leave these lazy old possums to sleep." Chenoa got to her paws. "We can ride the fast currents."

Lusa swallowed. *Ride the fast currents!* Did that mean swimming in the middle of the river? She hadn't been deeper than the shallows yet. She looked past the trees at the rushing water.

Chenoa headed toward the shore. "Don't worry. You'll love it."

Lusa trotted after her. She felt less confident as Chenoa waded deeper and deeper into the river. When the water lapped her shoulders, Lusa paused. "Chenoa?"

Chenoa glanced back. "What?"

"It's a bit deep." Lusa could already feel the current tugging her paws.

"Don't worry!" Chenoa ducked underwater and vanished, leaving a trail of bubbles on the surface.

Lusa stared at the foaming waves. What was Chenoa doing?

A moment later, the black bear bobbed up. Her shoulders pumped as she churned the water with her paws. She was clearly at home in the swollen river and swimming easily in the current. "I see some rocks you can stand on while I teach you."

Lusa scanned the surging water. She couldn't see any rocks. "I can't—" Before she could object, Chenoa nudged her forward. Lusa scrambled to keep her footing as the water snatched her and dragged her downstream.

Chenoa grabbed her scruff. "Reach with your paws," she puffed through Lusa's pelt.

Lusa flapped her paws, feeling the drag of the current, relieved as her claws hit rocks jutting up from the riverbed. "Found them!"

Chenoa paddled hard and kept her grip on Lusa's scruff while Lusa found a pawhold.

"Ready!" Lusa planted herself firmly, and Chenoa let go.

Lusa braced herself against the current. It buffeted her legs and dragged at her fur.

"Watch me!" Chenoa let the swirling water grab her.

Lusa gasped as the river swept the other bear downstream, fast as a leaf. Powerful eddies swirled Chenoa this way and that until she flipped over and began to swim back to Lusa. "Try it!"

Lusa swallowed. "How do I stop?" What if the currents carried her all the way back to the Melting Sea?

Chenoa pointed her nose along the fast-moving channel. "Do you see where the fast water turns to slow water?"

Lusa narrowed her eyes. The frothing channel Chenoa had ridden was edged by smoother waves. "I see!"

"Swim toward the slow water when you want to stop."

Chenoa nudged Lusa off the rock. "I'll keep up with you!"

Lusa hardly heard Chenoa's words. A blast of water shot her downstream. Her legs swept beneath her, held stiff by the current. Water rushed up her nose. "Help!" She fought to stay upright, but the river twirled her around, dunking her snout beneath the waves. She splashed out blindly. "Chenoa!"

A black shape surfaced beside her. Lusa pushed against the current and reached out a paw, thankful to feel Chenoa's warm pelt. She grabbed it. Relief swamped her as she felt Chenoa's steady paddling.

"Relax!" Chenoa shouted above the rumble of the water.

Lusa forced her stiff legs to move with the flow. Suddenly the water seemed to cradle her instead of fighting her. It carried her so smoothly that Lusa relaxed even more. The sensation of floating at the same speed as the river was breathtaking. *This is how eagles must feel when they soar.* Tentatively, she loosened her grip on Chenoa and floated free. Sticking out her paws, she lay on her back and let the river weave her around eddies and swoop her up and down, through waves and troughs.

"Come on!" Chenoa held out a paw and guided Lusa toward smooth water.

Released from the current, Lusa slowed and began swimming, her legs churning beneath her. "That was great!"

"Let's swim back and do it again!" Chenoa turned and headed upstream. Excited, Lusa splashed after her.

By the time they'd reached the start, Toklo was standing on the shore. Lusa swam for the shallows till her paws hit the riverbed. Standing up, she called to Toklo, "We're river riding!"

"What?" Toklo padded to the water's edge.

Chenoa bounded out to meet him. "Come and play!"

Toklo followed her into the water, frowning. "What's river riding?"

Lusa splashed back toward the racing currents. "You'll love it. Chenoa taught me." She swam through the smooth water to the edge of the rapids. Chenoa and Toklo caught up.

"Do you see the fast current?" Chenoa pointed out the frothing channel to Toklo.

"You swim in that?" Toklo looked uncertain.

"You don't *have* to swim!" Lusa spluttered as she swallowed a mouthful of river water.

Chenoa puffed a warning at her. "Careful, Lusa. Don't forget the river's way bigger than us, and it doesn't care if you sink or swim."

Lusa spat out the water, undaunted. "Can we try a faster channel?" She looked beyond the one they'd already ridden. Another current swept even more swiftly beyond it.

"Let Toklo try this one first." Chenoa nudged the brown bear forward. "I know you're a good swimmer, Toklo, but it's easier if you don't try to swim at all. The river thinks it's fighting you and makes it hard. Just trust the water to carry you."

Toklo blinked at her, water washing around his scruff. "You mean float?"

"Exactly!" Chenoa flicked her snout, drops spraying from her muzzle.

With a grunt, Toklo launched himself into the fast-moving stream. The current snatched him away. With a yelp of surprise, he was swept downstream.

Lusa watched his paws flail. "Will he be okay?" Alarm

flashed though her as she watched him struggle against the current. Then she saw his head rise above the frothing waves. He stopped floundering and slid fast over the water.

"He's got it!" Chenoa huffed as Toklo sailed smoothly away.

"My turn!" Lusa dove forward, through the fast channel and beyond. The river snatched her and dragged her downstream, so fast that she gasped.

"Lusa!" Chenoa's shout alarmed her. It was edged with panic.

Lusa jerked her head around, fighting the current. Was Chenoa all right? She glimpsed a wide yellow shape at the corner of her vision.

"Rafts!" Chenoa bellowed.

Lusa twisted, fighting the current to see behind her. Huge yellow shapes were racing across the top of the water. Flatfaces peered over the sides, bundled up in colorful pelts. They were dipping broad-ended sticks in and out of the water, steering the yellow rafts. One of them was heading straight toward her.

Lusa floundered, struggling to escape the channel. Paws churning wildly, she pushed for smoother water, but the current was ferocious. She couldn't break free. The raft was gaining on her.

"Toklo!" Chenoa's roar sounded faint through the rumbling of the river.

Lusa's heart pounded in her ears. The raft bore down on her till all she could see was water and yellow. Terrified, she took a gulp of air and dove underwater. The raft thumped her spine as she pulled herself down. She spun, dazed. Water rushed up her nose and into her mouth. It filled her ears and dragged at her fur. Lusa struggled for the surface, but it had disappeared in a storm of bubbles.

Her lungs ached for air. *River spirits, help me!*

Strong teeth pinched her scruff. Firm claws snagged her pelt. She felt fur swirl softly against hers. She let herself fall limp. In a moment she was above the surface as stout paws pushed her through the churning channels into smooth water. *Ujurak?*

"Lusa!" Toklo's growl sounded in her ear. "Are you okay?"

Lusa blinked water from her eyes. Chenoa and Toklo were bobbing around her, their gazes anxious. Slowly she began to stroke her paws through the water, swimming gently, relieved by the smoothness of the water washing around her. Chenoa let her go, then Toklo.

"Thanks," Lusa gasped.

"I thought the flat-faces had drowned you!" Toklo's eyes were round with horror.

Lusa gazed downriver, feeling dizzy. The yellow rafts were bobbing away over the rapids. The flat-faces stared back, openmouthed as the river washed them downstream.

"Come on." Chenoa nudged Lusa toward the shore.

Lusa paddled in, relieved as her paws scraped pebbles. She waded from the river and shook out her pelt. Toklo circled her anxiously. "Are you sure you're okay?"

"She's fine." Chenoa nosed him away. "It was an adventure, wasn't it, Lusa?"

Lusa looked into Chenoa's sparkling gaze. It hadn't felt like an adventure when she'd been fighting for her life. But now that she thought back, it did seem exciting. She'd been out in the rapids and escaped a flat-face raft. The exhilaration of being swept along by the current sent a fiery tingle through her paws.

Toklo pushed past Chenoa. "She won't be doing it again."

"Doing what again?" Kallik's call surprised Lusa. The white bear was hurrying along the beach toward them, Yakone at her heels. "You look half-drowned. What's happened?"

"Lusa just escaped a flat-face raft," Chenoa told her proudly.

"What?" Kallik stopped beside Lusa and sniffed her. "Are you hurt?"

Lusa realized that her wolverine bites were throbbing. Had she grazed them on the riverbed when the river had tossed her around? "I'm okay," she reassured Kallik. She didn't want to be fussed over.

But Kallik was already hustling her toward the trees. "Let's get you tucked in your nest." She growled under her breath. "There are too many flat-faces around here."

"I'm fine," Lusa insisted.

"She's been riding the river," Chenoa announced.

Kallik paused. "Doing *what*?"

Toklo nudged Lusa on. "It doesn't matter," he muttered. "She's safe, and she won't be doing it again."

"Why not?" Chenoa sounded offended as Kallik led them through the bracken. "She was a natural. And I was there to look after her." She touched Lusa's head with her snout. "I won't let you get washed away, little one."

Lusa shook her off. "I'm not little!" she snapped.

Kallik scrambled down into the sleeping hollow and started brushing pine needles to make a nest for Lusa. "Snuggle down here before you get cold," she ordered.

Lusa met her gaze, ready to argue. She didn't need to be treated like a cub! But tiredness pulled at her paws. Her fur felt heavy and her wound throbbed. "Okay." Sighing, she slid into the nest that Kallik had made. She looked up at Chenoa. "I don't always need rescuing," she told her firmly. Chenoa had saved her from the wolverines, and now she'd helped save her from drowning. "I've traveled a long way."

Chenoa's gaze grew serious. "I know, Lusa." The young she-bear padded down into the hollow and curled around Lusa. "You're way braver and stronger than I'll ever be. You've seen more things than I could imagine."

Lusa nestled into the warmth of Chenoa's thick pelt. "I have, haven't I?" she murmured, closing her eyes. She rested her muzzle on Chenoa's flank. How much more was she going to see before the journey was over? And when it was, what would happen next? With her thoughts growing hazy with exhaustion, she let herself drift into sleep.

CHAPTER THIRTEEN

Toklo

Toklo glanced up at the sky. White clouds were sailing across a sea of blue. Beside him, sunshine shimmered on the crystal river. In the days since Lusa had recovered enough to walk, the weather had grown steadily warmer. Toklo relished it. For the first time since leaving the Melting Sea, he felt warm to his bones. Lusa and Chenoa were clearly enjoying the sunny weather, too, charging ahead on the grassy slope that threaded between the forest and shore.

"Don't wear yourselves out!" Toklo called as they dodged back and forth, play-hunting each other to break up the monotony of walking. "I want to keep going till sundown."

Behind him, Kallik and Yakone were wading into the river. Toklo glanced at their dripping pelts as they sent water spraying up around them. He knew that the sun was hard on the two white bears, and it was not even at its strongest. They should be traveling in the shade of the forest, but Yakone still resented the snagging roots and branches and the angry buzzing of flat-face beasts that hummed in the distance as though colonies had built hives deep in the forest.

So they followed the river. Its constant murmur was reassuring. Besides, Kallik and Yakone could cool off when they chose. Toklo heard them now, splashing through the shallows. Soon they were swimming against the current in deep water.

Toklo saw their white heads bobbing through the waves. He checked upstream for yellow rafts. His belly still fluttered with fear as he remembered Lusa disappearing under the flat-face raft. For a moment he thought she'd drowned. He pushed the memory away. They were so close to the end of their journey; they had survived so much already. Nothing bad could happen now.

Chenoa scrambled down the grassy slope and stopped beside a thick clump of weed. "Look, Lusa!"

Lusa hurried down to see. "It's just sedge."

"No, it's not." Chenoa pulled out a pawful. She wafted it under Lusa's nose.

Lusa's eyes brightened. "What a strange scent! Can I eat it?"

"Yes."

Lusa chewed on a stalk, ears twitching with surprise. "That tastes weird, but nice."

Chenoa waved a few leaves at Toklo. "Do you want some?"

"No, thanks," Toklo called back.

"It's delicious," Chenoa promised.

"Then let Lusa have it." Roots and grass were fine when a bear was starving, but forest prey was rich, and with five bears hunting together, it was easy to catch food before their bellies started to rumble. Toklo would save grass for when he had no choice.

Kallik splashed through the shallows toward him. Yakone was still plowing upstream, keeping abreast of Toklo despite the current. Toklo watched him, impressed. White bears were skillful swimmers. How come they couldn't walk through a wood without tripping? Of course, they must wonder why he swam so awkwardly when he could plunge so effortlessly through leafy undergrowth.

Kallik caught up with Toklo, her pelt glittering wet.

Toklo made room as she fell in beside him. "Are you cool now?"

"Yes, thanks." Kallik glanced at Yakone. "But I don't know if he'll ever feel cold enough when he's not on the ice." She pointed with her snout toward Chenoa and Lusa. The two she-bears had stopped chewing leaves and were scampering along the edge of the trees some way ahead. "I'm glad they get along so well," she rumbled.

"Wow! A bear spirit!" Lusa stopped and pointed at an old pine. She huffed and hurried on, pointing to another.

"They're like littermates," Toklo agreed warmly. The high spirits of the two younger bears made up for the dark cloud Yakone seemed to carry with him. The white bear had stopped complaining, but it was clear that he wasn't happy traveling inland. *Was* I *such a sore-paw when I was on the ice?*

Kallik interrupted his thoughts. "Isn't it great to have friends traveling with us?"

"You mean Chenoa?"

"And Yakone."

"Sure." Toklo glanced at Kallik. Was she worried that he was still annoyed the white bear had joined them? "They're both great." Yakone wasn't exactly fun, but he was easy to hunt with, loyal, and strong.

Kallik sighed. "I miss Ujurak. I know he's back where he belongs, but I wish he was still with us."

Toklo grunted. *Back where he belongs.* Was it true that Ujurak had never been a *real* bear? That he came from the *stars*? Toklo's head buzzed, and he shoved the thought away.

"Look!" Lusa's excited bark sounded ahead. She was pointing to a flat-face pelt-den planted on the shore upstream.

Toklo bristled. Flat-face scent tinged the air. What if they were waiting inside the den with firesticks? He motioned Chenoa and Lusa toward the woods, where thick undergrowth spilled out.

As they scrambled up the bank, Toklo called to Yakone, "Flat-faces!"

Yakone waded from the river, shaking water from his pelt. He caught up with Toklo as the grizzly bear pushed through the thick bracken crowding the edge of the forest. "Is there any place *without* flat-faces?"

Chenoa was waiting with Kallik and Lusa underneath the pines. Her eyes were round with worry. "Did you see them?"

Toklo shook his head. The pelt-den fluttered in the breeze—he could see it through the trees—but there was no sign of flat-faces.

Lusa tasted the air. "I can't smell any." Her eyes were bright. "But I *can* smell their food."

Chenoa's pelt spiked. "Let's get out of here."

Toklo shifted his paws uncertainly. The thick smell of flat-face treats was making his mouth water.

Lusa opened her mouth. "It smells delicious!" She began to creep nearer to the pelt-den. Toklo followed.

Behind them, Yakone growled. "Careful."

Kallik shushed him. "Let them look."

"Look?" Lusa blinked. "Let's take it."

"No!" Chenoa stiffened. "You remember what happened last time we tried to steal flat-face food." She glared at Toklo.

Lusa blinked. "But I'm great at raiding flat-face dens. Just watch!" She charged forward, but Toklo caught her tail.

"Hold on."

Lusa scowled at him.

"Let's see if there are any flat-faces in there." He lifted his muzzle and roared. Then he peered at the den.

No flat-faces rushed out. No flicker of movement at all.

"Kallik, Yakone." Toklo pointed his snout toward the trees. "Can you check for flat-face trails?" Kallik grunted, and they headed away.

Sniffing the ground, Toklo padded toward the shore. Lusa and Chenoa crept after him as he pushed through the thick bracken at the edge of the trees. The pelt-den was a few bear-lengths away.

Lusa nosed in beside him. "Let me go first."

"Lusa, be careful." Chenoa's voice trembled.

"She's done this before," Toklo reassured the black she-bear. "But we'll wait for Kallik and Yakone to report back."

As he spoke, fur swished through the undergrowth behind.

"We followed a flat-face trail," Kallik hissed.

Yakone twitched his ears. "It was heading into the woods. It's quite stale. They left some time ago."

"They'll be deep in the forest by now," Lusa pleaded.

Toklo glanced at Kallik. "What do you think?" He licked his lips. The scent of flat-face food filled the air.

Kallik's nostrils twitched. "Let her try."

Lusa huffed with excitement and darted from the bracken. Beside him, Toklo felt Chenoa stiffen as their friend galloped to the side of the den and, quick as a fox, slit open the pelt with her claws. She slid inside.

"She'll be okay," Toklo promised Chenoa, praying it was true.

A few moments later, Lusa popped out, dragging a bundle. She hauled it back toward the trees.

"Let's get out of here!" Toklo nodded upstream and broke into a run. He veered past the pelt-den and raced beside the river. Behind him, he could hear pawsteps, and Lusa's bundle swishing against her legs.

As the river curved around a corner, Toklo slowed to a halt on a stretch of sandy shore. Yakone and Kallik slowed behind him, panting hot breath on his haunches. The pelt-den was hidden behind trees. Lusa dropped the bundle and ripped open the covering. Bright shapes tumbled out.

Chenoa approached them, nostrils twitching. "What prey is that?"

"Wait and see," Lusa declared.

Toklo licked his lips, remembering the sweet and salty

morsels Lusa had stolen from flat-face dens before.

Kallik clearly remembered, too. She padded toward Lusa, eyes bright with excitement. "What did you get?"

Lusa ripped open a bright red shape and scattered round, yellow flakes onto the shore. They looked like pale crispy leaves. Kallik grabbed one delicately between her teeth and passed it to Yakone. Lusa nosed a few flakes toward Chenoa. Toklo leaned forward and lapped up a tongueful, leaving plenty for Lusa. The salt tasted delicious on his tongue, and he crunched and swallowed the flakes eagerly.

Lusa was already ripping the shiny skin from another treat. She tasted it, snuffling with delight, then turned to another and began scooping out sweet-smelling goo.

Toklo's belly rumbled. Each new flavor tasted better than the last. He watched Yakone and Chenoa, guessing they'd never tasted flat-face food before, and huffed with pleasure as he saw their wary gazes light up.

"What's this?" Chenoa rolled a shiny cylinder beneath her paw.

Yakone sniffed it. "It doesn't smell like food."

Toklo recognized the shape. "You have to open it. Like clams."

Yakone pulled the cylinder away from Chenoa and examined it. "There's no place to get your claw in."

Toklo reached for a stone. It slipped in his claws, and he curled them more firmly around it. Concentrating hard, he dragged it toward him. "Put the shiny clam down on the sand."

As Yakone dropped the cylinder, Toklo hit it with the stone. The cylinder exploded, spraying hissing orange water over Yakone. Yakone jerked away, his pelt stained.

Kallik snorted with laughter and began lapping at Yakone's fur. "It's like honey," she told him between licks. "You should taste it."

Yakone growled, his pelt bristling on his shoulders. Pulling away, he stamped to the river's edge and plunged in. Toklo watched him go, feeling a stab of sympathy. No bear liked losing his dignity.

As the shiny litter fluttered down the beach, Chenoa sat back on her haunches. "That was delicious, Lusa! How did you learn how to find food like that?"

Lusa burped. "When I first left the Bear Bowl, flat-face food was all I could find."

Toklo nudged her with his nose. "Gathering it was a good skill to learn." He turned to Chenoa. "Lusa saved us from starving more than once by stealing flat-face food. Didn't she, Kallik?"

"Huh?" Kallik wasn't listening. She was watching Yakone rinse his pelt in the shallows.

Toklo followed her gaze. Was Kallik wondering whether they'd made the right decision about coming so far inland? *So far.* The thought of the long journey behind them sparked thoughts of home. Toklo stood up. *We should get moving.* They'd lingered too long.

"Come on." Toklo jerked his nose upstream. "Let's go."

CHAPTER FOURTEEN

Toklo

Lusa scrambled to her paws and headed off with Chenoa. Toklo watched them go, their heads bobbing as they chatted happily. "Are you coming?" he called over his shoulder.

Kallik was still watching Yakone. "I thought the food might cheer him up," she sighed.

Before Toklo could answer, Lusa called back to them. "Hey, Kallik! Chenoa wants to know if flat-face food tastes better than seal."

Kallik dragged her gaze from Yakone. Toklo nudged her forward. "Go with Lusa," he murmured. "I'll wait for Yakone. He'll feel better once he's clean."

Kallik dipped her head and hurried away.

Toklo met Yakone as he waded out. "Okay?"

Yakone grunted and headed along the shore. Toklo fell in beside him. They padded on in silence, Yakone swinging his head. Beside them, the forest began to rise. The grassy verge turned to rocks, then cliffs on either side. Soon, they were following the river through a deep gorge.

Toklo glanced at Yakone. His eyes were dark. "Didn't you like the flat-face food?" he ventured.

"It tasted good," Yakone conceded. "But it's not bear food, is it? Can you imagine having to eat it every day?"

"Not every day," Toklo commented. "But once in a while's fun."

"Bears should eat prey they share territory with," Yakone huffed. "That's why it's there. It's unnatural, eating flat-face rubbish."

"I guess you miss seal and saltwater fish." Toklo glanced at Yakone. "I used to miss woodland prey. So I know how you feel. Perhaps you'll be more used to it by the time we reach the end of our journey."

Yakone swung his head around. "When will that be?"

"Chenoa's shown me the mountains on the horizon," Toklo told him. "Once we're there, I just need to find a good place to mark out my territory." He could imagine woodland, stretching like a pelt over the mountainside. He pictured marking boundaries beneath the trees. His heart quickened. It wouldn't be long now.

"What about Lusa?" Yakone pointed out. "Will we have to find her home, too?"

Toklo's pelt started to prick. "You didn't *have* to come—"

"No, I didn't," Yakone growled. "Kallik and I had found our own home on the Melting Sea. But she insisted on coming with you. Did you think I'd let her travel by herself?"

"I'm glad you *did* come," Toklo confessed. "It would have been hard on Kallik to come so far inland and then travel back to the ice alone. It means a lot to me and Lusa that you're traveling with her."

Yakone looked at him. "Really?" He sounded surprised. Toklo studied him. Did Yakone think they didn't want him there?

"Yakone! Toklo!" Kallik trotted toward them. "Have you seen that?" She gestured upriver with her snout. Ahead of them, just visible around a curve in the gorge, a wall of water pounded down into the river, abruptly ending it.

Toklo blinked. He had to tip his head right back to see the top of the water, which loomed above them. The sides of the gorge were even higher here, taller than several trees end to end.

Yakone stood still. "It's like a glacier come to life," he whispered.

"No, it's a waterfall!" Toklo stared, suddenly realizing that the cliffs were ringing with its roar. Rainbows rose from its spray. It was a spectacular sight, but Toklo felt disappointment drag at his belly. The river had led them to a dead end, but the water had to be coming from somewhere. The river must continue on the other side of the falls. "We'll have to go back and climb through the forest," he said heavily.

Kallik's eyes clouded. "You mean, go back to where the gorge starts? It'll be a long way around."

Yakone had walked farther upstream and was staring at the tumbled rocks on either side of the waterfall. "Couldn't we climb up there?" he said.

Toklo narrowed his eyes. The rocks shone like silver, slick

with spray. "We'd never get a grip on that stone." Their claws weren't meant for digging into rock. What if one of them fell?

"It'll take an extra day's walking to go around," Yakone pressed.

Kallik caught Toklo's eye. "Let's at least get closer and see if there's a way up the cliffs."

Toklo studied the distance. It wouldn't take that long to walk to the falls, and if there truly was a way up the side, it would save retracing their steps. The tug in his belly toward the mountains made Toklo feel it would be physically painful to turn back in search of a different route. "Okay, we'll take a look," he grunted.

They trekked in single file along the narrow strip of shore. The water came right up to the sides of the gorge in several places, meaning they had to splash through, resisting the pull of the current. The river grew more and more turbulent as they neared the end of the gorge, splashing and frothing until the bears' pelts dripped and they had to screw up their eyes against the spray. The noise of the falling water was so deafening that they couldn't speak to one another. Toklo started to wonder if they'd even make it to the bottom of the cliffs.

Then Yakone, who was ahead of him, stopped abruptly. Toklo almost crashed into the white bear's haunches. He peered around Yakone's bulk and saw they were as near to the cliffs as they could get without being lost in the tumultuous falling water, which filled the entire width of the gorge. The bears huddled together on the tiny patch of shore. They had to bellow to make themselves heard above the roar of the falls.

Kallik tipped back her head and stared at the rocks that were visible above the mist of tumbling water. "I think we could do it!" she barked. "I can see plenty of pawholds."

Toklo followed her gaze. The gorge rose in a steep face beside the falls, but there were lots of ledges and jutting stones.

Chenoa stroked the wet stone under her paws, smoothed by countless moons of spray. "It's more slippery than ice," she warned. "And we'll be right inside the falling water for the first half of the climb."

Toklo squinted through the mist. He could just make out the end of the gorge where their climb would start. It would be worse than rain; it would be like being underwater. *Will we* drown? he wondered. "It's going to be dangerous," he said. "Yakone, what do you think?"

He shifted sideways to let the white bear move up. Yakone stared at the cliff. "Without the water, it wouldn't be too difficult," he commented.

"We've been wet before," Kallik pointed out. "I vote for trying."

Toklo looked at Lusa. "What about you?"

Lusa bristled and lifted herself to her full height. "I'll be fine! Kallik's right, we've been soaked to the skin before."

Chenoa leaned close to the little black bear. "And I'm here to help you," she reminded Lusa.

Lusa snorted. "I think you'll find that *I'm* here to help *you*!" The black bears huffed with amusement.

"If we're going to do it, there's no point waiting any longer and getting even wetter," Kallik said. "Come on." She started padding into the spray. Her white pelt was almost instantly swallowed up.

Chenoa and Lusa bounded after her, dark shadows inside the mist. They slipped past Kallik and launched themselves at the rock face. Toklo hissed, but Yakone said, "Let them lead. That way we can keep an eye on them, and they can set the pace."

Chenoa scrambled up the first few rocks, finding pawholds on the pitted stone. Lusa followed closely, using the same nooks to pull herself up. Kallik took a slightly different route, able to use pawholds that were farther apart. Toklo hesitated by the foot of the cliff, tipping his head back as he strained to see the top. It was clouded in spray and seemed farther away than the clouds. He felt Yakone nudge him.

"Go on," the white bear grunted. "We'll be okay."

Toklo heaved himself onto the first rock and stretched up for pawholds. The stone felt perilously slippery beneath his pads, but suddenly his paws lodged in a smooth-edged crevice and he was able to pull himself quite easily up to the next jutting boulder. He tried not to look at the falling water thundering past him a bearlength away. Its speed made him dizzy. His ears throbbed at the sound. He fixed his gaze on the rock immediately above him and concentrated on keeping his balance and finding new pawholds—front paws, then back paws, front, then back.

Before long, his claws ached as he pulled himself up, from ledge to ledge. He lost sight of the others in the spray, but he could hear the black bears calling encouragement to each other. Chenoa was leading them through a zigzagging route across the rock, but she was finding firm ledges with easy pawholds. Just above Toklo, Kallik was silent, only letting out the occasional grunt as she heaved herself up. Toklo realized that the black bears were finding this easier than the others because of their lighter bodies.

Suddenly his head emerged above the cloud of spray. The air was still soaked in tiny droplets, but he could see the trees beside him more clearly now. He risked a glance upward. They were nearly at the top! The cliff ended abruptly just a few bearlengths ahead, giving way to gray, sullen sky. Lusa was hopping from rock to rock as though they were branches. Chenoa was just above her, swarming up the cliff like a lizard.

Toklo focused on a pawhold a muzzlelength above his reach. Pushing off with his hind legs, he sprang up and clamped his forepaws around the ledge and dragged himself up. Relieved, he tumbled onto a wide shelf of rock and stopped to catch his breath. It was much quieter here. His pelt dripped and his paws stung. *Not much farther,* he told himself, over the sound of his racing heart.

There was a shriek from above. "We made it!" Chenoa cheered.

"Come on, slow slugs!" Lusa called down.

Toklo hauled himself to his paws and studied the last stretch of rock. The quickest route was directly upward, using the overhanging lip above his current ledge. Leaning back, Toklo could just see Kallik vanishing over the very top of the cliff. He heard yelps of delight from the black bears. Looking over his shoulder, he saw Yakone scrambling up closer to the edge of the forest, his paws slipping on loose stones.

"Careful!" Toklo warned. Yakone just grunted.

Toklo reared up on his hindpaws and stretched his front paws over the edge of the lip above him. His claws sank into the tiny grooves on the surface of the rock. He lifted his hindpaws briefly, testing his weight, then took a deep breath and pushed as hard as he could. For a moment, his body swung in empty air, and Toklo caught a glimpse of the pounding mist far below. His claws slipped on the ledge, and he let out a snarl. Digging in once more, he heaved his belly over the lip and rolled sideways onto the rock. He looked up, panting heavily, to see Lusa and Chenoa peering down at him. Their eyes were huge with terror.

"Did you think you could fly?" Chenoa squeaked.

Toklo was too out of breath to speak. He scrambled over the last rocks and pulled himself onto the cliff top. Just a bearlength away, the river was as smooth as a trout as it slid over the edge of the cliff.

"That was fun!" Chenoa bounced on her paws.

"Are you okay, Toklo?" Lusa sniffed him.

"Fine," Toklo puffed. He padded away from the edge and sat beside Yakone, who had arrived a few moments before him. "We made it," Toklo breathed.

Yakone nodded. "I knew we would."

The river looked wide and peaceful beside them, slipping gracefully toward the waterfall before it tumbled down. Toklo wondered what happened to the fish. Did they know there was a drop, or did the river just sweep them over?

"Come on." He felt uneasy being so close to the edge. The others jumped up, complaining mildly of sore claws and scratched pads, and followed Toklo upriver. The shore was hard going, the uneven rocks jolting his legs as he hopped down one boulder, then climbed the next. He glanced back, checking on the others. Chenoa and Lusa were helping each other, steadying, nudging, and sidestepping as they scrambled along the beach. Kallik and Yakone walked in single file. Yakone's gaze was dark as he brought up the rear; he was concentrating hard on every step, on a surface that couldn't have been more different from cool, smooth ice.

Toklo wrinkled his nose. He could smell the fragrant tang of flat-face food, tinged with BlackPath stench. He stopped, pelt twitching. The trees were retreating from the shoreline, leaving a wide-open space, and he could make out a herd of bright pelts farther upstream.

Flat-faces.

He stopped. "Look," he hissed over his shoulder.

Lusa caught up with him. "Why are they here?"

Ahead, the shore was swarming with flat-faces. They crowded right to the edge, wrapped against the chill in thick, colorful pelts, pointing at the river as it disappeared over the falls. Bright white flashes exploded among them, curiously silent apart from shrieks from the flat-faces.

Toklo flinched. "They've got firesticks!"

"No." Lusa pressed against him. "There's no noise, is there? And the lights are much smaller. The flat-faces who came to the Bear Bowl made flashes like that," she explained. "They come from flash boxes."

Toklo stared. "What are flash boxes?"

"Dunno," Lusa snorted. "But they seemed to make the flat-faces happy. They flashed at everything. Now they're flashing at the waterfall."

"Everywhere we go, we trip over flat-faces!" Yakone stopped behind them. "It's not like the ice."

"I know," Toklo agreed. "Perhaps we're crossing their migration path."

Beside the flat-faces, a wide stretch of BlackPath was crowded with firebeasts of every size and color.

Kallik reached Yakone, ears twitching. "A flat-face colony, guarded by firebeasts!"

"How will we get past it?" Yakone growled.

"We could head into the woods and circle around," Toklo suggested.

"No!" Chenoa gulped. "There'll be BlackPaths all over the woods if that many firebeasts are here." She began to back away, as if she was seriously considering retracing her route down the cliff.

"It's okay." Lusa nuzzled her.

"But she's right," Yakone muttered. "There's probably a tangle of BlackPaths through there, all full of flat-faces and firebeasts."

"What are we going to do?" Kallik asked. "There's no way past them."

Toklo gazed across the river. The far shore was empty.

It was wider and more pebbly than where they stood now, though not as wide as where the flat-faces stood. But that meant the trees were closer to the water, offering good cover if they needed to hide, and a source of prey. "It would be better if we could travel on that side of the river," Toklo pointed out. He studied the flat, shining surface of the river. "We could swim across."

"I don't know. The currents are probably stronger than they look," Kallik warned. "And it's a long way to swim when we're tired."

"There are rocks showing above the water." Lusa pointed out wide, smooth stones dotting the river. "We could use them to rest between swims."

Toklo's gaze flicked from one boulder to the next. They were widely spaced, but they reached right across. The water moved swiftly around them. He narrowed his eyes, judging the distance from the boulders to the edge of the waterfall. Kallik and Yakone were strong swimmers; Chenoa was young but had been raised by the river and knew its currents better than any of them. But would Lusa be strong enough?

"Lusa?"

She whipped around, dragging her attention from the water.

"Do you think you can make it?"

"Yes, I really do." Lusa lifted her muzzle. "The water's moving steadily. It'll be like swimming from the ice to land."

"But not as cold," Kallik put in.

That's true. Toklo knew that Lusa had faced greater dangers than this. "Let's aim for that boulder first." Toklo flicked his snout toward a flat-topped rock a few bearlengths out. "There won't be room for all of us at the same time, so you two go first. If you think the currents are too strong, let us know." He glanced from Kallik to Yakone. "Okay?"

Yakone nodded and began wading into the river.

Upstream, flat-faces started hooting and pointing. Toklo ignored them. "Then head for the second rock there." With a flick of his muzzle, he showed Kallik a boulder farther out.

"I see it." Kallik headed into the water. "We'll stay one boulder ahead of you until we reach the far shore. That way we can swim back if you need us."

"Go on, Lusa," Toklo urged. But the black bear was already following Chenoa into the river. Toklo waded after them. He pushed off into the stream, his belly tightening as he felt the heavy pull of the current. It was stronger than he'd expected. The falls were dragging greedily at the river, hungry for more spray, more roaring water.

Yakone and Kallik were already plowing toward the second boulder. Chenoa reached the first and hauled herself out. She turned and grabbed Lusa's scruff, helping her onto the stone.

Toklo reached them a moment later, relieved to escape the current. "You're doing well," he told Chenoa and Lusa.

"The current's strong, but it's not impossible." Lusa studied the next boulder. Yakone and Kallik were swimming past it, heading for a rock farther upstream. The water was growing choppy around them. Currents clashed as rocks broke up the flow. Branches and leaves bobbed past, caught in the stream and carried over the falls.

"Come on." Chenoa plunged in and followed the white bears.

Lusa blinked at Toklo, water dripping from her ears. "Which boulder are we aiming for?"

Toklo nodded to the nearest, but Chenoa was swimming around it, pushing on after Kallik and Yakone.

Toklo's heart quickened. What was she doing? She should rest before tackling the difficult water. "Come on." He plunged in and swam after her, looking back to make sure Lusa was on his tail.

Lusa splashed into the river after him and swam to his side as he moved steadily through the water. A broken branch flashed past, missing them by a muzzlelength. "Chenoa's heading for the wrong rock," Lusa puffed.

"Let's catch up with her." Toklo pushed harder, making sure Lusa stayed close. Her pelt brushed his. He could hear her spluttering. "There's a rock soon," he promised.

A jagged boulder rose from the white water upstream from Chenoa. Toklo headed for it, calling to the black she-bear, "Over here!" Her head jerked around and followed his gaze toward the rock. Turning, she headed toward it.

The water frothed as the currents grew more chaotic, pulling this way and that like wolves fighting over prey. Kallik and Yakone had reached a boulder near the far shore. Toklo pushed on for the jagged rock in the middle of the river. Chenoa was almost there, her paws sending up spray as she fought the tumbling water. Toklo reached it, slapping out a paw and heaving himself out of the water. He turned and grabbed Lusa. As he pulled her close, Chenoa caught up and nosed Lusa onto the rock.

"Thanks—"

Chenoa's head jerked backward as a branch bounced past her. It crashed into her hind legs and dragged her away from the rock. Her bark choked into silence. She spun away with a yelp and vanished under the water.

Toklo leaned forward in horror.

"Chenoa!" Lusa gasped.

Chenoa fought her way to the surface, paws flailing, eyes glazed with shock. There was no strength in her paddling, no sense of balance as she rolled over and ducked underwater again. The river tossed her one way, then the other, as it swept her closer to the waterfall.

Lusa stiffened beside Toklo, eyes wide. "The stick hurt her!"

Panic pounded in his ears. *What can I do?* Chenoa was too far away to reach if he stayed where he was. But the currents would be just as strong for him if he tried to swim after her. He crouched on the edge of the rock, staring wildly.

Suddenly, Lusa lunged past him.

"No!" Toklo sank his claws into her pelt. "You can't go after her! You might be swept over!"

She stared at him. "What about Chenoa?"

He scanned the water, heart lurching. "Where is she?"

Kallik's bellow sounded from the far boulder. "Chenoa!"

Toklo whipped around, almost losing his footing on the rock. A black head was bobbing at the edge of the waterfall on the far side of the river. Paws thrashed against the rush of water for a moment, then disappeared.

Toklo stared, his belly hollowing, as Chenoa vanished over the edge.

CHAPTER FIFTEEN

Kallik

"She's gone!" Kallik's breath stopped as water splashed over the boulders onto her paws. This wasn't supposed to happen.

We were only crossing the river!

Yakone shifted beside her. "Chenoa?" He was staring at the empty space where the black bear's head had appeared a moment before she was swept, flailing, over the edge. "Chenoa!" His voice rose to a roar before he plunged into the river.

Kallik gasped, her breath flooding back. "Yakone! It's too late!" She stared, stiff with shock as Yakone swam toward the falls. "It'll drag you over, too! Come back!"

"Yakone!" Toklo howled. "Don't be a fish-brain!"

The current swept Yakone closer to Toklo's boulder. Fear flashed in the white bear's eyes. The current had grabbed him. He struggled against the water.

Don't let him fall! Kallik pleaded with the spirits.

As Yakone thrashed, Toklo leaned out and grabbed for his pelt. He caught Yakone's scruff in his teeth and threw his weight backward, trying to pull him out of the river.

Don't let go! Kallik's heart pressed in her throat.

Toklo heaved and Yakone flailed. Suddenly, a wave threw him against Toklo's rock, and with Toklo's teeth still locked in his fur, he managed to haul himself out of the water. Kallik stared, numb with shock.

Toklo bellowed at her, "Get to the far shore! We'll climb down and find Chenoa!"

Does he think she might have survived? Kallik froze for a moment, trying to picture a small black shape falling through the water and splashing harmlessly into the river below. Chenoa was an excellent swimmer. Maybe it was possible that she had been washed up, winded but unhurt, on the shore below the cliffs. Toklo was right; they had to go look for her! Kallik dove from her rock and swam for the shore. Jaws clenched, she reached the bank and waded out.

She turned and saw that Toklo was moving swiftly through the water toward her. Yakone followed, Lusa's scruff in his jaws. The small black bear held her head above the waves as Yakone carried her through the rapids, struggling free as soon as her paws reached the riverbed.

"We have to get down there and find her!" Lusa raced past Kallik.

"We will," Kallik promised. She glanced past Lusa to Toklo. He was staggering from the river, hollow-eyed. Yakone shook the water from his pelt as he padded through the shallows.

Lusa hurried for the cliff edge.

"Wait!" Kallik caught up with her. She peered down. On this side of the river, the forest reached the waterfall. Trees clung to the sheer cliff, while rocky soil edged the steep slope. It looked as though the forest was sliding into the gorge. In fact, the presence of roots and soft earth would make for an easier climb than the slippery rocks on the other side. *It's a good sign!* Kallik told herself. *Chenoa must be down there alive!*

Lusa began to climb down, threading herself through the branches. Kallik lowered herself after her, hindpaws first, hanging on to a branch and letting her pads slide over crumbling earth until they reached solid rock. She let herself drop onto the ledge, then slithered down, reaching again with her legs until she felt a stiff branch blocking her way. Clinging onto brambles, she called down to Lusa, "Are you okay?" She could just make out Lusa's small shape sliding from branch to rock, sending earth showering down.

"Yes!" Lusa called without stopping.

"Slow down!" Kallik warned.

"Chenoa needs us!" Lusa barked back.

Kallik stared at the relentless wall of water, pounding into the pool at the bottom, then looked up. Grit sprayed her muzzle. She blinked it away and saw Yakone's white pelt heading toward her. Toklo was above him, his claws stripping bark as he skidded downward.

Kallik started moving. Climbing down was much quicker than climbing up. Grabbing a branch, she let her haunches drop. As her hindpaws bumped down the cliff face, the branch dipped and lurched in her claws. Kallik gasped in terror as it cracked and broke. She dropped, heavy as a deer carcass. Stone scraped her pelt as she thumped down the rocks. She hit a ledge with a jolt. Grunting with shock, she grabbed for branches and steadied herself. *Thank the spirits!* Catching her breath, she slid gently down onto a boulder sticking out below. Bracken brushed her cheek as she scrambled tail-first down the last few bearlengths. She could see Lusa though a haze of spray, already racing over the rocky shore.

"Can you see her?" Kallik bellowed over the roar of water.

"Not yet!" Lusa waded through the shallows.

There was no sign of a black pelt among the mossy boulders edging the pool. Kallik felt a tingle of hope. "She must be farther downstream."

Yakone landed heavily beside her. His pelt was stained with mud and stuck with pine needles. Toklo leaped down from the lowest ledge and stared across the water.

"We can't see her," Kallik told him.

Yakone glanced at Kallik, his gaze dark. "Do you think she survived the fall?"

Kallik flinched. She didn't want to answer that right now, when the water was crashing down beside them loud as thunder, heavy as rocks. Instead, she followed Toklo as he clambered past the boulders to where the pool flowed over a ridge and became a river once more. Lusa was a few pawsteps ahead, her head swinging back and forth as she searched the shore.

"Chenoa! Chenoa!" Panic edged her cry.

Kallik brushed past Toklo and caught up to Lusa, who was stumbling, eyes glazed. Tufts stuck from her pelt where brambles had snagged her. Kallik smelled blood. Lusa's pads were leaving red stains on the rocks. Kallik pressed against her, propping her up as she staggered along the river.

Yakone padded into the shallows. Nostrils twitching, he passed Kallik, Lusa, and Toklo and launched himself into the river. Swimming fast, letting the current carry him, he pulled ahead, his head turning as he scoured the edges. As the walls of the gorge gave way once more to forest, he turned and headed toward the riverbank. Emerging from the water, he padded ashore.

Kallik's pelt pricked along her spine. Yakone had seen something. His nostrils were twitching and his ears were flat. He was heading toward boulders, where a dark shape was wedged in the shallows.

"Chenoa?" Kallik quickened her pace.

Lusa bounded forward. "Chenoa!" She reached Yakone first. "Chenoa!"

"Wait!" Toklo darted after her, pulling her back.

Kallik's heart lurched as she saw the dark shape. A sodden pelt lay half in, half out of the water. The river tugged at Chenoa's limp paws, making it look as if she was trying to swim away.

"Wake up!" Lusa struggled free from Toklo. She crouched beside Chenoa, nudging desperately at her cheek. "We're here now! You'll be okay!"

Kallik saw a deep gash above Chenoa's closed eyes. The blood had been washed away, leaving the flesh clean and pink. Kallik hoped that the blow had come quickly, stunning Chenoa before she could feel any pain.

Toklo reached his paw out and pulled at Lusa's shoulder. She shook him off. "Chenoa! Wake up!"

"Leave her." Kallik nudged Toklo away. She raised her eyes, meeting Yakone's gaze as he stood in the shallows. He stared back darkly.

"Wake up, Chenoa! We've found you! You're safe now!" Lusa's agonized cry rang around the walls of the gorge.

Toklo leaned forward. "There's nothing we can do to help her, Lusa."

Lusa turned on him, eyes blazing. "You should have let me go after her!" She was trembling. "She always rescued me! Why didn't you let me rescue her?"

Toklo blinked, his eyes sharp with grief. "I'm so sorry," he murmured.

Lusa turned back to Chenoa. "Another lost bear," she wailed.

"It's not your fault, Lusa," Kallik told her.

"No." Toklo's growl cracked.

Kallik caught his eye and saw panic glittering in his gaze.

"It's not her fault," Toklo repeated. He turned and stalked up the shore.

Kallik's belly tightened. *He blames himself for Chenoa's death!*

Yakone splashed out of the shallows. "Toklo!"

"Let him go, Yakone." Kallik shook her head. "He needs time alone."

She leaned past Lusa and grabbed Chenoa's pelt between her jaws. Yakone hurried to help, lifting Chenoa's flank with his muzzle. Tugging hard, they freed the she-bear and pulled her close to the tree line. They laid her out gently. Water drained from her pelt and streamed over the stone, carrying her blood to the river.

Lusa pushed past Kallik and crouched beside Chenoa, beginning to lap her pelt like a mother washing her cub. "Don't be cold."

Kallik watched her, feeling hollow. *You can't warm her up, Lusa.*

Yakone gazed into the forest where Toklo had disappeared. "We should bury her," he growled. "Unless you want wolverines picking at her pelt."

Kallik hushed him with a warning glance, but Lusa hadn't heard.

She was murmuring to Chenoa. "You nearly made it! You nearly found your own home. But you'll be safe now. You'll make your home beside your mother."

Grief rolled through Kallik, hardening in her chest until she was aware of the weight of every breath. The shadows lengthened, and she felt the sudden chill of evening as the sun dipped down behind the forest.

The undergrowth swished, and Toklo appeared from the trees. "I've found a place for her," he announced. "She'll have a proper burial."

Kallik searched his eyes for grief or rage, but they were clear and steady. He nudged his snout beneath Chenoa's damp pelt. With a grunt, he rolled her up toward his shoulders. Yakone helped haul Chenoa across Toklo's back. Together, they carried her into the forest.

Lusa stood trembling on the stones. "It's too soon to bury her. I need to see her."

Kallik rested her muzzle on Lusa's head. "We'll build her

a safe place to rest. Away from scavengers." She nudged the black bear forward into the forest. Yakone's white pelt flashed ahead of them. Kallik guided Lusa until the trees opened into a small clearing. She gasped when she saw that the undergrowth had already been scraped away and broken branches were heaped beside a pile of rocks. *Toklo's prepared her burial place.*

Toklo knelt and let Chenoa slide from his shoulders. As Yakone gently lowered the dead bear to the ground, Toklo began to dig in the place where he had exposed the dark brown soil. Yakone joined in. Together, they heaped up pawfuls of earth. Kallik nosed in beside them and helped.

They dug until the hole was deep enough to hold Chenoa's body. Wordlessly, Toklo grabbed Chenoa's scruff. Kallik saw his muddy paws buckle with the effort. She leaned closer and grasped the she-bear's cold pelt between her teeth, and together, they heaved her in. Chenoa slid into the bottom of the hole.

Lusa backed away, her fur on end. Her eyes were round with horror. "Chenoa." The word came in a sob.

Kallik padded to Lusa's side. "She'll be safe here," she murmured.

Toklo pawed earth onto Chenoa's body. "Sleep well, Chenoa," he whispered. "May your spirit hear the wind in the trees and taste the scents of the forest."

Yakone bowed his head. "May you find good hunting and feel the sun warm on your back."

Kallik stepped forward and scraped more soil into the hole. The black she-bear looked as small as a cub, curled in the bottom. Her soaked pelt was disappearing beneath the coat of earth. "We will meet again in the stars," Kallik promised. She glanced over her shoulder. "Lusa?" Was she ready to say good-bye to her friend?

Lusa blinked back at Kallik, her eyes misted. Then she darted forward and leaned into the hole. "I should have rescued you! I'm so sorry! This is all my fault. I wanted to be your friend forever."

Toklo paced around the edge and nudged Lusa softly away. "We have to bury her now. Before scavengers scent her death." He turned and dragged a branch from the pile and laid it over Chenoa. Yakone covered her with another. Then they began to pile the rocks on top. Kallik padded across the clearing and lifted a heavy, flat stone. She placed it carefully in front of the mound, a marker if she ever came back here. Lusa sat and watched.

They worked in silence until Chenoa was hidden under a heap of stones, earth, and branches.

"No one will disturb her now." Toklo backed away, his pelt dusty. He dropped to his belly and rested his nose on his paws. "I'm sleeping here tonight."

Kallik's heart ached. She swung her head around and caught Yakone's eye. Yakone stretched out his muzzle and touched hers. "Let's all rest," he whispered. Padding to Toklo's side, he settled down and pressed close to the brown bear.

Kallik turned to Lusa. "Come on," she huffed softly. "Let's rest beside Chenoa."

Lusa stared blankly as Kallik curled around her. "Rest,

Lusa." She pulled Lusa down into the warmth of her pelt. "Sleep. Dream of Chenoa."

Lusa did not move.

Kallik looked up. The sky showed in tiny slivers, dark between the treetops. Moonlight streamed down into the tiny clearing. She could see stars, glittering. "Take care of Chenoa," she whispered to her mother. "Keep her safe until we meet again."

Lusa hardly spoke in the days after Chenoa's death. During the second long, weary struggle up the waterfall and all the sunrises since, she'd walked alone, her eyes on her paws. When they hunted, she sat on the shore and watched. Yakone brought her roots, but she only nibbled at them. Her pelt grew dirty and unkempt.

"I'm worried about Lusa." Kallik fell in beside Toklo as he marched along the shore. They'd trekked all day, and now the sun was sinking behind the trees. She could hear Yakone splashing through the cool shallows behind them. Lusa was trudging along a few bearlengths ahead.

Toklo didn't look up. "She's grieving over Chenoa."

"She can't go on like this," Kallik pointed out. "She's not eating properly or washing."

"Did you think I hadn't noticed?" There was anger in Toklo's growl.

"But we need to help her."

"How?"

"We need to make her understand that it's not her fault."

Toklo flashed her a glance. Kallik veered away, shocked by the rage glittering in his eyes.

"It's *not* her fault," he hissed. "It's *my* fault!"

Kallik blinked. "How?"

"I persuaded Chenoa to come with us." He kicked angrily at the pebbles. "I should have left her where she was. Traveling with us is too dangerous."

"But she *wanted* to leave Hakan!" Kallik argued. "She was so happy to be with us. You gave her a chance to find a new life."

"What a great new life I gave her!" Toklo snarled. "It didn't even last a moon!"

Kallik felt his grief and rage like a wall of stone around him, shutting her out. "Be gentle with yourself," she whispered, and hurried to catch up with Lusa. "We should stop soon, Lusa," she told her briskly.

Lusa ignored her.

"Toklo's sad about Chenoa, too," Kallik ventured. "But I know her spirit is watching over us." She jerked her muzzle toward the woods. "Have you seen her spirit yet? In a tree?"

"No." Lusa's growl was hard.

Kallik refused to be pushed away. "But you were such a good friend to her," she persisted. "And Chenoa was so fond of you. She'll know you'll be looking for her."

"But I'm not," Lusa snorted.

"Perhaps you should," Kallik suggested.

Lusa stared straight ahead. "I don't want to see her being dead!" she snapped. "Why don't *you* look? Or Toklo? Let's *all* look. I'm sure one of us will find her. She'll be *so* pleased.

Playing hide-and-seek is the best part about being dead."

Kallik was shocked by the harshness in Lusa's growl. "Please, Lusa, don't be angry. It's not your fault Chenoa died, any more than it's Toklo's." She felt despair swamp her. "Chenoa knew how brave you are. She knew you would have saved her if you could. But the river's too powerful. There was nothing you could have done."

"But I'll never know that!" Lusa's growl turned into a wail. "I didn't even *try*! I let her down when she needed me most!"

Kallik fought the grief rising in her throat. She hated to see Lusa in so much pain. "We're here if you need us," she murmured. She slowed down, letting Toklo pass, and waited for Yakone to catch up.

He bounded from the water and stopped beside her. "Couldn't you cheer them up?"

Kallik sighed. "I've seen Toklo in one of his dark moods before, but never Lusa."

"This is something they're going to have to work through by themselves," Yakone warned her. "You can't fix everything."

"I can try."

Yakone pressed his cheek against hers.

"We should stop and rest for the night," Kallik suggested.

Yakone nodded. "Toklo! Lusa! We're stopping!"

The woodland bears halted and peered back.

"Who wants to help me find a good den in the woods?" Yakone headed for the trees.

Kallik felt a rush of gratitude for her friend. Yakone *hated* sleeping in the forest.

Lusa shrugged. "Don't bother," she called. "I'll find my own nest." She headed into the trees farther upstream. Toklo settled down on the shore where he'd stopped.

Kallik stared at them.

"Come on, Kallik." Yakone's white muzzle poked out from the shadowy trees. "Let's sleep."

Kallik gazed at Toklo. Lusa had disappeared. "But—"

Yakone cut her off. "Let's sleep," he repeated firmly.

Kallik followed him into the woods, heart aching. Why did Chenoa have to die? She was just beginning her new life. She'd been so eager to explore, always rushing to be first around the next bend in the river. Hadn't she deserved more happiness before she died? Hadn't they all suffered enough grief?

CHAPTER SIXTEEN

Lusa

Lusa barged through a line of ragwort into the forest. Evening light streaked the leaf-strewn earth. She growled under her breath. The others could sleep where they liked. She wanted to be alone. She was sick of Kallik trying to cheer her up and Toklo pretending it was all his fault.

I'm so sorry, Chenoa.

She wandered through the trees until dusk softened into night. The air grew chilly. Lusa scanned the branches above her head. The aspen and birch trembling around her reminded her of the way Chenoa shook with laughter. Lusa padded to a trunk and scrambled up it, nestling in the low branches. The bark scraped her fur. The branch was twisted and knobbly. This tree would be no good for sleeping.

She clutched the trunk with her forepaws and lowered herself to the ground. A birch nearby had thicker branches. She clawed her way up, past the lowest branches to a sturdier bough. Curling in a cleft where the branch arched from the trunk, Lusa nestled down. The bark was smooth and the tree cradled her. As a breeze swished through the tree, Lusa listened to the sighing of the branches. She felt comforted by their gentle creak. Safe in their embrace, she closed her eyes and burrowed into sleep.

The river swept through her dreams. Suddenly, she was back at the waterfall. She was balancing on the rock, water swirling around her.

Chenoa!

Her friend's eyes were dazed with shock as she stared back from the edge of the falls. Lusa froze in horror as Chenoa floundered desperately against the current.

"Chenoa!" The scream stuck in her throat. Her chest seemed to burst as Chenoa slid from view.

She can't be dead! She can't be!

Lusa struggled in her sleep, trying to escape her dream, but another flooded in. She was on the shore, the waterfall thundering in the distance upriver. Dread filled her as she padded toward the boulders where Yakone stood. She knew what he'd found, even before she saw it. But the shock of seeing the limp black pelt, snagged on the rocks, slammed into her like a firebeast. She struggled for breath.

Next moment, Chenoa was lying in the shallow pit Toklo had dug with Kallik and Yakone. They were heaping dirt onto her, then branches, then rocks, one by one. *How will she breathe?* Lusa wanted to scream as they covered her friend's body. Suddenly, she was in the pit alongside Chenoa. *But I'm not dead!* Darkness pressed in with the weight of the rocks. She struggled to push them off, but they were too heavy. She clawed at the branches, trying to scream, but earth showered into her mouth.

"Help!" She woke with a shriek, relieved to feel the cool night air ruffling her pelt. She was safe in her tree. Moonlight filtered through the branches, glowing on the silvery bark. It seemed to pool on one particular part of the trunk, delicately picking up shadows and coils in the surface of the tree.

Lusa stiffened as a swirl in the trunk close to her muzzle seemed to take on a familiar shape.

"Chenoa? Is that you?" She sniffed at the whorls in the bark. There was no tang of sap, just the soft scent of her friend. Lusa jerked backward, eyes wide. The shape in the trunk seemed to be looking straight at her. "Chenoa! It *is* you!" Lusa wrapped her paws around the trunk and closed her eyes. She'd tried not to look for her friend, scared of any reminder that Chenoa was dead. But Chenoa had found *her*! Her spirit had found its way into the tree. Even though she was dead, she was still in the forest. Lusa suddenly felt warm and safe.

"Thank you for finding me," she whispered. Clinging to the tree, she closed her eyes and drifted deep into sleep.

A buzzing noise woke her. Lusa opened her eyes.

Sunshine glittered through the branches. *Where are the others?* She jumped to her paws, realizing with a jolt that she wasn't in a nest or a den but in a tree. She clung to the trunk to stop herself from falling. Chenoa's scent touched her nose. Gasping, Lusa remembered and sat back on the branch. In the warm sunlight, she could see Chenoa's face clearly picked out by the rippling bark: her broad muzzle, her neat ears, her warm eyes.

"Hi, Chenoa!" Lusa huffed in delight.

The buzzing noise broke into her cheerfulness. It was the same angry buzzing they'd skirted before in the forest, the one that sounded like all the firebeasts in the world gathered together. She'd better find the others.

Lusa climbed down from the tree and glanced around, trying to remember which way she'd trekked from the river. Nothing looked familiar in the morning light.

"Toklo?" she called. "Kallik?" She pricked her ears, but only the buzzing answered.

She looked up at Chenoa. "Which way should I go?"

The swirl in the bark looked down solemnly.

"I need to find the others." Chenoa must understand that she had to leave. Lusa backed away, feeling sadness tug in her belly. "I'll always remember you." She turned and set off through the woods. Was that a glimmer of water flashing through the trees? The river must be this way, and the others would be on the shore. She quickened her pace, ducking under bracken and pushing past knotweed until the birch gave way to pine. The buzzing hummed louder until it grew to a screech. Lusa flattened her ears. What was making the noise? Was it coming to hurt them? Her heart began to pound. Why had she left the others last night? She had to warn them.

A harsh scent touched her nose. It smelled of BlackPath and flat-faces. *And wood dust!* She could taste the freshness of sap on her tongue. In a flash, she remembered watching firebeasts carrying trees away.

No!

A crack split the air. Branches clattered and swished. Somewhere nearby, a tree thumped to the ground.

With a gasp, Lusa scrambled forward. *What's happening?* Fear spiked her pelt. She ran blindly, panicked. "Toklo! Kallik!" Where were they? She burst into a clearing and, terrified, stumbled to a halt. Stumps jutted before her, glistening with fresh sap. The bodies of trees lay between them.

Lusa's eyes watered as wood dust and firebeast stench washed her muzzle. As tears welled, she saw the blurry shapes of flat-faces stalking between the stumps. Moving stiffly, in thick yellow pelts, they lifted long, shiny paws, which screamed as they swished through the air. *The buzzers!* The flat-faces had brought them! Lusa flattened her ears against the agonizing screech. A flat-face moved toward a towering pine. He lifted his shiny paw and pressed it against the trunk. As the paw sliced into the tree, wood dust sprayed like blood.

"No!" Lusa roared. She was sure she could hear a bear spirit wailing. The tree tottered as the flat-face freed his paw and stepped away. He yelped a warning to the other flat-faces as slowly the tree began to fall. Lusa watched, breathless, as it folded and crashed to the ground. It bounced, then lay as still as Chenoa when they'd pulled her from the water.

Lusa raced back through the forest. Blind with horror, she pelted through the pines and crashed past the birch. Bracken whipped her muzzle and brambles snagged her fur, but she kept running. Her paws burned as they skidded over the earth. She tripped and tumbled, the sky flashing overhead as she fell out onto the shore. The wide river stretched ahead of her. Jerking around, she searched the shoreline. With a rush of relief, she spotted a white pelt shambling along the rocks.

Kallik! And Yakone! He stood in the river, the water washing his back. *Where's Toklo?*

As Lusa scrambled over the rocks, Toklo padded out from the trees.

"I can't even find her scent," he called to Kallik. "The whole forest stinks of flat-faces and BlackPaths."

"Toklo!" Lusa wailed. "Come quickly!" Her heart beat in her throat. "They're killing the trees!"

"Lusa!" Toklo's eyes widened as she skidded to a stop beside him. "We've been worried. Where have you been?"

Lusa fought for breath. "I've seen them! The buzzers! They're big, shiny paws. The flat-faces are using them to cut down the trees."

Kallik galloped to meet her. "Calm down. Tell us exactly what you saw."

Lusa stared at her. Didn't she understand what was happening? "The flat-faces are killing the *trees*!" She swung her head from Toklo to Kallik.

Toklo's eyes went round in sympathy. "I saw the wounds they'd left in the forest when Chenoa showed me the mountains."

Yakone huffed. "There are too many trees here anyway."

Lusa gasped. "But we *need* them! For prey and food and—"

She broke off and swallowed. "Where will my spirit go if there are no trees left?"

Yakone shifted his paws. "I'm sorry, Lusa." He twitched his ears toward the distant sound of buzzing. "I didn't think."

Kallik touched her muzzle to Lusa's head. "Flat-faces kill trees wherever they go, Lusa. There's nothing we can do."

"But it's horrible! You have to see!" Lusa tore away from them and plunged into the woods. She glanced back to make sure Toklo and Kallik were following, relieved when she saw them charging after her.

Yakone raced after them. "Hey, where are you going?"

Lusa followed the path she'd beaten in her rush to the shore. The buzzing grew louder.

"We shouldn't be heading this way!" Yakone bellowed.

"Lusa!" Kallik thundered behind her. "There's nothing we can do."

"You have to see!" Lusa called back. If the others saw the trees dying, they'd have to do something. After all, they'd stopped flat-faces from destroying things before. She raced faster as the buzzing turned to screeching. She ignored the pain piercing her ears. "There!" She stopped a muzzlelength from the tree line, where the forest opened onto the stump-filled clearing. "Look!"

Toklo crept forward. Lusa watched his ears quiver as he peered past the trunks. Kallik followed him, Yakone pushing in beside her. Wood dust shimmered in shafts of sunshine. The air was filled with choking firebeast stench. A huge black-pawed firebeast rumbled at the edge of the clearing, while another picked up the dead trees with a gigantic dangling claw and loaded them onto its back.

Lusa slid next to Toklo and watched the flat-faces. The clearing was swarming with them. One was slicing into a fresh tree. Lusa's pelt stood on end as she heard it scream. Another tree cracked. Lusa snapped her head around. A flat-face held up his shiny paw triumphantly and yelped as a tree toppled away from him. The far edge of the clearing seemed to sway as tree after tree collapsed like grass bending beneath the wind. "They're cutting them *all* down!" Lusa gasped.

Toklo pressed against her and steered her away. "There are too many flat-faces," he breathed into her ear. "We can't stop them."

Kallik touched her nose to Lusa's head. "I'm sorry, Lusa. There's nothing we can do."

"What about Chenoa?"

Toklo froze. "Chenoa?"

"I saw her, in the bark of a tree. Her spirit's over there." Lusa pointed with her muzzle. "What if they cut her down, too?"

Kallik's eyes clouded with pity. "Oh, Lusa."

Yakone padded away from the clearing. "Her spirit will find a new home."

"You don't *know* that!" Lusa gaped at him. "What would happen to white bear spirits if flat-faces melted all the ice and stole all the stars?"

"Come on, Lusa." Toklo began to hustle her away. "We can't stay here. It's not safe." His ears were twitching.

"And it's too noisy." Yakone headed back toward the river. Kallik trotted after him, glancing anxiously at Lusa.

"I wish we could help." Toklo steered her forward. "But what can we do?"

Numbly, Lusa let Toklo guide her. She'd let the river sweep Chenoa away. Now she was leaving her spirit to be destroyed by flat-faces. She'd been too small to help her friend when she was alive, and Lusa was still too small to save her spirit now.

CHAPTER SEVENTEEN

Toklo

As they reached the shore, Lusa pulled away from Toklo. He watched her anxiously as she headed along the riverbank. The black bear weaved, stumbling over the stones, as though half-blind with grief.

Toklo forced away a groan of despair. There was nothing he could do. Surely Lusa understood? How could he protect Chenoa's spirit tree?

Kallik hurried to catch up with Lusa, reaching her just in time to steady her as a loose rock turned beneath her paw.

"Dumb stones!" Lusa snarled, flinching away from Kallik.

Toklo stared into the forest. There seemed to be as many flat-faces as prey here; first the rafts, then the herd by the falls, and now the tree cutters. The bears had to keep moving, find a way to a less crowded place.

The morning passed slowly. Clambering over the rocky shoreline was harder than before, with looser pebbles to challenge weary paws. Stones shifted and teetered underfoot. Toklo's forepaw slipped off one moss-covered rock and hit another. He winced, glancing at the wide, flat beaches on the far shore. It looked like easier walking on the other side, but he couldn't be sure there weren't flat-faces there. And he knew he couldn't suggest crossing the river again.

Dark, fat-bellied clouds rolled from the horizon, and as the bears pushed on, the breeze lifted, ruffling their fur. Rain began to spatter Toklo's muzzle, falling more and more heavily until the treetops disappeared in a gray haze. Toklo clung to the tree line, sheltering beneath branches, but soon they dripped cold droplets along his spine. He shivered, shaking off the rain.

"It wasn't your fault." Yakone's growl took him by surprise. Toklo jerked his head around to see the white bear fall in beside him.

"What wasn't?"

"You gave Chenoa a real chance to find her own place in the forest." Yakone kept his gaze fixed on the shore ahead. "She would never have been happy staying with Hakan."

Grief stabbed Toklo's heart. Was a short glimpse of happiness enough? "We'll never know," he muttered.

As the rain poured, the river began to churn. Swelling, it thundered past, snatching at the shore. Rain dripped faster through the branches. Before long, Toklo was drenched.

Ahead, Kallik shook raindrops from her muzzle. "We need to stop."

Lusa slowed beside her, head low, gaze dull.

"Lusa needs a break." Kallik lifted her snout. "And food."

Toklo nodded. "You stay here with Lusa. I'll hunt."

"I'll come with you." Yakone headed into the forest.

Kallik nudged Lusa toward the shelter of a thick pine. "Don't let Lusa go chasing after any more bear spirits," Toklo warned Kallik.

Lusa flashed him a look.

Yakone was waiting for him in the shadow of the trees. "Let's split up," the white bear suggested. Water dripped from every branch, but there was more shelter here than on the shore.

"Okay." Toklo gazed into the shadows. He smelled the rich, damp scent of prey. His belly rumbled.

As Yakone lumbered away, Toklo followed a scent trail. It led him straight to a raccoon. It was sitting among the roots of a pine, gnawing on a shoot. It didn't even have time to run as Toklo lunged and killed it with a bite. He headed back for the shore and dropped the raccoon at Kallik's paws.

She wrinkled her nose. "Woodland prey."

Toklo snorted impatiently. "I can catch you a fish if you want."

Kallik glanced at the river raging past. "Let's wait for the water to calm down. I don't want you washed away—" She stopped, her gaze flicking toward Lusa.

"It's okay," Lusa grunted. "We can't ignore the river forever."

Yakone pushed his way through bracken upstream and bounded onto the shore. A fat grouse dangled between his jaws; a root, wedged behind it, stuck out from the side of his mouth. He picked his way across the loose rocks and laid the grouse beside the raccoon. The root tumbled after it and landed on the warm prey. "It smelled sweet." Yakone nosed the root toward Lusa. "I thought you might like it."

Lusa took it, her eyes brightening. "Thank you."

Toklo felt his shoulders loosen. Was Lusa starting to feel better? He rested on his haunches and watched her nibble the root. Yakone settled beside Kallik and tore a chunk from the grouse. Toklo bit into the raccoon, savoring the taste. It had been moons since he'd tasted raccoon. The flavor brought memories flooding. Oka had caught a raccoon once and shared it with him and Tobi. She'd nudged Toklo away as she tried to persuade Tobi to eat some. Had she been scared he'd steal his brother's share?

Lusa's growl cut into his thoughts. "Why didn't Ujurak save Chenoa?"

Toklo glanced at Kallik. Did she have an answer? He'd wondered the same thing himself. Ujurak had saved each of them before, one way or another. Why had he let the river take Chenoa?

Kallik dodged his gaze. "I don't know," she confessed.

"Isn't he watching us anymore?" Lusa persisted.

"Of course he is." Kallik stared at the grouse in her paws.

Lusa tipped her head on one side. "Perhaps he didn't like her traveling with us."

Anger flared in Toklo's belly. "Don't be a fish-brain!"

Lusa's eyes widened. "I just wondered if—"

Yakone interrupted. "*I'm* still here, aren't I?"

Toklo blinked at him.

"Ujurak would have stopped me from getting this far if he didn't like other bears traveling with you." Yakone puffed grouse feathers away from his nose.

"How could he stop you?" Toklo barked. "Ujurak wouldn't hurt a bear!"

"But he didn't save Chenoa," Lusa fretted. "Perhaps he trusted us to save her ourselves."

Toklo swallowed. The raccoon flesh scraped his throat and hit his belly hard as stone.

"There was nothing we could have done," Kallik reminded her.

"Then why didn't *he* save her?"

Kallik touched her nose to Lusa's head. "Ujurak can't save every bear in the world."

"I'm not asking him to!" Lusa snapped. "Just Chenoa."

Toklo pushed the rest of the raccoon away. His mind was whirling. Had Ujurak really seen Chenoa struggling and decided not to help her? Toklo's heart burned. Perhaps he hadn't known Ujurak as well as he thought.

The rain eased as they set off again, and slowly the river calmed. They trekked through the day, and by dusk, it was running smoothly once more. And the shore had widened. As they reached a stretch of pebbly beach, Yakone slowed. "Let's stay here for the night." He gestured with his muzzle to the river. "It looks like a good fishing spot."

Kallik started snuffling among the boulders at the top of the beach. "I'll get some bracken and make a nest here."

Toklo sat down, relieved to rest his aching paws. He

watched Lusa pad into the shallows and stare at the water washing around her paws. Did she really think Ujurak had let Chenoa die?

Yakone splashed past her and dove into deeper water. A moment later, he surfaced, a fish in his jaws.

Toklo stared at the setting sun. A breeze lifted his fur as it slid behind the trees.

"Don't you want some fish?" Kallik called from the beach.

Toklo shook his head. "Not hungry."

Kallik curled her lip. She must have noticed that he'd eaten hardly any of the raccoon. But she didn't question him. Instead she lumbered into the forest. She returned quickly with a bundle of bracken in her mouth. Carefully, she used the stalks to line a hollow among the boulders at the top of the beach.

"It's getting dark," she warned as Lusa and Yakone padded to join her. "Are you coming to sleep, Toklo?"

"In a while." Toklo watched the clouds tearing open to show the moon. The river raced past, and soon he could hear Yakone snoring. The stars glittered across the sky. Toklo picked out the sparkling needle-prick shapes of Ujurak and his mother. "Are you still watching us?" he whispered. Wind whisked through the trees. "Why did you let Chenoa die?"

Gravel crunched beside him, and fur brushed his pelt. Toklo stiffened as the scent of Ujurak warmed the air.

"Please don't doubt me."

Toklo jerked around. "Ujurak?" He couldn't see his friend, but he knew he was near.

"I'm sorry Chenoa died," Ujurak murmured in his ear. "I wish harm to no bear. But I cannot promise that your journey won't be dangerous. Have courage, dear Toklo. You'll get home someday."

The air suddenly smelled of pine and water once more. Ujurak had gone.

Toklo's pelt bristled. *You didn't tell me why!* He dropped to his belly and thrust his nose on his paws. *Why did you let her die?* Staring at the river, he flexed his claws. *This journey is taking forever. I just want to get home.* Toklo's belly suddenly fluttered with fear. *But what will happen when I get there? Am I leading my friends into more danger?*

"Come on, Lusa!" Yakone galloped along the wide beach. "Race me!"

Kallik huffed in Toklo's ear. "It's sweet of him, trying to cheer her up."

Toklo grunted. "Yeah." Lusa was ignoring the white bear as he bounced around her encouragingly.

The river had narrowed. It crashed past, churning over rocks. White water foamed, throwing sparkling spray into the sunshine.

Kallik nudged Toklo. "Do *you* want to race?"

Toklo stared ahead. Why wouldn't Ujurak tell him *why* Chenoa had to die? "No, thanks."

A shriek pierced the air.

Toklo halted. "What was that?"

Kallik was already sniffing. "Flat-faces."

Toklo jerked around. "Where?" As he spoke, a shape appeared on the river upstream.

Lusa and Yakone hurried toward them. "Flat-faces," Yakone warned.

Kallik nodded. "We know."

Lusa pointed to the shape rushing downriver. It bounced over the waves.

Another shape followed, then another, then more. Toklo narrowed his eyes. The flat-faces were riding in brightly colored logs. Each log held one flat-face. Pointed at each end, the logs skidded over the water faster than birds. The flat-faces squealed, waving broad-headed sticks in their hands and dabbing them in the water as they guided their logs past jutting rocks.

A disapproving growl rumbled in Yakone's throat. "What in all the spirits are they doing now?"

"At least they're not killing trees," Lusa muttered.

Logs carrying small flat-faces scudded toward them. Kallik stared in disbelief. "They've brought their cubs."

Yakone flicked his nose toward the trees. "Let's get out of sight."

Toklo nodded and headed upshore. Kallik sprinted after them. "Hurry up!" she barked over her shoulder. Lusa was still on the pebbles, her gaze fixed on the bobbing flat-faces.

"What are you doing?" Toklo barked. Alarm pricked him as the excited squeals of the flat-faces sharpened into terror. He saw one of the brightly colored logs roll sideways as it hit a crosscurrent. It tipped its flat-face cub into the water and slid away. The cub tumbled downstream, flailing and screaming as the churning water battered it. The other flat-faces started shouting and beating the waves with their sticks, trying to get closer to the cub, but the current swept it away too quickly.

Lusa raced to the waterline. "Spirits save it!"

Toklo charged after her. "Stop!" He snapped at her scruff with his teeth and hauled her back before her paws hit the water.

Lusa's eyes brimmed with panic. "Don't let the river kill anyone else!"

Toklo met her gaze. "I won't." He flicked his muzzle toward Yakone. The white bear had bounded up to him, Kallik at his side. "Stay here, Yakone, and keep Lusa out of the river." The rapids were fierce. His pelt lifted along his spine. "Kallik, will you come with me?"

Kallik headed for the water. "What's your plan?"

The flat-face cub was being swept closer, squealing.

Toklo flicked his snout toward it. "Grab the cub if you can," he told Kallik. "Then dump it on the far shore." Unable to keep pace with the cub, the flat-faces were crashing their logs into the bank opposite. They leaped out and began waving and screaming at the cub in the water. "Can't flat-faces swim?" Toklo growled, wading through the shallows. They weren't even trying to reach their cub.

"I want to help!" Lusa wailed from the shore.

"No!" Toklo roared over his shoulder. "We'll save it, I promise. You don't have the strength for these currents." Ignoring her protest, he dove into the river, pushing out into the fierce stream. Kallik appeared beside him, her paws churning.

The cub swirled toward them, terror glittering in its wide blue eyes.

Kallik lunged toward it. Toklo fought the rushing tide, ready to help. As he watched, a powerful wave hit the white bear and knocked her sideways. He gasped as Kallik spun away toward a rock that jutted out midstream. Toklo swam after her, but she hit it and bounced away.

"Kallik!" Yakone roared from the shore.

Toklo looked back, searching the foaming water for the flat-face cub. Who should he go after? Kallik or the flat-face cub?

The cub hurtled past. It twirled in the current, then disappeared beneath the waves. Its paws shot up into the air, flailing as it struggled for the surface.

A white pelt flashed downstream. Kallik had reached another rock and was hauling herself out.

The cub!

Toklo dove after it. He felt a fast current catch him and rode it, just as Chenoa had taught him. It swept him past the cub. The cub's face froze in horror as its gaze fixed on him.

Don't be scared of me! Toklo willed it to understand. "The river's your enemy, not me!" As he roared across the water, the cub flailed harder. On the bank, the flat-faces screamed louder.

Fish-brain! I'll scare him more if I bellow. Toklo clamped his jaws shut as the river carried him past Kallik. She stared, dazed and dripping, her pelt pink with blood.

Toklo spotted a wide, smooth boulder farther downstream. *No jagged edges!* The cub might be able to grab onto it without getting hurt. Toklo ducked beneath the water and swam for the cub. Nudging it with his muzzle, he steered the cub toward the rock. The cub kicked, but Toklo pushed harder until he slammed against the boulder. He surfaced, gasping for breath. Pain seared his flank.

Relief swamped him as he saw that the cub was pinned to the boulder by the force of the river. It scrabbled at the stone with its forepaws, struggling to climb up. The flat-faces on the bank hollered as Toklo bobbed around the rock. Menace edged their panic. *They think I want to hurt it.* What if they brought firesticks? He had to save the cub quickly.

Shoving his muzzle under the cub's flank, he heaved it up onto the top of the boulder. The cub lay on its side panting, coughing up water.

Toklo held still against the rock. The rushing water pushed hard, nudging him downriver. He glanced back. Kallik was signaling, her gaze clear once more. The flat-faces pelted along the shore, waving at the cub as they neared. They'd never be able to reach it across the wide channel of roaring water.

"You're safe," Toklo huffed at the cub.

The cub scrambled backward, a scream gurgling in its throat.

"I won't hurt you!" Toklo promised desperately.

The cub stared at the water, then back at Toklo. Uncertainty shone in its eyes.

He's going to jump!

"No!" With a snarl, Toklo ducked around the far side of the rock to block it. The current snatched him and tried to drag him away. But Toklo fought it, gripping onto the rock. Anger surged through him. The river was trying to kill him, just as it had killed Chenoa!

"Leave us alone!" Toklo roared at the water.

The cub screamed as Toklo flung his paws over the edge of the boulder and gripped on hard. Toklo froze.

Stop.

Swallowing back his rage, he heaved himself around the rock until the current pushed instead of pulled. Then he tried to look kindly at the cub. *I won't hurt you.*

The cub met his gaze.

I want to help you. Keeping quiet, Toklo willed the cub to understand. Where was Ujurak? If he were here, he could change into a flat-face and explain.

Ujurak's not here anymore.

The flat-faces screamed. Toklo could see them pointing and waving, their brightly colored pelts flashing at the corner of his gaze. But he didn't take his eyes off the cub.

Trust me.

The cub lost the stiffness of cornered prey.

That's right, Toklo urged. *You'll be safe with me. I promise.*

Slowly, the cub crept nearer. The water battered Toklo's spine, but he ignored it. He tipped his head, softening his gaze like he used to when he was begging Tobi to play with him. He held his breath as the cub lifted a paw and reached out toward him.

The flat-faces screeched like trapped foxes. Toklo forced

himself to ignore them, holding still as the cub touched his snout. *Come on.* His heart felt close to bursting, but he didn't move. The cub's eyes were round with hope. Its fingers crept gently over Toklo's snout and touched his head. Slowly, Toklo hunched his back until it was clear of the water, pressed alongside the cub's boulder. He saw the cub's eyes flick along his spine.

He's wondering whether to climb on. Toklo held still. *Come on,* he pleaded. *You understand. I know you do.*

Gingerly, the cub slid a pink paw across Toklo's shoulders. Toklo didn't breathe. The little flat-face slithered like a snake over his pelt. Then, with a rush, the cub clambered onto his back. Toklo felt a surge of relief as the cub's claws dug into his fur and gripped on. He felt its hind legs pressing hard against his flanks. The flat-faces leaped wildly around the shore. Toklo took a breath, steadied himself, then launched away from the boulder.

The current hit him hard, and he tipped sideways. The cub gripped tighter as Toklo fought to right himself. Paws churning, he pulled himself forward, fighting the river, his gaze fixed on the shore. He hit a trough in the waves and dropped. Shock knocked out his breath. The cub's grip loosened, and with a jolt of horror, Toklo felt it slide from his back. Whipping around, he lunged and grabbed at the cub with his jaws a moment before the current snatched it away. Snagging its loose pelt in his teeth, he dragged it close. The river pulled, but Toklo held firm, his paws aching as he fought the tide. The cub twisted in his grip, then grabbed Toklo's pelt and hauled itself onto his back once more.

It held harder this time, its claws dragging at Toklo's pelt. Toklo hardly noticed. The cub could tear out a whole clump of fur, just so long as he got it to safety. He forced his way on until suddenly the current eased. Toklo fell limp as he hit smooth water, swimming in steady strides till the riverbed scraped his paws. He waded into the shallows and padded from the water.

The flat-faces were howling a few bearlengths away. Toklo scanned them for firesticks. He couldn't see any. The cub slid from his back and raced toward its kin. Toklo backed away. If they had firesticks, they'd use them now. He tensed, but the flat-faces only stared. Their hostility had gone. One caught his gaze, its eyes wide with wonder. Another grabbed the cub and hauled it into a frantic embrace.

Warily, Toklo backed into the water, then turned and swam for the far shore. The river pushed him downstream once more. He didn't fight it; instead he focused on moving forward until, exhausted, he felt pebbles beneath his paws.

As he heaved himself from the river, Kallik, Yakone, and Lusa galloped toward him. Lusa reached him first, sending him staggering as she rushed into him. "You saved the cub!"

Toklo glanced at Kallik, relieved to see her safe on the shore. "Are you okay?"

"Just a bump," she answered, lowering her head so he could see the swelling behind her ear. "It'll mend."

"It'd mend quicker if Chenoa was here to find herbs." Toklo scowled at the river. "You didn't get the cub," he hissed under his breath. "That's one life you couldn't take."

CHAPTER EIGHTEEN

Kallik

Kallik's head throbbed. She stumbled after Toklo as he headed for the trees, Lusa at his heels. He was still dripping from the river, while the flat-faces squealed and hooted on the far shore.

"You shouldn't have risked your life for a *flat-face*!" Yakone called behind her.

She turned to look at him. "I risked my life to make sure Toklo was safe."

"Toklo didn't need your help!"

"How could I know that?" Kallik sighed and closed her eyes. Her side ached. Her flank had hit the boulder harder than her head. It hurt when she walked, and she didn't dare cough. She'd hacked up water after reaching shore, and the pain had made her eyes sting.

Yakone caught up with her. "I'm sorry." He touched his muzzle to her cheek. "I was just worried about you." His breath grazed her swollen ear.

Kallik met his gaze. "I couldn't let a cub drown. Not even a flat-face one. I couldn't let Lusa see another death, not so soon after Chenoa."

"I know." Yakone swung his head and watched Lusa and Toklo disappearing among the trees. The flat-faces were pointing from the other bank. "Let's get out of sight."

Kallik let him guide her up the beach and into the forest. The shade eased her throbbing head, but a root tripped her up, and the jolt sent pain shooting through her flank.

"Great spirits!" Yakone cursed as he stumbled behind her.

"We can head back to the shore soon," she promised. "Once we're away from the flat-faces."

A bit later, Yakone waded through a sea of quillwort, heading for the river. He paused at the tree line and called over his shoulder, "It's clear."

Undergrowth parted and Toklo appeared, Lusa on his tail. "What's up?"

"The flat-faces are gone." Yakone pushed through bracken onto the rocky shore.

Toklo shrugged and followed. Kallik hesitated, catching her breath.

Lusa stopped beside her. "Are you okay?"

"Just bruised," Kallik told her.

"You can lean on me." Lusa pressed gently against her as they padded from the trees.

The sun was beginning to slide toward the treetops, but it was a while before dusk. There was still plenty of time to walk. Kallik's heart sank. She wanted to rest.

"I'm hungry," Yakone announced as she reached him.

"Already?" Kallik stared at him. His belly never started growling until sunset.

He leaned forward and whispered in her ear, "I want to give you a chance to rest."

"Thanks." Kallik pulled away. "But I can speak for myself."

"But you won't, will you?"

Kallik was surprised by the anger in his tone.

Yakone turned his back. "Do you want to come fishing, Toklo?"

Toklo squinted upstream, where the river curved between hills. "We shouldn't be wasting time."

"Kallik needs to rest," Yakone told him bluntly.

Lusa frowned. "Why didn't you say so, Kallik?"

"She shouldn't need to," Yakone muttered. "She nearly drowned back there."

Kallik stretched her nose toward Lusa. "I'm fine," she promised. She didn't want Lusa to worry.

Yakone stalked away. "Are you coming, Toklo?"

Toklo's eyes darkened as he looked at the river. "I'll hunt in the woods," he growled, heading for the trees.

Lusa scampered after him. "I'll find some roots."

Kallik watched Yakone splash into the river. Weary, she sat down, relieved to be resting. Her vision softened and blurred as she watched Yakone fishing. His white head popped up, then disappeared. Every now and then he'd carry a fish to the beach, drop it, and head back into the water.

Bracken swished behind her, and Kallik scented Lusa. The black bear's paws crunched over the pebbles.

"Birch root." Lusa settled beside Kallik and began chewing on an earthy stem. Kallik listened to her in sleepy silence.

"You were really brave," Lusa commented.

"When?" Kallik turned.

"Trying to save the flat-face cub."

"Toklo saved it."

"But you tried." Lusa chewed her root a little more. "I was so scared when you hit the rock. Did Ujurak help you climb out of the water?"

Kallik paused. Would Lusa feel better if she believed Ujurak *had* helped? She shook the thought away. She should be honest. "No," she confessed.

Lusa gazed into the distance, the root in her paws. "Perhaps he was helping Toklo."

Kallik sighed. "Maybe."

Lusa looked at her sharply. "You don't sound sure. Do you think Ujurak has abandoned us?"

"Of course not!" Kallik lied. Her chest tightened. "Why would he?"

"But what if he has?" Lusa fretted. "We might be going the wrong way and we'd never know!"

Kallik pressed gently against her. "This is Toklo's journey now," she told her. "He knows where he's going."

"I hope so." Lusa swallowed a piece of the root. "He deserves to find his home."

"We all do." Kallik's thoughts flicked back to the Melting Sea. She could see Taqqiq charging across a wide stretch of ice. Her paws tingled, imagining the delicious coldness of snow. She remembered swimming through smooth, bottomless ocean.

The stones rattled as Yakone padded toward them. His jaws were filled with a good catch of fish. He dropped them at Kallik's paws. Kallik scooped up a trout, her belly rumbling in anticipation. "Thanks, Yakone."

He settled beside her and reached for a salmon.

Toklo called from the trees. "Poor prey here." He bounded across the shore, empty-pawed.

Lusa blinked at him. "You didn't catch *anything*?"

Kallik pushed a fish toward him. "Yakone caught plenty."

Toklo shook his head. "I'm not really hungry."

Kallik took another bite of her trout and watched the sun slide toward the trees. *Had* Ujurak helped Toklo save the flat-face cub? She glanced at him hopefully.

Toklo was staring into the distance, lost in thought. He looked weary. A frown creased his brow. Kallik sighed. If Ujurak had been with him when he rescued the cub, she was sure he wouldn't look so worried.

Kallik woke into darkness. Something was wrong. She shifted in the wide nest they'd lined with bracken. There was a space beside her. Alarmed, she sat up. Toklo and Lusa were fast asleep, but Yakone was gone. Her heart lurched. She scanned the moonlit shore.

As she got to her paws, she spotted his silhouette in the distance. Yakone was sitting on a wide boulder in the middle of the river. Water flowed smoothly around him, glittering with starlight. Kallik hurried across the beach and slid into the river. The chill of it reached to her bones.

She swam to his rock and hauled herself out. "Yakone?"

He tipped his head. "I thought you were sleeping."

"I was." She shook out her pelt. "What are you doing?"

"Thinking." Yakone lifted his muzzle and gazed at the sky.

Kallik sat beside him. "About what?"

Yakone gestured toward the stars. "Which one is Ujurak?"

Kallik looked up, surprised. It wasn't like Yakone to think about stars. "You see that bright one?"

Yakone frowned, then nodded.

"That's his tail. Can you see the stars near it, making the shape of a bear?"

He squinted. "Not much like a bear."

"Enough to imagine."

"That's *Ujurak*?" Yakone sounded unconvinced.

"You don't have to believe he's up there, watching over us." Kallik looked at Yakone. "But I believe it."

Yakone jerked his snout toward her. "Believing isn't enough."

Kallik stiffened. "What do you mean?"

Yakone's growl hardened. "You could have died today. And for what? So you could save a flat-face cub?"

Kallik stared at him. "But I didn't die."

"Not today!" Yakone's eyes flashed in the moonlight. "But what about tomorrow? Or the day after? How many more flat-face cubs are you going to risk your life for? Or brown bears, or black bears, or any creature that's passing?"

Kallik flinched away, shocked by his anger. "But that's part of the journey," she exclaimed. "We face danger together!"

"Together?" A growl rumbled in Yakone's throat. "Who do you mean? I thought *we'd* planned a future together! I thought we were going to watch the burn-sky sun and build ice-dens when snow-sky came."

"We can still do that—"

Yakone cut her off. "You say danger is part of the journey, but it's not *your* journey anymore, is it?" He glared at her. "This is Toklo's journey. And Lusa's." He flicked his muzzle toward the forest. "We don't belong here! Tripping over bushes, fishing in rivers, melting in the sun! What if something does happen to you? I'll be alone. I'll have to travel back to the ice by myself. And what about the plans we made? You promised we'd live together on the ice." He was quivering. "I know they're your friends, but I'm scared for you. And for me! This isn't our home, and every pawstep takes us farther from where we belong."

Kallik caught her breath, astonished. Was he really that unhappy? "I'm sorry," she murmured. "I'm sorry you feel this way. I can't wait till I'm on the ice again, with you. But I've lost too many bears. First Nanuk, then Ujurak and Kissimi. Now Chenoa. I can't turn my back on Lusa and Toklo." She searched his gaze. Was he really so heartless he couldn't understand?

"You're not the only bear who's lost someone!" he snarled back. "I left my entire *family* for you."

Kallik's fur spiked. How dare he throw that at her? *Don't you know how important this journey is to me?* "Don't make me choose, Yakone," she warned. "Taqqiq made me choose once, and I nearly lost him forever." She remembered with a pang how she'd left Toklo and Lusa to travel home with Taqqiq. But she hadn't been able to carry it through. She'd had to return to her friends. And she'd do the same this time.

Yakone's eyes widened. "You'd choose them over me?"

Pain seared Kallik's heart. "I'm sorry, Yakone. I care for you, truly. I'd hate being here without you. But I *have* to see Toklo and Lusa to the end of their journey."

"Even if you die trying?" Yakone's question was hardly more than a whisper.

Kallik closed her eyes. "Yes."

Yakone dove into the water and headed for shore.

"They'd do the same for me!" Kallik called. "I know they would!" As she watched him pad ashore, fear sparked beneath her pelt. "Are you leaving?" She stared at him as he shook the water from his pelt. "Are you going back to the Melting Sea?"

Yakone gazed at her across the water. His eyes shone like stars. "No, Kallik. I'll stay with you."

Her shoulders drooped with relief.

"For now." Yakone turned away and padded back to their nest.

Kallik stayed on the boulder until dawn lit the distant horizon. Then she swam back to shore and settled quietly on the bracken beside Yakone. Ears pricked, she listened to him sleep. His breath rose and fell steadily, rumbling as he snored. She rested her muzzle on her paws, her eyes drooping as tiredness pulled at her. What if Yakone left while she was sleeping? He mustn't go back to the Melting

Sea without her. But how could she leave Toklo and Lusa? They were more than friends now; they were family. She wriggled, fidgeting in the nest, trying to get comfortable until finally, she slid into sleep.

She awoke with a start. Sun streamed onto the shore. Lusa was beside her, nibbling leaf dust from her pelt while Toklo stretched at the side of the nest.

Yakone?

Kallik jerked up her head. There he was. Sheltering in the shade of the trees.

"Are you okay, Kallik?" Toklo's growl surprised her. She turned and saw worry in his gaze.

"I'm fine." She sat up briskly. "Who's hungry?"

She fished, catching enough for them all. Yakone ate in silence, then trekked upriver without a word. Toklo and Lusa exchanged looks as they padded a few bearlengths ahead. They had to know that something was wrong. Kallik wished she could explain, but what would she say?

Anger surged through her. *I want to go home, too!* She kicked at the pebbles as she walked. *I hate this stupid terrain. I hate the trees and the sun. We're so far from the ice, and I don't know how far we have to go!* Every day they were moving farther from where she belonged. But she *belonged* with Toklo and Lusa. Her mind whirled. How could she leave them?

As the shore narrowed, Toklo halted. The river was curving away toward sunset-sky. Lusa hurried on, heading to where the forest reached the water's edge. She climbed over the line of rocks edging the trees and peered farther around. "There's no shore for ages," she called back. "Just forest."

Kallik scraped her claws against the ground. They were going to have to travel through the woods. She glanced at Yakone. *He'll hate it.* She bristled. *What can I do about it?* Was she supposed to apologize? It wasn't *her* fault the shore disappeared!

Huffing, she followed Toklo through the sedge and into the forest. Lusa trotted ahead. The two woodland bears moved easily between the trees, following trails as though they'd traveled this way every day of their lives.

Yakone pushed through a bramble, leaving hunks of white fur snagged in its thorns. "I'm sure I can smell firebeasts."

"You're imagining it." Kallik could only smell sickly sap scent. She followed him through the thorns, growling as a tendril tore her pelt.

Yakone's back dipped suddenly, and he lurched. "Great spirits!" His paws had disappeared into watery peat. Scrambling out of the boggy soil, he tripped on a tree root. Kallik darted forward to steady him.

"If firebeasts or flat-faces don't kill us, the forest will!" he complained.

A pine twig jabbed Kallik's sore flank. She gasped with pain. "There are no firebeasts here," she hissed through gritted teeth. "The forest is too thick."

"We should be swimming upriver, not trekking through this stuff," Yakone growled.

Kallik swallowed back anger. Yakone was miserable. She'd chosen her friends over him. "We can't swim all the way," she reasoned gently. "Lusa wouldn't be able to fight the current for that long." She froze as a distant rumbling touched her ear fur. Yakone pricked his ears.

Lusa came charging toward them. "There's something big ahead." She skidded to a halt, Toklo at her heels.

Kallik listened harder. Had Yakone been right about the firebeasts? A deep, ominous rumbling throbbed through the forest. She opened her mouth. Sour air touched her tongue.

Toklo struck off into thicker undergrowth. "We should head around it."

"Great," Yakone growled.

Kallik plunged into the bushes, screwing up her eyes as twigs lashed her snout.

Ahead, Lusa slowed her pace. "It's getting louder."

The rumbling shook the air. The trees seemed to tremble around them.

"I thought we were avoiding it," Yakone muttered.

"It's everywhere." Fear edged Toklo's growl.

Kallik barged through a clump of bracken. Suddenly the air was thick with firebeast stench. The roaring came from every side. Her belly tightened as the ground shook beneath her paws.

Lusa's fur stood on end. "What's happening?"

Toklo swung his head, scanning the forest.

Trees creaked, howling through the thunder of firebeasts. Lusa's eyes widened in terror. "The trees are screaming!" she wailed. "They're all screaming!"

Yakone marched ahead. "Let's find out what's going on."

"Be careful!" Kallik hurried behind him. Toklo and Lusa

crowded at her heels. Light streamed through the trees. The noise was coming from a clearing.

Yakone stopped, and Kallik slid in beside him. In front of them, tree stumps rose like a bed of thorns, stretching away toward the riverbank. Flat-faces pointed and shouted, signaling to massive firebeasts.

Kallik swallowed. The firebeasts were huge—bigger than she'd ever seen. They churned through mud on fat, black paws. Their long, flat backs were heavy with the bodies of trees, stacked high like fresh prey. Rumbling like thunder, one rolled toward the riverbank. With a terrifying roar, it lifted its shoulders and let the trees slide from its back. The trees tumbled into the river, crashing together as they splashed down into the water.

Lusa moaned in horror. "They'll drown." Her words were no more than a gasp. "The bear spirits will drown and be lost forever!"

Kallik closed her eyes. Was this how their journey was going to be forever? This world was filled only with horror and grief. She longed for the ice more desperately than ever, wishing she were back there, with Yakone beside her.

CHAPTER NINETEEN

Lusa

Lusa charged forward, her mind blurring with panic.

Teeth snagged her scruff. "Lusa! No!"

She gasped as Kallik hauled her back.

"Get off!" Lusa scrabbled at the ground, struggling to free herself. "I have to save the trees!"

Toklo loomed over her. "Lusa! How are you going to fight that many flat-faces? Look at those firebeasts! They'd crush you! And what if the flat-faces have firesticks?" His eyes blazed.

Lusa stopped struggling and fell limp in Kallik's grip. "But the spirits," she wailed. "The flat-faces have cut down their trees, and now they are *drowning*!"

Kallik gently let her go. "We can't help them."

Lusa stared at her friends. Were they really going to let the spirits drown?

Yakone headed away. "Let's look from the shore."

"Will that help?" Lusa hurried after him. Did he have a plan? Toklo and Kallik swished through the undergrowth behind her.

They skirted the clearing and emerged from the forest a little way downstream. The riverside sloped away from them, sandy underpaw, with great boulders lying here and there. Yakone padded past them, slowing as he reached a stretch of beach where the flat-face clearing opened onto the river.

A firebeast was turning at the top. It hunched its back and tipped another haul of logs down the slope. They rolled into the water, clattering against the mass already jammed between both shores. Lusa stared, horrified. The river was hidden under countless logs.

"Why don't they wash downstream?" Kallik wondered.

"They're trapped." Yakone pointed his snout toward a gleaming vine, as thick and shiny as a water snake. It looked like a silvery strand of whatever firebeast pelts were made of. One end was fastened to a boulder on the shore, snagged by a fat, shimmering claw that had been driven into the stone. The other end spanned the river.

"It's holding a web!" Lusa could see tight silver mesh flashing beneath the surface, as though woven by a giant swimming spider. It held the floating mass of trees in place, stopping them from being carried downriver by the current.

The logs creaked as they pressed against the web. "They're trying to break free!" Lusa gasped. She scanned the bark. Faces showed among the knots. How many bears' spirits were trapped here? She glanced from one log to another, seeing faces everywhere. Their eyes pleaded with her, their jaws gaped wide in noiseless terror. Lusa's pelt prickled with alarm. "We have to help them!"

Before she could dart forward, another firebeast emptied its load at the top of the bank. The logs tumbled down, spraying her pelt with bark chips as they clattered past.

Kallik pulled her away. "We need to get out of sight."

"What about the spirits?" Lusa wailed.

Toklo steered her toward the trees and pushed her through a clump of ragwort. In the shadows beyond, she stared at her friends. Their pelts were ruffled. The firebeast roar thundered behind them. "What are we going to do?" Lusa demanded.

Toklo shook his head. "I don't know. We've got to think of a way to get past the floating trees."

"Get *past*?" Lusa tried to ignore the shrieking of the bear spirits as it shrilled through her ear fur. "We've got to save them!"

Toklo curled his lip. "Impossible!"

"Is it?" Kallik tipped her head. "There's only vine holding that web in place. If we could break it, the trees would be free."

Lusa nodded frantically. "Oh, please, please, set the trees free. The bear spirits need us!"

"But it's *flat-face* vine," Toklo pointed out. "How are we meant to break it?"

"At least we could try," Yakone rumbled. "We haven't tested its strength yet."

Hope sparked in Lusa. "What if we all pushed against the vine? We might snap it."

Toklo seemed to flinch. "You want us to wade into the river? Did you see how many trees are pushing against the web? We'll get crushed or drowned. Besides, if the trees can't break through, how can we? I'm sorry, Lusa, but the flat-faces have trapped them for whatever reason, and we can't change that."

Lusa stared at him. Wasn't Toklo even going to try to save the bear spirits? He was usually ready to try anything. She noticed his gaze glitter as he eyed the water. "Are you *scared*?" she snapped.

Toklo looked at his paws. "Of course not."

Kallik narrowed her eyes. "The current's not fierce here, Toklo. It's not like when we rescued the flat-face cub. Couldn't we try?"

"With the place full of flat-faces?" he argued.

Yakone shifted his paws. "Let's get away from this noise and wait until dark," he suggested. "Perhaps we can take a closer look when the flat-faces are sleeping."

Kallik nodded. "Good idea."

Lusa flattened her ears against the screaming of the bear spirits. "Okay," she agreed, trembling.

Toklo headed back through the forest. He wove between pines, following the path of the river, which glittered beyond the trunks. Lusa followed Kallik and Yakone, dragging her paws. Every hair in her pelt screamed at her to run back to the bear spirits, but she forced herself to keep up with her friends. She let out a sigh of relief when Toklo stopped in a clearing. The roaring had eased to a distant grumble. Kallik sat down while Yakone sniffed the undergrowth.

How can they carry on like nothing's happening? Lusa paced beside a clump of brambles, the shrieks of bear spirits echoing in her ears. She couldn't believe so many were suffering, bobbing helplessly in the water. Why were the flat-faces trying to drown them?

"Are you hungry?" Yakone asked her.

Lusa continued pacing, hardly hearing him.

"Let's fish," Kallik suggested.

As the two white bears headed for the river, Lusa glanced up through the branches. The sun was still high. Such a long time until dark! Impatience pricked in her paws. When Kallik and Yakone returned with fish, she wrinkled her nose at the smell. Her gaze flicked toward the sky, tracking the sun as it slid with agonizing slowness toward the horizon.

At last, day eased to dusk and dusk turned to night. "Can we go and look now?" she demanded.

Toklo cocked his head to listen. "It sounds like the flat-faces are still awake." The air trembled with the distant roaring of the firebeasts. Harsh white light flashed through the trees.

"I'm going to look." Lusa marched toward the shore. She wouldn't let anyone stop her this time. Her heart twisted in her chest. The bear spirits must be terrified, trapped in the river, not knowing what was happening to them. What if their faces had disappeared from the bark? Where could they go? Who would watch over the forest? She heard pawsteps behind her and flexed her claws. "You can't stop me," she growled. "I have to see the spirits. I have to know if they're still there."

"I know." Kallik caught up with her. "I'm not going to stop you."

Lusa padded onto the shore and headed upstream. Kallik

fell in beside her. "When I was a cub, I used to worry about white bear spirits trapped beneath the ice. I wanted to help them find their way out."

"But you knew they'd find their way to the stars eventually," Lusa pointed out. "Black bear spirits aren't supposed to be in the water. They need to feel roots beneath them and know they are still part of the forest."

Kallik's fishy breath billowed in the night air. "Every creature needs to feel connected to the land they were born in," she murmured. Her pelt glowed like the moon against the dark shore.

Moving closer to Kallik, Lusa padded on in silence as they neared the flat-face clearing. A firebeast rumbled at the top of the slope as it tipped a fresh load of logs into the river. Lights flared so brightly that Lusa had to screw up her eyes to see. "Don't they ever stop?"

"They may, if we wait." Kallik sat down.

Lusa flinched as more logs tumbled down the slope. Bark screeched as it ripped away from the soft heart of the trees. "Look!" With a fresh jolt of horror, she spotted a firebeast on the far bank. A spindly leg lifted from its spine. Its spiked paw reached for the logs. With a howl, it snatched a bunch out of the water and scooped them into the air. The whole leg swung around and dropped the trees onto the flat back of another firebeast. There was a deafening rumble, and the newly laden firebeast pulled away into the forest.

Kallik leaned forward. "This must be how flat-faces move trees across the water when there's no bridge."

"Move trees?" The words choked in Lusa's throat: "They're stealing *spirits*! We can't let them do this!"

Kallik jumped to her paws. "Let's get the others."

Lusa shook her head. "I'm not leaving them."

Kallik held her gaze for a moment, then turned away. "Wait for me to get back," she warned. "Don't do anything fish-brained."

As the white bear charged away, Lusa crept forward. Her eyes were adjusting to the harsh glare of the flat-face lights. She squinted up the slope, watching a firebeast roll away. Leaning forward, she noticed how long it took for another to appear and fling its load into the river. They were slowing down. The gaps between were longer each time. Were the flat-faces and firebeasts growing tired at last?

Bear spirits, I'm going to save you. I promise. Lusa pelted forward and ducked under the silver vine. Splashing into the river, she lunged for a log and hauled herself onto it, wobbling as it spun beneath her paws. She ran with the roll, keeping upright, heart pounding as she scrambled onto the next trunk, then the next. A knot in the bark frowned up at her. "I'm sorry!" Lusa landed too close to the end of the log and bobbed down into the water. Her pelt fluffed up in alarm as water washed her paws. She threw herself forward, clinging to the next log.

"Forgive me!" she wailed to the bear spirits. She was trampling all over them. But she had to see them for herself, and let them know that she was here, that she hadn't abandoned them to the flat-faces. She dodged out of the glare of the white lights as she headed across the logs. They were jammed tighter here, near the middle of the river; it was easier to keep her balance. The river swirled, black, beneath them, whispering as it lapped the logs.

"I can hear you!" Lusa called to the spirits. They sounded frightened, their anxious sighs lifting into the breeze.

Lusa felt a jolt run through the pack. She turned as another load crashed into the river. The trees around her creaked and moaned. "I'll save you!" Lusa bounded back toward the shore. Her paw slid from a log and splashed down into the water. She crashed, muzzle-first, onto the bark. Pain jabbed through her jaw and she clung on, dizzy with shock. The log held still beneath her. "Thank you!" she whispered to the spirit inside. The log held firm as she heaved herself to her paws and stepped gingerly onto the next log. She blinked as she reached the flat-face light. No one must see her. She hurled herself forward and managed to scramble to shore.

She pelted downstream. "Kallik! Toklo! Yakone!"

Shapes moved in the moonlight. She recognized a flash of white pelt. They were coming. Lusa scampered to meet them, panting. "We have to save them! They're wailing!"

Toklo skidded to a halt and glanced nervously at the water. "We can't," he growled.

"You're scared!" Lusa accused him.

"The river tried to kill me when I rescued that flat-face!" Toklo snapped.

Frustration surged through Lusa. There wasn't time to be scared.

Kallik's pelt brushed hers. "The river is strong, Toklo, but we're with you. We won't let it hurt you."

Toklo ignored her. "Let's just wait for the flat-faces to go to sleep and get past this mess."

"Mess?" Lusa stared at him. "I can't believe you're giving up! Aren't you even going to try to save the spirits?"

"We're not strong enough," Toklo insisted.

"We won't know unless we try!" Bear spirits were trapped! They had to release the logs! It was the only chance the spirits had of escaping. They could reach the shore, far away from the flat-faces, and find new homes. Logs crashed behind her, and Lusa spun as the next load bounced into the river.

"Please, Toklo. We must help—" Her words caught in her throat as she spotted silver bark among the dark pine. "Chenoa?" she whispered. Splashing through the shallows, Lusa raced toward a birch as it rolled into the river. As the birch bobbed in the water, Lusa saw Chenoa's face etched in the bark—broad muzzle, neat ears, warm eyes. *"Chenoa!"* The face gazed back at her.

Lusa turned to the others. "How did she get here? We left her days ago!"

Kallik looked somber. "The firebeasts must have carried her here."

"We have to save her!" Lusa stared desperately at Toklo.

"Is that really Chenoa?" The brown bear peered, blinking, at the birch.

Lusa grabbed Chenoa's tree and dragged it toward shore. "We can haul her out!" she puffed.

"Move!" Yakone roared.

Logs clattered down the bank. Lusa froze as she watched them bouncing toward her. Claws grabbed her flank and ripped her away as a huge pine crashed past.

"That was too close!" Kallik hugged Lusa against her belly.

Lusa struggled free. She stared at Toklo. Bark chips specked his muzzle. "You saw her, didn't you? You saw it was Chenoa! We can't leave her here!"

Toklo's eyes glittered with fear. "She's with the other tree spirits. She's not alone."

Yakone flexed his claws. "Let's get out of here before someone gets killed."

"No!" Lusa barked. "There are *spirits* in the trees!" She swung toward Kallik. "Did I ever doubt that *your* ancestors were beneath the ice?"

Kallik shifted her paws.

"They're trapped! In the water! They'll drown if they stay here!" Lusa jerked her snout to the clawed firebeast on the far shore. "Or that monster will take them somewhere worse!"

"She's right," Kallik murmured. "We can't walk away from this."

Lusa fixed her gaze on Toklo. "I abandoned Chenoa before," she growled. "I'm not doing it again."

The flat-face lights blinked out. Lusa gasped as darkness swallowed her up. As she strained to adjust to moonlight, the roaring rumbled to a halt. Lusa's heart soared. The firebeasts had stopped. "We can save them! We must!"

"Okay." Toklo lifted his muzzle. "We need to break that vine." He padded to where one end was hooked into the rock.

Thrusting his weight against it, he grunted with effort. Sighing, Yakone padded to join him. Kallik followed.

Lusa rushed to help. She grabbed the vine with her paws. It felt hard as stone, and slippery. Straining, she pushed beside Kallik. "It's not moving."

"Let's bite through it." Yakone clamped his jaws around the vine and tugged hard.

"Careful." Kallik stiffened. Dark patches were spreading through the white fur around Yakone's muzzle. "Your mouth's bleeding!" He let go, spitting out blood.

Lusa wrapped her paws tighter around the vine and pulled harder. It held firm. She glanced along its length, following it down to where it tethered the web. "It might be easier to break in the water." She splashed into the river. There was no room between the press of logs and the web. She scrabbled over the floating trees, digging her claws deep into the bark to steady herself. "I'm sorry!" she whispered to the spirits. Balancing on a pine, she pushed at the web. It was as tough as the vine! Panic bubbled in her belly. "I can't move it!"

On the shore, Toklo gnawed at the claw holding the vine. He backed away, blood dripping from his jaws. "It's too hard."

"We're not strong enough!" Lusa wailed. She scrambled back to shore, her pelt dripping. "What do we do—" As she spoke, a shadow cut across her path. She looked up with a gasp.

A huge moose gazed down at her, its wide antlers framed by the moon. Its gaze caught hers, its blue eyes pale as ice. A flame flickered deep within them. And inside Lusa's head, a voice said, *I can help you.*

Lusa froze. "Ujurak? Is that you?"

The moose turned toward the river. It padded down to the water and waded in. Lusa gulped. It left no hoofprints in the sand. The moose moved through the water without a ripple and the logs shifted, opening to let it pass.

Lusa felt pelts brush around her. Kallik, Yakone, and Toklo were staring at the huge animal.

"Is it Ujurak?" Toklo whispered.

"Yes." Lusa's eyes widened.

"I thought he was a bear." Yakone sounded puzzled.

"I told you, he changes shape," Kallik murmured.

The moose sniffed at the mesh, then waded out of the river. It touched its nose to the vine, following it up to the boulder.

"We can't break it," Toklo explained.

The moose gazed at him wordlessly.

I've missed you, Ujurak. The words sprang from Lusa's heart.

The moose seemed to hear. It jerked its soft muzzle around. *I am always with you, my friend.*

Lusa felt the words like warm sun through her pelt. She stared, joy rising in her chest, as the moose walked back into the water. Once more, the logs cleared a path. The moose beckoned with a flick of its antlers, and Kallik waded in behind him. Yakone followed and grabbed hold of the web. Lusa glanced at Toklo. He was hesitating at the river's edge. Stiffening, he splashed into the water, screwing up his eyes like a cub.

Lusa scampered after, staying in the shallows where her hindpaws could get a grip on the riverbed. She lifted her forepaws and gripped the web. Its tough threads dug into her pads.

"Push!" Kallik gave the order.

Together, the bears heaved. Lusa felt her muscles burning. Her hindpaws slipped, and she splashed underwater. Coughing, she surfaced and caught hold of the web once more. The vine creaked. Were they shifting something? Lusa pushed harder. *We can do it!* Toklo grunted beside her. Kallik's eyes bulged. A roar rumbled in Yakone's throat.

The moose watched them work, his pale blue eyes full of encouragement.

Lusa plunged her muzzle into the water, pushing with all her might. Something thumped her back, and she tumbled beneath the surface. Glancing up, she glimpsed silver bark through the water. Chenoa was nudging her! Lusa surfaced with a splash. "I'm pushing!" she promised. Heaving her shoulder against the web, she quivered as she strained.

Suddenly the vine shifted. With a crack, the claw pinning it to the rock gave way. The web folded beneath Lusa's paws as the vine snaked down the bank and disappeared into the water.

"Get out of the way!" Kallik roared.

The sea of logs sailed toward them. Lusa splashed from the water and scrambled onto the bank. Toklo landed beside her, panting.

The spirits were free! The river was unblocked! With a gasp, Lusa saw that Kallik and Yakone were still in the water. "Hurry!" Lusa barked as Kallik splashed toward the shore.

Wood cracked and bark splintered as the current swept the logs closer to the white bears. With a bellow, Yakone threw himself against a log and held it back with his shoulders. Trunks piled up behind, and his face twisted with effort. Kallik bounded toward the shore. She exploded out of the shallows and skidded to a halt beside Toklo.

"Yakone!" Her panicked cry echoed across the river.

Yakone let go of the log and lunged for the shore. A trunk bashed his rump, knocking his paws out from under him. He began to spin away, logs crowding toward him. Kallik darted forward and snapped at his scruff. As she grabbed him, his paws hit the riverbed and he scrambled from the water, logs clattering behind.

Lusa's heart soared. They were safe! And she could hear the trees sighing. The spirits were singing as they slid downstream. "Good-bye, Chenoa," she whispered, a lump rising in her throat. "You're free now to join your mother." She dug her claws into the sand. *I'll be alone soon.* The future she'd imagined with Chenoa slipped away with her spirit.

She stiffened. *The moose!* Where was he? Just before the mesh gave way, he'd been standing in the middle of the river. "Ujurak!" She scanned the mass of trees skimming past.

Toklo raced to the river's edge. "Ujurak!"

The moose had disappeared. Was it lost beneath the logs?

Something flashed at the edge of Lusa's vision. She whirled and saw a beaver haul itself onto the bank. It shook out its heavy fur and gazed straight at Lusa. Its eyes burned brightly in the moonlight.

Ujurak! She knew it was him. "Thank you!" she called.

A voice whispered in her mind. *Chenoa is free now. Travel on, my friends. I'm watching over you.*

The beaver turned to go.

"Wait!" Lusa called. "Why did she have to drown? Couldn't you save her?"

The beaver looked back. *I can't change every bear's destiny.*

Lusa blinked, her eyes misting.

The beaver slid into the water and, with a flick of its powerful tail, disappeared beneath the ripples. *I grieved with you.*

CHAPTER TWENTY

Toklo

Toklo watched the logs slide away. They rode the current, rolling and bumping, glittering with starlight before disappearing into darkness. *We set them free!*

Lusa stood wide-eyed beside him, her wet pelt spiked up in alarm. Toklo pictured the river filled with black bear spirits. They would be swimming, free as fish, among the brown bear spirits that already flowed through the endless stream. Relief flooded Toklo. Perhaps the river didn't hate him after all. It fed him and cooled him and rinsed the dust from his fur. And when he died, it would carry his spirit to the sea and to freedom.

Good-bye, Chenoa. The silver birch tumbled away, its bark shining among the dark pine trunks. *You'll be free soon.*

Lusa bounced beside him. "Ujurak came!"

"He helped us!" Kallik exclaimed.

"We couldn't have done it without him." Toklo had recognized Ujurak-moose the moment he'd appeared. He felt at peace. Their friend was still with them. "He set Chenoa free."

Yakone turned away. "We'd better get moving."

Toklo nudged him gently. "You still don't believe?"

Lusa scampered around the white bear. "But you saw him with your own eyes."

"I saw a moose," Yakone grunted.

Kallik's eyes flashed with amusement. "A very helpful moose." She headed along the shore, Lusa on her heels. Yakone shambled after them.

Toklo dipped his head to the river. "Thank you," he whispered, and hurried after his friends.

They trekked quickly past the log-rolling slope and followed the river. The shore became rocky, the river narrow and choppy. Foam flashed in the moonlight, and boulders sparkled. Before long, Toklo's paws grew heavy. Every muscle ached. But they couldn't stop yet. They had to get clear of the flat-faces and their firebeasts.

At last, the horizon paled as dawn pushed into the sky. Squinting, Toklo could make out the purple peaks of the mountain range Chenoa had shown him. The river chattered as it passed. It drew him on, pulling him toward the rising sun. He trusted the river. It carried a faint scent that tugged at his heart; it was leading him home.

As dawn melted the darkness and streaked the clouds pink, Toklo slowed. Lusa was limping. Kallik and Yakone tottered and tripped over the rocky shore.

"We should rest," Toklo called.

Kallik turned, her gaze soft with relief. "I'll make a nest near the trees."

Toklo's belly rumbled. "Let's hunt first."

Yakone headed for the river, wading into the shallows. Lusa bounded after him, splashing through the water.

"Don't scare the fish!" Yakone warned. "Or they'll hide in the deep channels."

Toklo rumbled with amusement. The white bear thought like a brown bear now. He watched as Yakone focused on the fast-flowing water, frowning with concentration. Swift as a fox, he slapped his paws down with a splash. He hooked out a trout and flung it to the shore. *He hunts like a brown bear, too.* Toklo remembered his days ice fishing. When they each reached the end of their journey, they'd have more skills than any other bears.

Lusa scampered after the fish, nosing it away from the edge and killing it with a bite. Kallik waded into the river a few bearlengths downstream. Yakone called to her without taking his gaze from the water. "Here comes another one."

Kallik stiffened, eyes fixing on the glittering stream, then pounced as Yakone's fish reached her.

Toklo turned away from his friends and headed for the forest to hunt. The river might be his friend, but he wasn't ready to get his paws wet again.

They slept through sunhigh, in the shade of the trees.

Toklo woke with a start. His pelt prickled. He sat up and glanced at the trees. Was something watching them? He got to his paws and shook out his pelt. He'd seen too many flat-faces; they'd set him on edge.

"Toklo?" Kallik lifted her muzzle, blinking away sleep. "Is everything okay?"

Yakone moved beside her. Lusa was still snoring.

"Everything's fine," Toklo promised. His fur lifted along his spine, but he forced it flat. "I'm just a bit spooked."

Yakone opened one eye. "Let's put some more distance between us and the flat-faces."

Toklo glanced up through the branches. The sky had cleared to a brilliant blue. There was plenty of walking time before sunset.

Kallik nudged Lusa with her nose. "Wake up, sleepyhead."

Lusa rolled on her back and stretched like a bobcat. "Can't we sleep some more?"

"Toklo and Yakone think we should keep moving," Kallik told her.

Lusa stumbled sleepily to her feet. "Okay." She rubbed her nose with a clumsy paw.

Kallik winced as she hauled herself up.

Toklo jerked his muzzle around. "What's the matter?"

"My flank got bruised trying to save the flat-face cub," Kallik confessed. "Freeing the logs woke the pain."

Yakone touched his nose to her side. "It feels a bit warm. Should we rest longer?"

Kallik shook her head. "I want to get as far away from those tree killers as I can."

Toklo kicked the bracken they'd lined their nest with, sweeping the brittle stalks into the undergrowth. "Let's leave as little trace as we can." He couldn't shake the feeling they were being watched.

Lusa's eyes widened. "Do you think the flat-faces will be hunting us?"

Kallik frowned. "They'll never guess we set their logs free."

"They'll think the vine snapped by accident," Yakone added.

"Let's hope so." Toklo padded between the trees and bounded onto the shore. The glare of the sun made him squint after the shade of the forest. Lusa bounced out beside him, Kallik and Yakone lumbering after.

Toklo headed along the shore. Wide stretches of boulders gave way, every now and then, to pebbly beaches. The river curved through the trees, narrower and quieter now after the noise and mayhem of the logs and waterfall.

As they leaped a stream running across the shore, Kallik caught up to Toklo. "Your pelt's ruffled," she commented softly.

"I don't like this part of the forest." Should he tell her about the unease he'd felt since he woke?

"I know what you mean." Kallik glanced into the trees. "I keep feeling like we're being watched."

"Me too." Toklo's heart lurched. He quickened his pace. The sooner they were out of here the better. A sharp, musky scent made him freeze. "What's that?"

Kallik stopped beside him. Her nostrils twitched. "I don't know, but I don't like it."

Yakone joined them with Lusa beside him. "I smell trouble," the white bear growled.

"Have you smelled that scent before?" Toklo searched his memory.

"Not exactly." Yakone twitched his ears. "But it feels bad."

Toklo swallowed. He knew what Yakone meant. Deep in his belly, he sensed danger.

Lusa's eyes glittered with worry. "Where's it coming from?"

"I don't know," Toklo admitted. "But the shore feels too exposed. We should head into the woods."

Yakone backed away. "If we stay on the shore, we can see what's coming."

"And *it* can see *us*," Kallik pointed out.

Toklo's gaze flicked from Kallik to Lusa, then Yakone. "Let's try the woods and see if the scent's fainter there."

Yakone frowned but didn't argue. They headed for the trees. Toklo led the way, nostrils wide. Sap scent drowned the musky tang, but he still felt uneasy. He glanced behind. Kallik and Yakone were watching their paws as they lumbered between the trees. Lusa leaped roots and ducked brambles, pulling quickly ahead. "Stay close," Toklo warned her. He scanned the undergrowth, trying to find deer trails that Kallik and Yakone could follow easily.

"Toklo!" Lusa's call made him jump.

"What is it?" He couldn't see her through the dense greenery. "What's wrong?" Heart thumping, he veered from the trail, leaving Yakone and Kallik to find their own way though the undergrowth.

Lusa had stopped in a clearing. "That smell's here."

Toklo sniffed. He stiffened as the musky odor bathed his tongue.

"I'm scared, Toklo," Lusa whimpered.

"We'll be okay," he promised, hoping it was true. "We just need to keep moving."

"But it feels like we're being hunted." Lusa's eyes were wide with fear.

"Of course we're not," Toklo huffed. "We're *bears.*" He dodged her gaze. She was right. It felt like something was tracking them.

A roar ripped through the air.

Toklo whirled around. "Yakone!"

Lusa charged past him, heading back along the trail. Toklo pelted after Lusa. His belly tightened as he heard the pain in Yakone's howl. The stone tang of blood filled the air. He skidded to a halt as he spotted Kallik and Yakone. "What happened?"

Yakone was writhing on his feet, kicking out with his hind-paws.

"Stay still!" Kallik ordered. "You'll make it worse." She stared down at his forepaw with white-rimmed eyes.

Toklo followed her gaze. He blinked, shock hollowing his belly.

One of Yakone's forepaws was clasped between gleaming, jagged silver jaws. Blood welled where they dug into his flesh and drenched his white fur.

Yakone's eyes rolled in agony. "Get it off me!"

"Hold still!" Kallik roared.

Lusa backed away.

"Stop!" Toklo ordered. "Everyone stand still. There might be more."

"What is it?" Lusa croaked.

"I don't know," Toklo growled. "But it looks like a flat-face left it here. It's made of the same stuff as that shiny vine."

Yakone was trembling.

"It's okay," Kallik soothed. "We'll get it off you."

"Why doesn't it let go?" Yakone hissed through gritted teeth.

"Don't move your paw," Toklo warned.

"There's another one over here!" Lusa called from behind a tree.

As Toklo turned his head, he spotted a pair of yellow eyes watching from the bracken, unblinking and cold. Toklo's pelt lifted along his spine. The musky odor that had scared them on the shore washed over him as the creature slid from the bracken, its brown-and-gray fur well camouflaged against the stalks. It was the size of a large dog, almost as big as Lusa, with a long back and scrawny, springy legs. Its narrow, pointed snout twitched toward Toklo. Its ears were pricked with excitement, and saliva glinted on its sharp teeth.

Coyote.

Toklo backed toward Lusa. She was sniffing the ground. "Come and look, Toklo."

Toklo checked Kallik. She was crouched over Yakone, soothing him. No one else had seen the coyote. He flinched as more shapes moved beyond the bracken, pacing low to the ground. Toklo could make out their pelts, thick as a wolf's. *They've been stalking us.* Toklo's throat tightened. *But we're bears!* Surely the coyotes didn't believe they could win a fight with bears?

The coyote lifted its snout and met his gaze boldly. Toklo saw confidence in its eyes, the same confidence he'd felt when facing up to Hakan. It must belong to a big pack. Toklo felt sick. *They* know *they can win.* How many were there?

He stared as the coyote turned away and disappeared through the bracken. Toklo hurried toward Lusa, blood thumping in his ears. "We've got to free Yakone." Trapped in the silver jaws, he'd be easy prey for the coyotes. Even if the bears stayed to protect him, they couldn't fight a whole pack forever. But if they pulled him from the silver jaws while they were still shut, Yakone might lose his foot. Then all the blood would drain out of him, and he'd die for sure.

Lusa was sniffing a bedraggled shape in the jaws she'd found behind a tree. "Look at this, Toklo."

The stench of death reached his muzzle. He slid past her and looked down at the rotting body of a raccoon. It was thoroughly mangled in the clamped silver teeth. "Flat-faces must put them here to kill things," Toklo said.

Lusa stared at him with round eyes. "Why?" She stared at the decomposing raccoon. "They can't want to eat it, because they haven't come to get it. So why kill it?"

Behind them, Yakone groaned.

"We have to get him out." Kallik's growl was tight with panic. "Before that thing bites his paw off."

Or the coyotes get him.

"There has to be a way of opening these things." Fighting

back fear, Toklo sniffed at the jaws holding the raccoon. His snout wrinkled. It smelled foul. Maggots crawled through its pelt. Warily he put out a paw and touched the edge of the jaws. A shiny twig jutted out either side. Toklo pushed down on one and the jaws started to tip toward him. Without thinking, he steadied them by putting his other paw on the opposite side. As he pressed both jutting pieces, the raccoon twitched.

"The jaws are opening!" Lusa gasped.

Toklo jumped backward, heart lurching.

"Press it again!" Lusa urged. "It was opening, I promise."

Gingerly Toklo put his paws on the hard sticks on either side of the jaws and pushed down. The jaws creaked open and the raccoon slithered out and flopped onto the pine needles.

Toklo let go. The jaws snapped shut. "I know how to free him!" He raced back to Yakone. "Lean back," he ordered. The white bear's eyes were glazing. He swayed away from Toklo, a tortured growl rumbling in his throat. Kallik stared at Toklo, her gaze sharp with terror.

"It's okay," Toklo said. "I know how to open it." He put his paws on either side of the teeth that had bitten into Yakone's paw. Steadying his breath, he pressed down slowly.

Yakone gasped as the jaws ripped from his flesh. Toklo pushed down harder. The shiny sticks jabbed, cold and hard, into his pads. "Get him out!" he hissed, straining to stop the jaws from snapping shut. *Spirits, don't let my paws slip!*

Kallik grabbed Yakone's scruff and dragged him backward. Yakone whined through gritted teeth. Toklo ducked as Yakone's bloody paw flashed past his nose. He let go of the trap and hopped out of the way as it snapped shut.

Lusa raced over. "Is he okay?"

Yakone lay on his side, flanks heaving. Kallik peered at his paw. Her muzzle wrinkled. "It's worse than any bite I've seen," she murmured, sounding ill.

Toklo sniffed at the silver jaws, which were clenched tight again. Sickness rose in his throat as he spotted two bloodied toes gripped between the shiny teeth. He told himself that it could have been worse; Yakone could have lost his whole foot. But would he be able to walk without those toes? And catch prey with fewer claws?

Kallik nudged the white bear. "Yakone? Can you hear me?"

Yakone struggled to sit up. "How is it?" he asked thickly. "My paw? Is it okay?"

"You've still got it," Kallik told him. Toklo could tell she was making an effort to stay calm. "But we need to clean it up and stop the bleeding."

Toklo pictured the coyote's eyes, flashing through the shadows. "We don't have time," he growled. "We have to keep moving."

Kallik's eyes widened. "Yakone can't walk!"

"He's going to have to." Toklo scanned the undergrowth, ears alert for the sound of pawsteps. *We're prey now.*

Toklo crouched beside Yakone and heaved his shoulder beneath the white bear. Straining, he pushed Yakone to his paws. Kallik raced to prop him up on the other side.

"Okay?" Toklo turned his snout toward Yakone. The white bear's breath was coming in gasps.

"Okay," Yakone croaked.

Lusa popped up in front of Toklo. "Shouldn't we let him rest?"

"There's no time," Toklo repeated. Yakone was going to slow them down as it was. He flicked his muzzle forward. "Lead the way, Lusa," he ordered. "Find the smoothest path and hold back any branches or brambles so we can pass easily." Lusa scampered ahead, sniffing for trails. She leaned against a bramble, pushing it clear as Toklo and Kallik helped Yakone past.

Toklo glanced down. Blood dripped, hot and fragrant, leaving a trail behind them on the forest floor. Toklo's heart sank. *It'll sharpen the coyotes' hunger and show them exactly where we are.* He fixed his gaze ahead. There was nothing they could do now but keep moving.

CHAPTER TWENTY-ONE

Kallik

Panting, Kallik heaved Yakone past Lusa as the black bear held back another bramble.

Yakone was mumbling, his voice slurred with pain. "Stupid bushes. Stupid trees. Can't see where I'm going."

Pain shot through Kallik's bruised flank, but she ignored it. Her mind was whirling. Just this morning, they'd been fine. Toklo had been nervous, but they'd been happy and healthy. *We just rescued Chenoa's spirit!* Yakone had made his jaws bleed trying to break the flat-face vine. Watching him fight to help their friends had made her heart soar.

Ujurak, why didn't you warn us? She glanced up through the branches. *Yakone doesn't deserve this.* The smell of his blood clogged her nostrils. Her fur was sticky with it. Yakone's mangled paw was still dripping. Kallik felt sick. On the ice, injured bears died quickly. *Is it the same in the forest?*

"Great spirits!" Toklo cursed as he tripped.

"Why don't we walk along the shore?" Kallik suggested. They were shadowing the river; she could see it through the trees.

"There's more cover here," Toklo puffed.

"Why do we need cover?"

As she spoke, Yakone lurched between them. Lusa rushed to help, ducking under Yakone's muzzle as it jerked forward.

Kallik could hardly breathe for the pain shooting through her flank. "We have to rest," she growled to Toklo.

"We can't stop," he hissed.

"But we're both exhausted!"

Yakone was growling under his breath, lost in a world of pain.

Please don't let him die. Guilt swamped Kallik. It was okay to risk her own life for her friends. But she'd asked Yakone to risk his, and now he might never make it home.

Yakone fell silent and slumped heavily between them. He was unconscious.

"We can't carry him any farther," Kallik grunted.

Toklo swung his head toward the trees. "There's a thicket over there." He jerked his muzzle to a bramble tangled between two pines.

Lusa ran ahead and sniffed it. "The earth's soft and clean."

Panting, Kallik guided Yakone toward it. Toklo pressed on, and between them, they hauled the white bear across the needle-strewn forest floor.

"Clear a path to the middle of the brambles," Toklo ordered Lusa.

Kallik frowned. "How are we going to get him in there?" She flicked her nose toward a tree a bearlength away. The earth was hollowed out between the roots. "He'd be much more comfortable there," she puffed. "And it'd be easy to lie him down."

"He'll be safer in here." Toklo shifted to let Lusa past.

"Safer from what?" Lusa asked as she tugged at the branches and pressed them aside with her rump.

Kallik narrowed her eyes. "Are you scared there will be wolverines?"

Toklo's gaze darkened. "The scent of blood might attract scavengers," he mumbled. "Help me get him in."

Kallik stumbled forward with Yakone. She could see a space just beyond the passage Lusa had made. Toklo squeezed into it and turned to grab Yakone's pelt in his jaws. He dragged the white bear inside, hissing with the strain. Screwing up her eyes against the twigs, Kallik shouldered her way in after him, shoving Yakone past the snagging thorns.

Inside the bramble thicket, they let him fall. The white bear collapsed on the soft earth, his head lolling sideways, his flanks barely moving. The branches closed around them, Lusa shut outside.

"Kallik?" Lusa called through the thorns. "Is he going to be okay?"

"I don't know!" Kallik smelled Yakone's breath. It had a sour tang. Blood was still pulsing from his paw. "We have to stop the bleeding."

Toklo blinked at her. "How?"

Lusa's black snout appeared under the branches. "We could pack it with mud."

"Mud might turn the wound bad," Kallik pointed out.

Lusa scowled, then brightened. "I know!" She began to squeeze out of the thicket.

"Wait!" Toklo's bark was sharp with fear.

Lusa froze. Kallik jerked her muzzle around. Toklo had sounded like he was scared to let Lusa go out alone. He'd always been protective of the young bear, but he knew better than to treat her like a helpless cub.

"I'm just going to get herbs," Lusa told him.

"I'll come with you." Toklo followed as she burrowed her way out. "Stay out of sight," he warned Kallik before he disappeared.

Kallik blinked. Why was Toklo being so cautious? Was there something he wasn't telling them? She curled around Yakone and began lapping the fur on his flank in long, smooth strokes. *Hang on, Yakone,* she begged. *We'll take care of you.* She listened to his shallow breathing, willing his flank to keep rising and falling. Lusa and Toklo were taking ages. Sunshine glittered through the branches, dappling Yakone's grubby pelt.

Hurry up!

Pawsteps sounded outside the bush. Kallik sat up, tasting the air.

"Toklo!" She pulled aside a pawful of branches, wincing as thorns pricked her pads. "Lusa!"

The black bear pushed through the thicket, herb scent rolling ahead of her. Kallik recognized it at once. "Chenoa's leaves!"

Lusa was clutching a bunch between her jaws. She spat them onto the floor of the makeshift den as Toklo squeezed in behind her. "They fixed my wounds." Lusa's eyes sparkled. "There was lots of it by the shore. We can grab as much as we need."

"We're not staying here longer than we have to," Toklo warned.

Kallik looked at him in surprise. "Why not?"

"We're just resting, then moving on."

Why was he in such a hurry to get them away from here?

Lusa was busy chewing up leaves. She spat the pulp onto Yakone's paw and began pressing it into the wide gap where his toes used to be. Kallik flinched away, feeling queasy.

Lusa lifted her head. "It's still bleeding." Her eyes glittered with worry. "The leaves aren't stopping it."

Kallik's belly tightened. The floor of the den was already red with Yakone's blood. If he lost much more, he would be dead.

Toklo nosed Lusa out of the way and inspected Yakone's paw. "We have to stop it flowing."

Lusa tipped her head. "Like blocking a river?"

Toklo narrowed his eyes. "But instead of stopping it flowing out, we can block it farther upstream."

Kallik blinked. "Like a beaver dam! But how?"

Toklo barged out of the bush and returned a moment later with a long, soft tendril of knotweed between his teeth. He lifted Yakone's leg with a front paw and felt along it with the other. "This is the softest place," he announced when his paw was halfway to Yakone's knee. He draped the knotweed over it. "Hold that," he told Kallik.

She pressed the stem in place, feeling it rigid under her pad, and watched curiously as Toklo used his free paw to wrap the trailing end around Yakone's leg. He drew the tendril up the other side, grabbing it with his teeth. "Keep pressing, Kallik," he mumbled. Kallik pressed harder, leaning out of the way as Toklo tugged the stem taut. Hooking it with his paw, he wrapped the tendril around Yakone's leg again. It flopped from his grasp.

"Stay still," Toklo ordered, reaching for the dangling end of the knotweed. He snagged it with a claw and pulled hard. The stem tightened, cutting into Yakone's pelt. Toklo leaned close and nipped the loops he'd made with his teeth, pulling hard enough to push the trailing end underneath with his claw. "That should hold." He sat back and cocked his head. "I hope."

Lusa leaned forward and peered at the white bear's paw. "The bleeding is slowing!" she barked triumphantly. Quickly, she chewed more pulp and wadded it into the wound.

Yakone stirred. "Where are we?" He tried to lift his head but fell back, panting.

Kallik lapped his cheek. "We've made a den for you," she murmured. "We're just fixing your wound."

He fell against her, his eyes closing as he drifted back into unconsciousness.

"Has it stopped bleeding?" Kallik asked Lusa.

Lusa looked up from his paw. "Yes."

Kallik felt her pelt smooth. Yakone was going to be okay. *For now.*

Toklo lifted his muzzle. Kallik could see him sniffing the air. Was he checking for something? "We'll give it time to dry," he growled. "Then we'd better get moving."

Get moving? He had bees in his brain! Walking might start the bleeding again! Kallik got to her paws. She had to find out what was bugging him. "Lusa, stay here with Yakone. I'm going hunting with Toklo."

Lusa stared at her. "Hunting?"

"We won't be much use to Yakone if we're half-starved." She began to push through the thick bramble wall. "Come on, Toklo."

"But—" He started to object.

She cut him off. "Come *on*."

Outside the thicket, Kallik shook out her pelt. It was specked with thorns. She'd be picking them out for days. "What's going on?" she demanded as Toklo nosed his way from the bush. "Why are we hiding in the world's prickliest den? And why do you want us to keep moving? Yakone's badly hurt!"

Toklo stalked away between the trees. "Keep your voice down!"

Kallik hurried after him. His gaze flitted over the undergrowth. He looked *hunted*. "Toklo," she began. "What aren't you telling me?"

He lowered his head. "I don't want to scare Lusa," he murmured.

"You're scaring *me*!" Kallik snapped.

Toklo swallowed. "We're being tracked by coyotes."

"Coyotes?" Shock jolted through her. "I didn't know there

were coyotes in the forest." She recalled seeing them in the distance when they were traveling across open plains, before they reached the Endless Ice. But never under trees.

"I've seen them," Toklo told her. "They look like wolves, and they're traveling in a pack."

"You've *seen* them? When?"

"When Yakone was stuck in the trap."

"Why didn't you tell us?" Alarm raged though Kallik.

"You had enough to deal with." Toklo met her gaze. "I didn't think it would help."

Kallik scanned the undergrowth, suddenly aware of every trembling leaf and twitching branch. "How many?"

"I couldn't tell, but one of them looked right at me." Toklo shivered. "I'm nearly twice as big as it was, but it just stared at me. It wasn't scared at all."

Kallik fought down a howl of panic. "There must be a lot of them."

"Yes." Toklo's gaze glittered with fear. "Normally, we could take them on. But Yakone can't fight and—" He hesitated.

Kallik understood. "We'd have to protect him."

"We couldn't fight properly with one eye on Yakone."

"So we have to keep moving."

Toklo nodded. "If we can get out of their territory, they might leave us alone."

Kallik glanced back toward the brambles. They'd left Lusa and Yakone. "We should get back."

As she turned, Toklo touched her shoulder with his muzzle. "They're safe for now."

"You can't be sure."

"We should hunt," Toklo pressed. "Like you said, we're not much use to Yakone if we're half-starved."

"Okay." Kallik wasn't hungry, but they had to keep their strength up. "Do you think we can outpace the coyotes?"

Toklo shifted his paws. "I hope so."

"What about Yakone?" She tried to read Toklo's gaze. "He can hardly walk." She knew that if it weren't for the wounded white bear, they could be clear of the coyotes' territory by sunup.

"We're not leaving him behind," Toklo growled. "We stay together until the end."

Kallik scuffed through pine needles, sniffing for prey. Budding leaves brushed her pelt. Trees blocked her view. Every bush might hide a coyote. Or a flat-face trap like the one that had hurt Yakone.

She pushed the thought away, tasting prey-scent. Toklo's brown back moved through bracken nearby. Kallik was anxious about losing sight of him, but she knew she must hunt. She forced herself to focus, spotting orange feathers flickering between waving fronds of quillwort. *Partridge.* Treading softly, she stalked it, her heart beating so loud she was sure it must hear her.

She stopped a bearlength away, scanning the ground for traps. The partridge strutted through stripes of sunlight, pecking among the needles. Hunkering down, Kallik fixed her gaze on its back. She tensed, and lunged. With a squawk of terror, the partridge fluttered into the air. Kallik reared and swiped it down with a paw. It fell, stunned, to the ground.

She nipped its neck between her teeth and carried it to Toklo, slowing as she saw him digging into the earth, his rump swaying as he rooted out prey.

"Toklo?" she hissed.

He turned, a dead rabbit in his jaws. "Wait!" He dropped his catch and began scooping rabbit kits from the hole, killing each with a bite. When he'd finished, he straightened and picked up the limp bodies in his teeth.

Kallik tensed. Prey-scent filled the air. What if it brought the coyotes? "Come on." She hurried for the den.

"Slow down!" Toklo's muffled growl sounded behind. "We need to make sure we aren't followed."

Heart lurching, Kallik scanned the undergrowth. Forcing herself to walk slowly, she kept her ears open. Partridge scent filled her nose. A coyote could be a bearlength away, and she wouldn't know. Or they might have sniffed out the den. Her heart quickened, and she broke into a run as she caught sight of the brambles. Panic rising, she burst through the branches.

Lusa jumped up, her pelt bristling. "What's wrong?"

Kallik dropped the partridge. "Nothing."

Lusa sat down again. "You scared me."

"How's Yakone?" Kallik touched her nose to his pelt. He felt warm, but his breathing had relaxed and deepened.

"The wound's drying," Lusa reported.

"Good." They'd be able to move him. Kallik nosed the partridge toward Lusa. "Eat this."

Lusa blinked at her. "I'm not hungry."

"You need to eat," Kallik told her. "We have to start walking as soon as we can."

Lusa's pelt rippled. "Why?"

Kallik paused. What could she say? Toklo pushed through the thorns behind her. He dropped his catch. There was no use keeping the secret any longer. "We're being tracked by coyotes."

Lusa leaped to her paws, ears flat. "Coyotes!" She glanced down at Yakone, sleeping. "We have to protect him!"

"We will," Toklo promised.

Kallik leaned down and touched Yakone's cheek with her muzzle. "Wake up," she whispered.

Lusa reached out with a paw and touched Kallik. "Don't tell him about the coyotes." Her eyes were round with fear.

Kallik shook her head. "I won't." She didn't want Yakone to know he was slowing them down. "Yakone?" He opened his eyes. "How are you feeling?" Kallik asked gently.

Yakone lifted his head. "My paw hurts."

He sounded lucid. Kallik nudged a rabbit kit toward him. "Eat this."

"I'm not hungry," he croaked.

"You need to get strong." Kallik's heart ached. "We have to leave."

"Already?" Yakone's eyes were misted.

"Yes." Softly, Kallik nosed the rabbit closer. Yakone snatched it up and swallowed it, groaning. Kallik tore a piece from the partridge and gave it to Lusa, eating a mouthful herself. Beside them, Toklo bit into a rabbit.

When they'd eaten, Kallik nodded to Lusa and Toklo. "Wait outside," she murmured. "I'll get Yakone to his paws." As they pushed through the brambles, she slid her nose under Yakone's shoulder. Heaving, she propped him up. "Come on, Yakone. It's time to go."

"Go?" he echoed groggily, letting her nudge him up. He winced as he put his injured paw on the ground.

"Try to use your three good legs," Kallik urged. She held the brambles aside and guided him out of the den.

He limped out, lurching heavily against her. Kallik braced herself against his weight, relieved as Toklo stepped forward to support his other side. Holding Yakone between them, they helped him hobble forward.

Lusa ducked into the lead. "Which way?" she asked.

Toklo scanned the trees. "Follow the moss," he ordered.

Lusa frowned at him. "Moss?"

"The mossy side of the trunks shows where we've been; the clear side will show where we're heading," Toklo told her.

Kallik glanced up at a trunk. Sure enough, one side was mossy, the other clear. "Where did you learn that?"

Toklo pushed Yakone forward. "Ujurak."

"What's the rush?" Yakone's words were slurred.

"It'll be sunset before we know it." Kallik tried to keep her voice light. "We need to cover some territory before then." What if the coyotes caught up?

Yakone lurched forward, holding his injured paw up and stumbling on three legs.

Lusa sniffed out the clearest path. "Deer track!" she called, finding another straight trail through the undergrowth. Her ears were pricked as she scooted ahead. Her eyes flicked from tree to tree, her pelt bristling along her spine. Kallik's belly churned. As a twig cracked behind them, she stiffened.

Toklo glanced across Yakone at her. "It was just a raccoon," he murmured. "I saw its tail."

The scents here were strange, each one new. Kallik walked with her mouth open, trying to tell one from the other, alert for the musky odor that meant the coyotes were closing in. The undergrowth darkened and grew lusher. The ground grew boggy underpaw. "Are you sure we're going the right way?" she hissed to Toklo.

"If we follow the moss on the trees, we'll be okay."

"Wouldn't it be better to follow the river?" Kallik longed to see open sky and hear the murmuring of the water.

"The shore is too open," Toklo told her.

Lusa called over her shoulder, "Yakone would never make it over the rocks."

Kallik's heart sank. They were both right.

"There's a clearing!" Lusa called.

Kallik looked up and saw the black bear waiting in a pool of light beyond the trees. She quickened her pace, shoving Yakone forward, until they broke into a clearing where budding shrubs and ferns crowded for the light.

Yakone suddenly shouldered her away. "I'll walk by myself for a while," he mumbled. He tested his wounded paw, placing it gently. He growled through clenched teeth. Kallik leaned down, stiffening as she waited to see if it started bleeding.

Lusa's pulp held firm. No red showed through the green.

"I think I can use it." Yakone swallowed and began to limp forward. Kallik exchanged glances with Toklo. Would Chenoa's herbs work on such a big wound?

Kallik watched him. *He's being so brave.* "You don't have to prove yourself," she barked as he began to totter across the clearing.

"I'm giving you a rest," Yakone growled back.

Kallik followed, her pelt brushing Toklo's as they padded after Yakone. Lusa dashed across the clearing, glancing at the sky. The sun was beginning to sink toward the trees. "Night's coming."

Kallik shivered at the thought of darkness. The coyotes could stalk them easily through a forest wrapped in shadow. She longed for the ice, where the sun never set in burn-sky; where she was the hunter, not the hunted.

Then the wind sharply changed direction, drifting over Kallik's fur and pulling her head toward a line of trees, just behind them on the edge of the clearing. Her heart lurched.

Eyes flashed from the shadows.

"Lusa, come here!" Her growl cracked with alarm.

Lusa charged toward them, stopping in front of Kallik. "What?"

Kallik whirled, scanning the undergrowth. Eyes glittered from behind every tree. "They're here," she murmured softly. She didn't want Yakone to realize the danger. Not yet.

Toklo bristled beside her. "There are four of us," he whispered. "And we're bigger than they are."

The eyes blinked around them. The coyotes didn't move.

Lusa slid in beside Kallik. "They're just watching," she hissed.

Had Yakone seen them? The white bear lumbered blindly on, head low.

"Let's just keep moving." Toklo hurried to catch up.

Kallik glanced over her shoulder. The eyes watched them leave.

"Why don't they attack?" Kallik flexed her claws. "Cowards!"

"Just keep *moving*," Toklo hissed over his shoulder.

They crossed the clearing and headed into the woods. Lusa peered back. "I can't see them." She hurried a little way ahead and disappeared up a tree, scrambling down a few moments later. "They're still following," she whispered in Kallik's ear. "They're like shadows in the bushes."

Kallik searched for shapes among the bracken. She saw nothing but jagged stalks. "What are they waiting for?" she growled. She smelled blood. Stiffening, she saw red staining the trail. "Yakone, you're bleeding again." She rushed to him. "Help me, Toklo!" She tucked her shoulder beneath Yakone's, taking his weight. Toklo did the same.

Yakone grunted but didn't argue. Lifting his paw, he limped onward.

The ground grew wetter, with boggy pools of peat tugging at their feet with every step. Kallik's paws sank deeper and deeper. The trees thinned, and sedges sprang up on every side. Before long they were trudging through a marsh, dotted sparsely with pine trees.

"Keep your wound out of the mud," Kallik warned Yakone. The stinking peat sucked at her paws, as if the earth were trying to swallow her. Every step was exhausting. She was burning beneath her pelt, struggling for breath. Yakone grew limper, finding each step harder until Kallik and Toklo were hauling the white bear along between them.

"I'll be okay if we just rest," Yakone grunted.

"There's no time," Toklo told him. He jerked his muzzle to a lightning-blasted tree rising from the marsh ahead of them. "Climb it, Lusa," he panted. "Tell us what you can see."

Kallik knew that he wanted her to check for the coyotes. Pain throbbed through her flank. Yakone was as heavy as stone. And silent. Was he unconscious again?

"I see them," Lusa whispered as she returned.

"How close?" Toklo asked.

"Same as before," Lusa told him.

"No closer?" Kallik frowned. A chill swept through her pelt as she realized what the coyotes were doing. She glanced at Toklo. His gaze looked haunted. He must have guessed the predators' plan, too. "They don't need to attack us," Kallik breathed. "They're waiting for Yakone to die."

CHAPTER TWENTY-TWO

Lusa

Lusa whipped around. "He's not going to die! I won't let him."

She saw Yakone hanging like dead prey between Kallik and Toklo. Drool dangled from his jaws. Turning back, Lusa heaved herself through the marshy soil. *Why do I have to be so small?* Gritting her teeth, she pushed on harder. "I'll find herbs! I'll get him well!" *Please, spirits, don't let him die!* With Chenoa and Ujurak gone, she'd have to save him herself. She plunged into a clump of sedge, sniffing the leaves. *Is this an herb?* She remembered the strange tang of the grass that Chenoa had shown her beside the river. This wasn't the same. Besides, what could *grass* do for a wound as bad as Yakone's?

A bright green weed sprouted beyond the sedge. Pushing her way through, Lusa grabbed a mouthful and splashed back to Kallik and Toklo. The leaves were fragrant and sharp on her tongue. They must be good for something.

She spat the leaves out at Toklo's paws. "Here!"

He halted and stared down at them, his ears twitching. "What's that?"

"Herbs for Yakone!" Lusa barked. "To make him better."

Kallik gazed at the pile of bruised leaves. "What are they?"

"I don't know." Lusa swallowed down a flutter of uncertainty. "But they smell like the sort of leaves Ujurak used to find."

Toklo gazed at her gently. "We can't give him stuff we don't know about."

"I'll find something else." Lusa bounded away. A prickly plant sprang from the mossy earth. Then a fresher scent touched her nose. A white-flowering bush was spilling over the soggy soil less than a bearlength ahead. "What about that?" she called back to Toklo. She darted toward it, the earth sinking beneath her paws. Mud seeped around her belly. Fighting her way up, she leaped forward, and sank deeper. She struggled to heave out her forepaws, but the mud sucked her down. Frustration surged through her. She had to get the leaves. They might save Yakone.

"Wait!" Pawsteps squelched behind. She glanced around. Toklo had left Yakone leaning against Kallik and was padding gingerly toward her. "You're doing great, Lusa, but let's wait until we're out of this marsh before we start collecting herbs." He leaned forward and grabbed her scruff in his jaws, dragging her from the bog.

She scrambled to find her paws as he gently lowered her onto firmer ground. Yakone's gaze was glazed and empty, and she could smell the hot tang of sickness. "But he needs herbs now!"

Toklo pointed his muzzle toward a tree-filled slope a little way ahead. Hills rolled behind it. "We can climb up there," he told her. "We won't be so exposed, and there'll be plenty of herbs."

Lusa's body tingled with hope. "I might be able to recognize one that Ujurak used, or find more hornwort."

"Can you find a safe path for us?" Toklo looked warily at the sodden peat stretching on all sides.

"Yes!" Lusa promised. She glanced past Kallik and Yakone. Had the coyotes gone? Perhaps they'd given up. She sniffed for them, stretching onto her hindpaws to taste the air. A faint musky scent touched her tongue, but she couldn't see any pelts in the shadows.

"Let's hurry." Toklo headed back to the white bears. "It'll be dark soon."

Lusa dropped onto all fours and snuffled the earth. The firmer soil had a sandy smell. She followed its scent, pressing with each pawstep to make sure it would take the weight of Toklo, Kallik, and Yakone. Where the trail threaded between clumps of sedge, she felt thin stems crisscrossing beneath her pads. The channels between them were firm underpaw where their roots knotted to make smooth walkways over the boggy ground.

She sniffed out a path, darting one way, then the other, until the peat turned to soil and sedge gave way to grass. The ground sloped up into woodland. Trees stretched toward the sky, bright with budding leaves. Birds twittered in the branches, announcing the coming of dusk.

Lusa scampered higher. Behind her, the other bears stumbled. "Can I help?" Lusa called.

"Just keep finding the easiest trail," Kallik puffed. Her paws were thick with mud from the marsh. Her belly fur was spiked and filthy.

The hill was short and steep. Panting at the top, Lusa peered back down, scanning the undergrowth for coyotes. She could see the marsh through the branches and narrowed her eyes as she spotted shadows moving at the edge.

Panic sparked beneath her pelt as her friends caught up with her. "They're still following us," she breathed.

"I know," Toklo growled. "Can you see the river?"

Lusa scrambled up a rowan tree and peered from the branches. Ahead rolled hill after hill, glowing orange in the setting sun. But there was no sign of the silver river threading between them. "I can't see it," she called down. She searched the horizon for Toklo's mountains. There was nothing but forest and sky.

Were they even headed in the right direction?

She looked back across the marsh. Beyond it, the sun was sliding toward the trees. *We must be going the right way.* She scooted down the tree and landed beside Toklo. "Follow me." She trotted over the crest of the hill, shivering as the forest descended into dusky shadow.

Shadows pooled in the valley like black water. Lusa reached the bottom first. Toklo, Kallik, and Yakone halted beside her, flanks heaving as they caught their breath.

Kallik glanced up the next hill. "I can't go on much farther."

Lusa's nose twitched. The stench of coyote rolled toward them. She bounded a short way up the next slope. Warm light bathed the summit. "Look," she called. "We're almost at the top."

Grunting, Toklo, Kallik, and Yakone pushed after her.

"You can do it!" She willed them on, wishing she was strong enough to help carry Yakone. "Not far to the top." She chased the sunshine farther and farther uphill, but shadow was following them, stretching up the slope as the sun slid toward the far horizon. By the time they reached the top, it had set.

Lusa's heart sank. The sky was purple beyond the trees as clouds rolled in. Soon it would be dark. She scanned the slope behind them, belly tightening as she spotted eyes flashing from the shadows. "Hurry!" she urged.

Her friends caught up with her, heat pulsing from them. The air smelled of blood. Lusa wrinkled her nose at its thick stone tang. Yakone's paw was oozing.

"Can you make it over another hill?" Lusa glanced anxiously down the slope.

Kallik nodded. Toklo huffed. Perhaps the next hill would give them shelter. Maybe they'd find a cave. That would protect them from the coyotes, wouldn't it?

Lusa led them over the top and headed down into shadow. The ground grew stony. Rocks slithered under her paws. She squinted to see ahead, but clouds had swallowed the last of the sun. No moon lit the forest. They were lost in darkness.

"Which way now, Lusa?" Toklo asked.

"I can't see—" Lusa yelped as her forepaw slipped from under her, spraying stones. She thumped to the ground, hardly feeling any pain as she heard pebbles clattering far below. Her pelt bushed in terror. "Stop!" she barked to

Toklo. "Cliff!" The earth dropped away beside her. Wind ruffled her pelt.

Toklo and Kallik stumbled to a halt, Yakone slithering between them, as Lusa lay, stiff with fear. *It's going to be okay.* She tried to calm herself, but her terror began to spiral. The air stank of coyote. "We're trapped!"

"No, we're not." Toklo was following the cliff edge. "There's a way down." He turned, his eyes shining in the darkness. "Yakone, I need you to walk this next bit."

Yakone growled.

"Can you do it?" Toklo asked.

Lusa got to her paws.

Kallik was breathing fast. "Can you do it, Yakone? Can you get down the slope?"

Toklo chimed in. "I'll be ahead of you, Kallik and Lusa behind. We'll steady you where we can, but the path's steep. Will you try?"

Yakone took a deep, shuddering breath. He lifted his muzzle, and Lusa saw his gaze harden. "Yes," he growled.

Lusa peered over the edge. The world disappeared into a pool of darkness. She had no idea how far the valley was below them. For a moment she thought of plunging over the edge, falling, falling, with the roar of water in her ears . . . *No! Don't think of Chenoa! Not now!*

Toklo was already heading down the path. As Yakone and Kallik moved off, Lusa followed. The path was stony, slippery underpaw. She spread her claws, digging them in where she could to get a grip. Kallik's rump swayed ahead of her. *Please let Yakone make it!* Cold air buffeted her side. Rock brushed her pelt. *Just keep moving.*

Toklo was taking it slow. Lusa saw his eyes flash every now and then, as he looked over his shoulder. "Are you okay, Yakone?" he called.

Yakone grunted.

"He's okay!" Kallik barked.

The path steepened. Lusa's heart pounded. How could Yakone grip with a wounded paw? She saw Kallik lean forward and hook her muzzle around Yakone's rump, pressing him against the cliff face.

Lusa blinked. The sky was clearing. Moonlight was glowing through thinning clouds. She could see a stream sparkling at the bottom of the cliff. Wide pebble beaches stretched along either side. Bushes dotted the shores, while plants clumped at the water's edge. Gnarled trees jutted from another cliff beyond. They were climbing down into a gorge. She glanced up, scanning the sky for Ujurak. *Are you watching?* A dark shadow caught her eye. The stones at the top of the cliff were moving. Lusa stared, puzzled for a moment. Then dread swept through her. Those weren't stones. The coyotes were watching.

No!

Eyes glinted against the starry sky.

"Toklo!" Lusa's voice trembled.

"I know," Toklo growled. "Don't look at them. They won't follow."

They're waiting for Yakone to die.

White fur flashed in front of Lusa, moving too fast for the slope.

"Yakone!" Kallik barked with terror.

Lusa froze. Yakone was falling!

Kallik thrust out her forepaws and snagged his pelt. "Help!"

Toklo whirled around and grabbed Yakone's scruff as the white bear tumbled over the edge. Panic jolted Lusa to life. She darted forward, squeezing past Kallik, and snatched at Yakone's pelt until she grabbed fur between her teeth. Her paws skidded on grit as his weight dragged her forward. Closing her eyes, she strained to pull him up. Stones showered down into the gorge as Kallik trembled beside her. A growl rolled in Toklo's throat as, together, they hauled the white bear back onto the path.

With a grunt, Yakone rolled limply toward the cliff face.

As Lusa collapsed, gasping for breath, she heard whining above. She looked up. The coyotes were pacing excitedly. Lusa bared her teeth. *He's not dead yet!*

Toklo heaved himself to his paws.

Kallik straightened and shook out her pelt. "Yakone?"

The white bear growled and stood up, his shoulders at an awkward angle as he tried to keep his weight off his injured paw.

"It's not far," Toklo told him. "Hang on to my tail."

Lusa steadied her breathing as they limped to the bottom.

Kallik stumbled onto the beach. "We have to stop."

"I know." Toklo's eyes were dull in the moonlight. He glanced at the cliff edging the far shore. "Let's build a nest against the rock."

Lusa saw Yakone sway on his paws. "I need to lie down," he mumbled.

Kallik brushed against him. "Come on." She steered him toward the stream. "Let's get a drink, then I'll make you a nest."

Yakone stumbled into the shallow stream and lapped at it blindly. Lusa padded after him, relieved to feel cool water wash around her paws. She dipped her muzzle in the stream and drank until her belly hurt. She hadn't realized how thirsty she was, or how tired.

When they'd drunk, Yakone rested against the cliff while Toklo, Lusa, and Kallik collected leaves and moss for a nest.

"Here, Yakone." Kallik tucked a large clump of water-weed beneath his head. Lusa peeled moss from a stone and dipped it in the stream. She laid it, dripping, beside Yakone's snout. "In case you get thirsty." His nose was dry and hot. Lusa frowned. Was the wound turning bad? She gasped, remembering. "I was going to find herbs!"

She dashed away, splashing downstream, sniffing from one plant to another.

Toklo caught up with her. "Don't run off by yourself," he hissed.

Lusa jerked up her head. "I promised to find herbs!" How had she forgotten something so important? Her heart thumped in her chest.

"Do you know what you're looking for?" Toklo scanned the water's edge.

Lusa shook her head. "I wish I'd listened harder when Ujurak was with us. He knew so much. I should have tried to learn."

Toklo sighed. "We didn't know we were going to lose him."

Lusa met his gaze. It was misted with grief. As sadness welled in her throat, a sharp, bitter scent touched her nose. "Hornwort!"

Chenoa's herb!

She splashed downstream and tore out a mouthful of leaves, then bounded back to Yakone. The white bear was asleep, his breath steady. Lusa sniffed his injured paw. The stream had washed it clean. Quickly, she chewed up the leaves and dressed his wounds.

As she admired her work, her belly rumbled. The long day's trek had left her hungry. "Did you see any fish in the stream?" she asked Toklo as he paced in front of the nest.

"Only minnows."

Kallik settled beside Yakone and laid her snout on his shoulder. "Come and rest, Toklo."

"Someone needs to keep guard." He glanced at the cliff they'd climbed down.

Lusa followed his gaze. The coyotes were still pacing at the top, silhouetted against the stars. "They won't attack while Yakone's still alive," she reminded him.

"But they might come to check," Toklo growled.

"I can take first watch," Kallik offered.

Toklo shook his head. "No, I'll do it. I'll wake you at moonhigh."

Lusa sat up. "What about me?"

"Kallik will wake you." Toklo turned and walked along the edge of the water.

Weary and anxious, Lusa nestled in beside Yakone. The

warmth of his fur soothed her, but the pungent smell of blood made her wince. Would it chase her through her dreams? She watched the stream sparkle as it passed, her eyes soon glazing. Exhausted, she drifted into sleep.

"Lusa." It seemed only a moment before Kallik was waking her with a gentle nudge. "It's your turn to keep watch."

Lusa stretched, her paws quivering. The predawn sky was milky white. Toklo was snoring beside Yakone. "Any trouble?" she asked Kallik.

"The coyotes started down the slope a few times, but turned back," she told her.

"They must know that he's still alive." Lusa glanced uneasily at Kallik. The white she-bear looked ragged with worry. "Go to sleep," Lusa told her softly. "I'll wake you if there's danger."

"Thank you." Kallik touched her nose to Lusa's head, then settled beside Yakone.

Lusa headed for the stream. She sat down, letting the water swish over her pawtips. The coyotes sat as motionless as rocks at the top of the cliff. Anger surged through her. *We can't live like prey for the rest of the journey!* Were the coyotes going to hunt them forever? *If Yakone could just get well, they would leave us alone.*

Lusa flexed her claws. She was going to find every plant Ujurak ever used. She'd recognize their scent if she found them. She lifted her muzzle and glared at the coyotes. One raised its head and gazed back, ears pricked against the dawn sky.

Cowards! Why don't you come and fight? You're like vultures, waiting to pick our bones. She growled. *You won't have him!*

The coyote watched her, unmoving.

I would fight you right now! Lusa leaped to her paws. *But you cowards don't come close enough! You'll only come near if Yakone dies!*

She paused.

If Yakone dies . . .

She hurried back to the nest. Yakone was awake. "How are you?" She leaned and sniffed his paw. The wound was dry and smelled of hornwort.

"Not bad," he rumbled. He blinked at her, his eyes weary but clear after a night's rest.

"Does your paw hurt?"

Yakone drew it closer to his chest. "It feels like it's on fire."

Lusa nudged his cheek with her nose, her heart twisting with pity. "I wish I could stop the pain."

"Lusa?" Toklo snapped awake. "Where are the coyotes?"

"It's okay, Toklo." Lusa glanced over her shoulder. "I'm just checking on Yakone."

Yakone hauled himself to his paws. *"Coyotes?"* He swung his head around, scanning the gorge. "Where?"

Toklo stood up and shook out his pelt. "We saw some in the area yesterday." He stretched slowly. "Nothing to worry about." He gave Lusa a warning glance.

"We're just keeping a lookout," she told Yakone. She padded away from the nest. "Toklo?" She willed him to follow, relieved when he did.

"I've had an idea," she whispered. She glanced back at

Yakone. He was sniffing his injured paw.

Kallik stirred beside the white bear. She stretched her muzzle closer to his. "How's your wound?"

"It's stopped bleeding," Yakone told her.

As Yakone lapped at it gingerly, Kallik looked up at Lusa. "Where are you two going? Is everything okay?" Heaving herself to her paws, she padded toward them.

"Lusa's got an idea." Toklo narrowed his eyes. "What is it?"

Lusa waited for Kallik to reach them. "We need to get those coyotes out in the open, right?" she whispered. "Close enough for us to fight them."

Kallik shook her head. "They won't come near unless—" She paused. "Unless one of us is dead."

Lusa met her gaze. "So, let's make that happen."

CHAPTER TWENTY-THREE

Kallik

"Make that happen?" Kallik stared at Lusa. "What do you mean?" A chill ran through her pelt.

"Not *really* make it happen." Lusa's eyes were bright. "But if Yakone *pretended* to be dead, then the coyotes—"

Kallik cut her off. "No way!" The thought made her quiver. Yakone was too badly hurt! How could Lusa even think of pretending he was dead? The coyotes would be on him like flies on a wound. They'd eat him alive!

Toklo leaned closer. "How would it work, Lusa?"

Kallik stared at him in disbelief. "You're not actually thinking of doing this?"

"We won't let them hurt him," Lusa insisted. "But if we could just get them to come sniffing around him, it would give us a chance to chase them away."

Kallik glanced at the coyotes, milling at the top of the cliff. She could hear them whimpering with excitement. Her pelt bristled as she imagined them closing in on Yakone. "He's not strong enough."

"He doesn't need to be," Lusa pressed. "*We'll* do the fighting."

"He can't do it!" Kallik showed her teeth. "He'll be *bait*!"

Toklo gazed at her steadily. "We can't keep moving with the coyotes tracking us. How will Yakone have a chance to heal? Isn't it better to lure them out and fight them? If we chase them off, we can move at our own speed, without watching our backs. Right now, we can't even hunt properly. We're scared to take our eyes off one another."

"And that's no good for Yakone," Lusa added. "He needs good food and rest to get better. He'll never get that while they're tracking us."

Kallik's head swam. "So you're saying he *has* to play dead for the coyotes."

"It will be his choice," Toklo told her.

Kallik flexed her claws. "You know he's too brave to say no."

Toklo gazed at her steadily. "If you don't want us to ask him, then we won't."

Kallik turned to watch Yakone. He had limped down to the stream to drink and was leaning over the water, lapping. She had to ask him. He'd never forgive her if she didn't give him a chance to help them.

Lusa shifted her paws. "What do you think?"

Kallik growled quietly. "I'll ask him," she agreed. Toklo was right. The coyotes would keep chasing them until Yakone collapsed from exhaustion. This was the only way they'd get rid of them. She caught Lusa's eye. "But we can't leave him long enough for the coyotes to hurt him."

"We won't," Lusa promised.

Toklo puffed out his chest. "I'll fight to the death to protect him."

Kallik took a breath. She knew Toklo meant it, and her heart lifted. But how could she ask Yakone to lie still while the coyotes closed in? She could picture their jaws snapping beside his pelt. They'd be close enough to really hurt him. They might even kill him. She shuddered.

"It's okay if he says no," Toklo said.

Of course he won't say no. Paws heavy, Kallik padded to the nest.

Yakone had returned to the soft leaves and was inspecting his paw again. It was dripping from the stream. His wound gaped, red and raw.

"Yakone?"

He didn't look up. "It's a bit of a mess," he huffed.

Kallik padded closer. "Yakone."

"What?" His gaze darkened as it met hers. "What's wrong?"

Kallik sat down. "Can you see the coyotes at the top of the cliff?"

Yakone jerked his head up, blinking. "Toklo mentioned coyotes. Are they the same ones?"

Kallik nodded. "They've been following us since you hurt your paw."

"I wondered what the foul stench was," Yakone muttered. "I thought it was Lusa's herbs."

"This is serious!" Kallik growled.

Yakone frowned. "You think I don't know that?" He held up his paw. "This is what they're following, isn't it? It's my trail of blood that they're tracking."

Kallik's throat tightened. "No one's blaming you."

"*I* am," Yakone snapped. "If I'd looked where I was going, I wouldn't be in this mess." He closed his eyes. "I've put you all in danger."

Kallik turned as paws rattled the pebbles behind her.

"We take care of one another." Toklo stopped at her side. "If one of us is hurt, the others protect them and help them heal."

Yakone's gaze flashed. "But I'm *not* one of you, am I?"

Kallik bristled. "Of course you are! You swam after Chenoa. You found roots for Lusa. You've learned to hunt like a brown bear."

Yakone dropped his gaze. "But now I'm a burden."

"Do you want to help us?" Toklo asked briskly.

"Yes." Yakone shifted on his rump.

"We need to shake off the coyotes."

Yakone leaned forward. "How?"

"We need to draw them out," Toklo explained. "But they won't come close until they think you're dead."

Kallik sat beside Yakone. Her chest tightened. "You don't have to do this."

"No, you don't," Toklo agreed. "But if you pretend to be dead, long enough to bring the coyotes to you, we can take them by surprise. Once they see we're ready to fight to protect you, they'll back off."

Yakone's pelt spiked up. "You want me to lie down like dead prey."

"Just long enough to bring the coyotes close." Kallik was

suddenly aware how frail Yakone looked, his eyes clouded with pain, his pelt ungroomed. Was it fair to ask him to put himself in any more danger?

Yakone looked at Toklo. Then his gaze flicked to Kallik and rested on her for a moment. Kallik gazed back at him. Every hair on her pelt trembled at what they were asking him to do.

"Okay," he growled at last. "We can't let them hunt us anymore. I'll do what I have to do."

Kallik pressed against him, nuzzling his cheek. "I won't let them hurt you," she murmured. "I promise."

The stones on the shore crackled as Lusa charged toward them. She was holding a wad of hornwort in her jaws. She dropped it and looked expectantly at Kallik.

Kallik guessed what she was thinking. "We asked him."

Yakone cleared his throat. "I'll do it."

Lusa nodded and began to chew the hornwort into pulp. "What's the plan?" she asked, green pulp dripping down her muzzle.

Toklo gazed along the gorge. Trees crowded the end, where the cliffs gave way to forest. "We'll need cover," he murmured thoughtfully.

"So we lead them along the gorge?" Kallik offered.

"Yakone can collapse near the end, in the open."

Lusa spat the pulp onto Yakone's paw. "And we can hide in the trees!"

"Exactly," Toklo agreed. "When the coyotes come sniffing, we'll be ready for them."

Lusa began licking pulp into Yakone's wound. Kallik watched him grit his teeth against the pain. "Do you think the coyotes will fall for it?" she asked.

"It's up to you to make it look real," Yakone hissed. "You'll have to act like I've really died."

"We know how to grieve," Toklo growled bitterly.

Kallik felt sick.

Toklo stared Yakone straight in the eyes. "This won't be easy for you," he admitted. "But we'll attack as soon as the coyotes are distracted."

As Yakone's eyes flashed with fear, Kallik pressed harder against him. *Spirits, protect him!*

He lifted his muzzle. "When do we do this?"

"Now," Toklo decided. "The sooner we chase them off, the sooner we can hunt properly."

Kallik was aware of the hollowness in her belly, but she couldn't imagine being able to swallow anything. Fear clouded her thoughts. She wasn't ready! What if the coyotes hurt Yakone before they could save him?

But Yakone was already on his paws. "Come on." He began to limp along the gorge. Toklo hurried and pressed against him.

Kallik slid in on his other side. "Are they watching?" she asked Lusa.

Lusa glanced up. "Like hawks."

Kallik didn't dare look back. She couldn't believe they were going to do this. But it was the best chance they had of shaking the coyotes. As they neared the woods, she tasted the sourness of sap. She longed for the cool, clean taste of ice. The walls of the gorge gradually shrank away, swallowed by forest slopes, and the stream widened and deepened, cutting a broad path through the pebbles.

"We do it here." Toklo gave the order though gritted teeth. Thick bushes rolled from the tree line a few bearlengths away. Kallik saw with a spark of relief that there was plenty of cover. They wouldn't have to go far from Yakone.

She glanced at Lusa from the corner of her eye. "Are they following us?"

Lusa circled nervously. "They're climbing down the cliff path."

Toklo scuffed his paws roughly over the pebbles. "Leave as much scent as you can," he hissed. "If we make it strong here, the coyotes won't notice our smell when we're hiding."

Kallik rubbed her pads across the stones.

"Ready, Yakone?" Toklo kept his gaze fixed forward.

"Ready," Yakone hissed. With a gasp, he staggered.

Kallik jumped away, shocked. This *was* just a trick, wasn't it? She stared in horror as Yakone dropped to his knees, then collapsed on his side.

"Yakone?" A yowl ripped from her throat. She crouched beside him, trembling. She felt his skin twitch under her paw. He was alive, which made Kallik even more terrified about what was going to happen next. "Yakone!" There was no way she could leave him here to be picked over by coyotes. What if she didn't rescue him in time?

Toklo dropped beside her and rested his head on Yakone's

shoulder. Lifting his muzzle, he let out a long howl of grief.

Lusa nudged Yakone's haunches with both front paws. "Get up, Yakone! Get up!" Panic edged her bark.

Toklo lifted his head and turned toward the black bear. "I'm sorry, Lusa. He's dead." He straightened and stepped away, dipping his head.

Alarm flashed through Kallik. She knew they were pretending. She could see Yakone's flank moving, just enough to take tiny breaths. But she couldn't leave him. "I'm staying!"

"There's nothing you can do." Toklo narrowed his eyes. "Come on."

Lusa pressed her head into Kallik's side and glanced back. "They're watching from downstream," she breathed.

Kallik couldn't bear to look.

"Let's wait," Toklo whispered. "We have to make this real."

Kallik pressed herself against Yakone, burying her muzzle into his pelt. "We won't let them hurt you," she whispered. She could feel the sun on her back. It was lifting high above the trees, beating from a blue sky. The stream swished past invitingly. Kallik felt thirsty at the sound of it. How would Yakone lie still in this heat?

Toklo circled Yakone, head low. Lusa crouched a bear-length away, her ears flat.

"Come on," Toklo growled suddenly. "We have to go."

"But—" Kallik glanced downstream. The coyotes were pacing in the distance, their eyes fixed hungrily on Yakone. She froze, suddenly unable to move. "I can't leave him," she whimpered.

Toklo curled his lip. "You have to." He padded away,

following the stream into the woods.

"Come on, Kallik." Lusa nudged her flank.

Kallik glared at the coyotes, furious at their confidence. *How dare you?* They paced silently, their gaze unmoving. She forced herself to her paws. Deep in her belly, she felt a tug of unease.

Lusa nosed her forward. "Just walk!" she hissed.

Numbly, Kallik followed Toklo into the woods. As she reached the shade of the trees, she glanced back. She could see the coyotes beyond the trunks. They held their ground, still pacing from side to side. "They're not coming." Her voice trembled.

Toklo was pushing through bracken beside the stream. "Keep walking," he ordered. "They have to believe we've gone."

Lusa fell in beside Kallik. "We'll go just far enough, then double back," she whispered.

Kallik pushed herself on, the pain of abandoning Yakone pricking like thorns in her heart. When she looked back again, trees and bushes blocked her view. "I can't see him!" she gulped.

"Keep going," Toklo insisted.

Kallik's breathing quickened. "Let's go back," she pleaded.

Lusa pressed against her. "Toklo?"

Toklo halted and looked back.

"We've gone far enough." Lusa blinked. "We promised we'd watch him."

Toklo grunted. "Okay." He veered away past a clump of brambles, avoiding the track they'd made through the wood.

Heading uphill, he circled away from the stream, climbing higher and higher.

"We're going the wrong way!" Kallik snapped. Her heart pounded in her ears.

"They might check our trail." Toklo pushed on until Kallik felt panic throbbing in her paws.

At last he turned and began to pad back toward the gorge. Kallik pushed past him.

"Be quiet," Toklo warned.

Kallik ignored him. She had to get back. She had to see Yakone. The stream chattered ahead, and she broke into a run. Toklo and Lusa followed, their pawsteps soft. As the forest lightened ahead, Kallik squinted through the trees. She glimpsed the pebble beach, scanning for Yakone.

He was exactly how they'd left him; hunched on the stones, muzzle flat against the ground. Sunlight drenched the gorge, blanching the stones white. *He must be burning up!* She moved closer, crouching as she reached the edge of the forest. Toklo ducked in beside her, Lusa keeping close.

"They're coming," Lusa breathed.

Gray shadows moved along the gorge. The coyotes were closing in. Kallik swallowed against panic, forcing herself to stay still. The coyotes stopped a few bearlengths from Yakone. Jaws open, they tasted the air. They glanced at one another.

"Can they smell that he's still alive?" Lusa hissed.

Toklo shrugged. "Let's hope not."

One padded closer, nostrils twitching. He stopped and

stretched his snout forward. Another padded to join him, tail flicking warily.

Lusa growled. "Rabbits would be braver!"

"Quiet!" Toklo silenced her as the largest coyote padded closer to Yakone. Stretching forward, it sniffed Yakone's fur. Its hackles lifted. Kallik tensed, ready to spring.

"Wait." Toklo moved a paw to hold her back.

The coyotes began padding around Yakone, seven gray pelts circling as silent as owls. Their ears were pricked, alert for noise. Their heads twitched back and forth, their gazes probing the forest. Kallik pressed herself closer to the ground. *How much longer?*

Suddenly, a coyote darted forward. Kallik saw its teeth flash as it snatched a bite at Yakone.

No!

As it jerked away, Kallik saw white fur in its teeth. She leaned forward, breath quickening. She couldn't see blood. It hadn't torn flesh. She looked at Yakone. He hadn't moved. Fear flooded beneath her pelt. The ground seemed to sway beneath her. *Is he actually dead?*

"Hold on, Kallik." Toklo brushed against her as she struggled to stay on her paws.

The coyote's eyes lit excitedly. Lifting its head, it barked a thin, harsh yowl that rang along the gorge. Its companions closed in on Yakone. The white bear's pelt disappeared as they fell on him.

"Now!" Toklo's roar rang through the trees.

Kallik lunged from the bushes, hitting the beach in a burst

of pebbles. The coyotes whirled around, their eyes wide as Kallik raced toward them. She hurled herself at the one nearest Yakone's head. Sinking her jaws into its spine, she flung it away. It thumped against a tree and dropped, limp, to the ground.

Kallik spun, growling at the next. It backed away as she glared into its startled gaze. Fury pumped through her. "You dare to threaten my friends? To track us like prey? You wait for him to die?" She reared and smashed her forepaws down. The coyote dodged away, but she caught its flanks and dragged it toward her.

Yakone stirred at the corner of her vision. Relief surged through her pelt. "Get to the woods!" she ordered. Yakone hauled himself up and began staggering toward the trees.

The coyote writhed in Kallik's paws. It twisted, its jaws glistening, and snapped at her throat. Kallik flung the coyote backward, pain searing as it tore a lump of fur from her neck.

"Help!" Lusa's panicked cry made her turn.

A coyote was on the black bear's back, slavering at her neck. Lusa bucked, trying to throw it off, but the coyote snapped its jaws around her spine. Kallik bounded toward her friend and sliced her claws along the coyote's back. Howling in pain, it let go of Lusa, and ripping it away, Kallik clamped her jaws around its scrawny neck. She bit deeper till it screeched, then dropped it. It glanced at her, eyes white-rimmed with fear, then fled, wailing, into the woods.

Teeth dug into her rump. Kallik whipped around and slammed her paw against a coyote's head. It reeled away, its stinking breath billowing around her muzzle. Toklo's roar sounded beside her. He was driving three coyotes back toward the woods. They snarled and snapped, showing their teeth as he reared in front of them. With a grunt, he crashed down onto one. Kallik heard its spine snap. It twitched, then lay still. Toklo turned on the others. One stared in horror before pelting away. Kallik watched it disappear into the undergrowth.

An ugly growl rumbled behind her. She turned slowly, narrowing her eyes. A coyote was pacing back and forth, glaring menacingly at her.

"Why haven't you run away yet?" Kallik tipped her head. "Aren't you scared?"

It growled again and leaped for her. She lashed out with a paw and batted it away. It twisted as it hit the ground, finding its paws and lunging for her again. This time Kallik grabbed it as it hit her, digging in her claws. It howled, struggling in her grip, its jaws snapping at her head. She felt teeth rip her ear and hurled it onto the pebbles. It landed with a yelp and stared up, eyes wide with shock. As she reared, snarling, it rolled away. Kallik slammed down her paws, sending pebbles showering after it as it pelted into the trees.

The gorge was suddenly quiet. Kallik turned her head to find her friends. Toklo panted at the edge of the stream. Tufts of fur hung around his neck.

Lusa limped toward Kallik. "Is that all of them?"

Kallik looked around. The coyotes had gone. "Let's find—"

A howl cut her off.

"Yakone!" Kallik raced for the trees, bursting through the

undergrowth. A coyote was dragging at Yakone's scruff.

Rage roared in her ears. She grabbed the coyote and sank her teeth into its rump. Yelping, it let go of Yakone, and Kallik dragged it through the bushes. It thrashed in her grip. A root caught her paw and she tripped and fell, rolling toward the stream. She landed with a splash, the coyote twisting between her paws. It snarled, trying to break free. Kallik held tighter. It clamped its teeth around her leg. Howling with rage, she shook it free. It scrambled up the bank, but she caught its leg and dragged it back. Pressing its head into the water, she held it down.

"Couldn't you leave him alone?" she snarled.

Anger surged inside her as it struggled. Bubbles rose from its mouth. Kallik pressed harder, feeling it weaken. *Don't kill it!* a voice hissed in her ears. Kallik paused. She never wanted to kill in anger. She let go and, hauling herself away, watched the coyote struggle to its paws and hare through the trees.

"Kallik?" Lusa appeared from the bushes.

Kallik looked up, panting. "Check Yakone." As Lusa disappeared, Kallik limped from the stream. *Please let him be okay.* She followed Lusa's trail into a clearing. Lusa and Toklo were leaning over Yakone's white pelt.

"Is he—?" The breath stopped in Kallik's throat. She watched the white bear's unmoving flank. Panic gripped her chest.

Then he twitched and slowly rose.

"Yakone!" Kallik rushed to him and pressed her cheek against his.

He pushed up with his hind legs and staggered clumsily to

his paws. "Are you okay?" His eyes were dark with worry.

She let out a long, slow breath. "Just a few scratches and bites." Looking along her flank, she saw red staining her pelt.

Lusa's cheek was swollen, her ear bleeding. "We did it!" Her eyes sparkled. "We scared them off!"

Together they limped from the trees. Two coyotes lay dead beside the river.

Toklo looked grim as he stared at the bodies. "We did more than just scare them."

Kallik flicked her snout toward the trails of blood disappearing into the woods. "We did what we had to."

"They won't come after us again," Lusa growled.

"I hope not." Toklo's gaze was dark. "Let's keep moving."

Kallik stiffened. "But Yakone needs to rest." Why else had they ambushed the coyotes?

"They were more aggressive than I expected," Toklo told her. "I didn't think they'd put up such a fight."

Lusa bristled. "Do you think they might still come after us?"

"I don't know."

Yakone lifted his muzzle. "I can walk."

Kallik heard the strain in his voice. "Are you sure?"

Yakone shrugged. "What's a few more scars?"

Kallik leaned close, her wounds stinging. "Thank you," she whispered.

Yakone pressed his cheek against hers. "We fought together today," he murmured. "We always will."

CHAPTER TWENTY-FOUR

Toklo

Toklo's ears pricked as he listened for pawsteps, or the swish of coyote pelts in the undergrowth. The bites on his flank stung. At least they weren't deep. He opened his mouth, tasting for musky scents. The coyotes hadn't traveled this way, but he was wary that they might still be nearby, watching for a fresh chance to close in on Yakone.

The white bear was struggling. He was trailing behind, Kallik steadying him. As the day wore on, he'd begun to stumble more. His pelt felt hot. His wound must be turning bad, and Toklo knew that a bad wound could kill him.

Toklo glanced through the branches, dazzled by flashes of sunshine glittering through them. Birds chattered; insects hummed. A gentle breeze ruffled his pelt. He could see Lusa's fur flickering through the bracken ahead. Perhaps she'd been right. Perhaps they'd chased off the coyotes for good.

"Toklo!" Kallik's bark made him jump.

He spun around, bristling. "What is it?"

She'd stopped. Yakone leaned against her, his head low, his flanks heaving.

Lusa burst from the bracken. "Yakone!"

"He's really hot." Kallik stared desperately at Toklo. "He needs to rest."

Yakone lifted his head. "I'm sorry."

"It's not your fault," Kallik soothed.

Toklo glanced back along their trail. They'd hardly traveled any distance since Yakone had been injured. His paws prickled. Home was tugging him hard. If he were traveling alone, he'd be there in a few days. He shoved the thought away. He would never abandon his friends.

Lusa paced around Yakone. "I wish I'd found more herbs." She touched his white pelt with her nose. "You'd be better by now."

Kallik dipped her head. "You've done plenty for him, Lusa."

Yakone grunted weakly. "If I could just rest for a while, I'll be able to go on."

Toklo closed his eyes. He couldn't risk Yakone getting sicker. He'd already said good-bye to too many friends on this journey. "Let's build a den."

Yakone huffed. "I'm sorry, Toklo. I know you want to get home."

Toklo swallowed back frustration. "Home can wait."

Lusa darted from shrub to shrub, stopping beneath a tree. "We could build a nest here." A wide branch arched, low to the ground. Grass sprouted in its shadow.

Toklo padded to her side. "It looks perfect, Lusa." He

glanced over his shoulder. "Will you fetch bracken, Kallik?"

Kallik was easing Yakone down onto the soft earth. She straightened. "Of course."

"I'll help!" Lusa charged away.

"I'll hunt," Toklo told Kallik. He tipped his head toward Yakone. "Will he be okay lying there while you build a nest?"

"I can answer for myself," Yakone grunted. "I'm *injured*, not deaf."

Toklo padded toward the white bear. "Sorry, Yakone." Heat was pulsing from Yakone's pelt. "Is it shady enough here?" Shafts of sunshine speared the forest floor.

"I'll manage until Kallik's built a nest." He twisted his head toward her. "Sorry I can't be any help."

"You rest," Kallik ordered. "Gathering bracken is easy."

Toklo headed away. "Stay close to him, Kallik."

She caught his eye. "Are you still worried about the coyotes?"

"They're probably far away by now." Toklo paused. "But let's not take any risks."

"Okay." Kallik began tearing bracken from a clump.

Toklo nosed his way through a patch of wild lilac. The ground crunched with leaves from last suncircle. It was good to be out of the dark pine forests. The air here already tasted of blossom. He followed the woods as they sloped upward. Hunting could wait. He wanted to see the mountains.

The slope steepened, rocks jutting here and there as he neared the top. Cresting the hill, he frowned. Trees blocked his view. How could he see the horizon from here? A leaf tumbled down and brushed past his muzzle. Toklo glanced up and saw a squirrel scampering through the branches of an oak. He'd seen Lusa climb countless times. Perhaps he could climb, too.

Gripping onto the bark, he hauled himself up. His claws ached with the effort, but the lowest branch was only just above his head. Digging in with his hind claws, he pushed higher and clasped the branch. His legs trembled, unused to the strain. He heaved himself up until he was straddling the branch. How did Lusa make this look so easy?

He scrambled onto the next branch, spotting a higher branch beyond. Spiraling around the trunk, he followed the pathway of branches upward until the ground swayed far below. *Don't look down!*

Toklo dragged his gaze away, dizzy. The next branch was just out of reach. He would have to jump to reach it. Swallowing, he crouched, then sprang, plunging across the gap like a clumsy squirrel. His forepaws slipped. He hung on, gasping. Digging in his claws, he began to rock from side to side, until with a grunt, he hooked one paw onto the branch. Blood pounding in his ears, he dragged himself up and sat, blinking with surprise as the world spread out before him.

The mountains!

There they were, smudging the horizon. Their purple peaks were veiled in clouds. And he could see the river, too, snaking away between rolling hills.

As Toklo breathed deep, tasting home, the air suddenly trembled. A distant rumble sounded far away. Toklo recognized the low roar of a powerful firebeast. A shrill hoot split the air.

He stiffened. He'd heard that sound before. He scanned the hills, searching for the familiar flash of silver tracks, and saw the long, thin body of a firesnake. It hooted again, smoke billowing from its head as it snaked along its pathway, following the line of the hills like a river flowing downstream.

Toklo's heart leaped. *It's the firesnake from home!* He used to eat grain spilled along its trail with Oka and Tobi. It could travel farther and faster than a bear could ever run. He didn't need the river now. He could follow the *SilverPath* home.

He squinted, trying to pick out a route to the SilverPath. He could see a patch of charred trees where the forest ended. A barren valley lay beyond, stretching toward a winding stream. Past the flashing water, the SilverPath glinted in the sunshine. Pelt pricking with excitement, Toklo scrambled down the tree, claws splintering bark, pads jagging on twigs. He reached the ground and galloped down the slope.

"Kallik! Lusa!" He barged through the wild lilac, bursting out beside the makeshift den.

Kallik looked up from laying bracken. "Are you okay?"

"I know the way home!" Toklo blurted.

"I thought we were following the river."

"We were," Toklo told her. "But now I've found the SilverPath, we can follow *that*!"

Kallik glanced at his paws. "Did you find prey?" she asked hopefully.

He blinked at her. "Prey?"

"You were going to hunt, remember?"

"Oh, yes. But don't you understand? The SilverPath leads *home*!"

"Great." Kallik padded away and stopped beside Yakone. The white bear had fallen asleep. "Let's get Yakone to the den."

Toklo hurried to help her. "Have you ever *seen* a SilverPath?"

"Yakone," Kallik whispered in the white bear's ear. "Wake up. We want to move you somewhere more comfortable."

Yakone blinked open his eyes. He tried to haul himself to his paws, but he floundered like a seal. Bristling with frustration, Toklo shoved his muzzle under Yakone's shoulder and pushed him up. Kallik steadied the white bear, and together, they guided him to the nest.

Yakone collapsed onto the bracken and Kallik began to pat spare fronds around him. "Is that better?"

Yakone grunted and closed his eyes. "Thanks, Kallik. I'll feel better once I've rested."

Toklo paced in a circle beside them. "It'll be easy walking," he told Kallik. "SilverPaths are flat and smooth."

Kallik didn't look up. "Like BlackPaths?"

"Not like BlackPaths at all," Toklo reassured her. "Only one firebeast uses them. And it's more like a snake than a firebeast, so I call it a firesnake. But you can feel it coming a long time before it appears."

Bracken rustled behind him. He turned and saw Lusa, her jaws full of herbs, her eyes round. "A firebeast that's more like a snake?" She dropped her herbs. "You want us to follow its path?"

"It's safer than following the river!" Toklo exclaimed.

"It's a *firebeast* path," Kallik argued.

"No, it's a *firesnake* path," Toklo insisted. "We scavenged on its trail when I was a cub, me and Oka and Tobi. It's easy to get out of the way, because it never leaves its path."

Lusa crouched over her herbs. "I think I've found an herb Ujurak used to use for fever," she told Kallik. "And something that should work on our coyote bites."

Toklo flexed his claws. Why weren't they listening to him? Toklo stared at Lusa as she nosed the herbs into two piles. "We should start moving," he urged. "I've seen the way to the SilverPath. It's easy."

Kallik sat down. "You told us we could rest."

"Yakone can't go on yet." Lusa poked one of her piles. "And I've got herbs for our wounds."

Toklo snorted. "I don't need herbs!" His pelt fizzed with energy. He felt like he could run all the way home right now. It would only take three sunups.

Kallik looked at him. "I know you want to get home," she told him softly. "But we need food and rest." She swapped glances with Lusa. "We can head for your home in the morning."

Grunting, Toklo turned away. "I'm going hunting, then." He stomped through the lilac, trampling it under his paws.

"Bring something back this time," Kallik called after him. "We're hungry."

Toklo kicked through grass and scanned the woodland for prey. *That's because* you *can't smell your home!*

CHAPTER TWENTY-FIVE

Toklo

The smell of dew woke Toklo. Excited, he slid under the branch and crept from the nest. His bites had stopped stinging. The herbs Lusa found had really worked. Pale light touched the trees and bushes. Birdsong rang through the woods. Kallik and Yakone were still snoring.

Lusa stuck her nose from beneath the branch. "Toklo?"

He leaned over the carcass of the deer he'd caught last night. "Hi, Lusa! Are you ready to travel?"

She stumbled sleepily out of the nest and stretched. "I guess."

Toklo peeled meat from a leg bone and chewed happily. "Are you looking forward to seeing my home?" He couldn't wait to show his friends where he'd been born.

"I guess." Lusa's eyes glittered with worry.

"What's wrong?" Toklo stopped chewing.

"What will happen when you get there?" she asked.

Toklo frowned. What did she mean? "Well, I'll be home," he told her.

"And Kallik and Yakone will go home and . . ." Her voice trailed away.

"Toklo." Kallik pushed her way from the nest. "Yakone feels hotter."

"Give him more of those herbs I found last night," Lusa ordered.

"I have." Kallik glanced back into the den. "His wound smells sour."

Toklo shifted his paws. He was hoping Yakone would be better today. "Once we get to the SilverPath, it'll be easy walking."

"Maybe we shouldn't travel," Lusa ventured.

The branch overhanging the den rustled, and Yakone limped out. "Yes, we should," he growled.

Kallik's eyes narrowed. "Are you sure?"

"I've held you up long enough." Yakone began to limp through the trampled lilac, following the trail Toklo had beaten the day before. "Let's get going."

Kallik hurried after him, slipping her shoulder beneath his to steady him.

Toklo huffed at Lusa. "I guess we're going." He caught up to Yakone, pressing in on his other side.

Lusa scampered around them. "So what is this firesnake thing you were talking about?"

"It's huge," Toklo told her. "Bigger than you could even imagine."

Lusa's eyes widened. "Bigger than the river?"

"Not *that* big, but much bigger than the firebeasts you see on BlackPaths."

"So why are we going to find it?"

"We're not going to find it," Toklo explained. "We're going to find its *path*. It'll show me how to get home."

"Oh." Lusa bounded ahead, then turned. "Do you want me to lead again?"

Toklo nodded. "You're good at finding easy paths," he told her. "I'll tell you which way to head." He could picture the route in his mind. He'd seen it from the oak. "First we have to get to the top of this hill."

Lusa found a zigzagging trail up, making it easy for Toklo and Kallik to guide Yakone. He was walking a little, but every now and then he slumped as his injured paw gave way.

By the time they reached the top, Toklo's pelt was prickling with excitement.

"Which way now?" Lusa paced in front of them.

"Down this hill, and up the next, then head toward the lightning trees." Toklo pictured them in his head.

Lusa tipped her muzzle. "Lightning trees?"

"A burned patch of wood—"

"Of course!" Lusa darted away. "I get it. Where lightning struck."

Toklo was the first to smell the scent of charred wood. It reminded him of Chenoa and the time she'd shown him the mountains from among the blackened tree stumps. Lusa waited while they caught up with her.

Yakone wrinkled his nose. "The ice is burning," he mumbled.

"He's stopped making sense," Kallik fretted. "That means he's too hot."

Toklo pictured the view from the oak. Thick forest, black charred stumps, parched yellow rock, then a glittering stream. "There's water ahead," he told Kallik. "That'll cool him down."

Lusa led the way, swerving over the ash-covered ground among the lightning trees. Leaving the forest behind, they followed Lusa until they reached a wide, treeless valley, then slowed as Kallik struggled to find her paws on the rocky terrain. Hills rose on either side, too high to see the mountains beyond. Toklo could see Lusa's pelt moving ahead, black against the pale yellow stones, as she sniffed out the stream.

"Am I going the right way?" she called.

"Yes!" Toklo answered.

She disappeared over a rise, then came charging back. "I can see trees."

"Good!" Toklo remembered that the stream ran through woodland.

Kallik stumbled beside Yakone as a rock slipped underpaw. "Will that mean we're near the SilverPath?"

"Yes." Stones crunched beneath Toklo's paws. His pads stung with the heat. Yakone must be burning up in the sun, even without a fever.

Toklo's thoughts drifted. If only they could reach his home. Yakone could lie in the wide, shallow river that Toklo had fished in as a cub. "The mountains will be cooler," he promised Kallik. "There's a river there where fish leap right out of the water. And the wind is fresh." He glanced up at the sun, searing in the pale blue sky. "And there are shady trees everywhere."

As they reached the top of the rise, Toklo saw, with relief, woodland stretching below. Water glimmered between the budding branches. "The stream!" He heaved Yakone away from Kallik, taking his full weight. "Let's hurry."

Yakone moaned beside him, his paws stumbling over the rocks.

"Nearly there, Yakone," Toklo soothed.

They threaded between the trees and staggered out onto the shore of a meandering stream. Lusa splashed into it, barking with happiness. "It feels great on my paws! Kallik, come and try it."

Kallik didn't seem to hear. She was sniffing at Yakone's wounded paw. As she leaned down, he collapsed, dropping away from Toklo like a stone.

"Yakone!" Kallik sniffed the white bear's breath. "He's really sick."

"I'll find fresh herbs." Lusa dashed from the stream and disappeared into the woods on the far side.

Kallik's eyes shone with panic. "What are we going to do?"

"He'll be okay," Toklo promised.

"You don't know that!" Kallik hissed. "What if he dies here? What if he never makes it back to the ice?"

Toklo's heart twisted. "He has to make it! He's come so far."

"Toklo!" Lusa's bark made him freeze. She pelted from the woods and splashed though the stream. "They're back."

Toklo froze. A chill washed his pelt. Kallik stiffened beside him.

Lusa's eyes were wild with panic. "The coyotes."

As she spoke, a snarl sounded beyond the stream. Eyes glinted from the undergrowth. A snout poked out. Toklo bared his teeth. The snout ducked away.

Lusa circled restlessly, her pelt fluffed up. "The forest stinks of them!"

Toklo swallowed. How many were there?

"And the scents are all fresh." Lusa jerked her gaze toward Yakone. "We have to get him moving!"

Kallik was already heaving Yakone to his paws. Toklo ducked in the other side and pressed his shoulder against Yakone's drooping flank. "We're following the stream," he told Lusa. He knew it crossed the SilverPath. If they could make it there, might a firesnake scare off the coyotes?

Scare them off? Nothing seemed to scare off these vermin! He pushed the thought away. They couldn't stay here, playing prey.

"Leave me," Yakone suddenly croaked, struggling between them.

"Don't be fish-brained!" Toklo told him sternly. "If you want to help us, try moving your paws!"

The stream flowed down the valley and followed the curve of the hill. Stumbling along the rocky shore, Lusa watched the woods. Toklo fixed his gaze on the trail. They couldn't fail now. They were so close!

Ahead, the stream ducked through a gully and disappeared into a hole in the ground. Toklo blinked with surprise. Two lines gleamed where the stream had vanished. *The SilverPath!* It flashed over the stream and curved away past the hills.

Toklo quickened his pace. "We've found it!"

Kallik stumbled to keep up. Yakone limped heavily.

"Come on!" Toklo heaved Yakone up onto the gray stones that lined the long silver tracks. He hauled him around and pushed him along the trail. "Just keep moving!"

"Toklo." Kallik's voice was soft with dread. "Look."

Toklo blinked. A pack of coyotes stood on the SilverPath in front of them. They showed their teeth, their eyes glittering greedily.

"Why are there so many?" Lusa pressed against Toklo until he could feel her shaking. "We killed two."

"They must have found more." Toklo glared at them. "Stay away!" he roared.

The coyotes held their ground, neither coming closer nor moving away.

"What do we do?" Kallik hissed.

"We go the other way." Toklo turned, hauling Yakone.

"But then we'll be heading away from the mountains," Lusa protested.

Toklo's belly hardened. *How will I ever get home?* "Watch our backs, Lusa," he growled. "Tell me if they come closer." He stumbled on, nudging Yakone along the SilverPath as his mind whirled in panic. *What do we do? Where can we hide?* Anger raged through Toklo. *I'm a bear! Not prey!*

Suddenly he felt the SilverPath tracks throbbing. He stopped and pricked his ears. They were humming!

"A firesnake's coming!" he barked.

"Spirits help us!" Lusa wailed.

Kallik started to steer Yakone off the path. "Let's hide in the forest!"

"No!" Toklo growled. "There's a bend up ahead!" He nodded toward a curve where the track disappeared around a low cliff. A rocky ledge jutted out halfway up the cliff. "I've got a plan."

"What?" Kallik's voice cracked with fear.

"They're getting closer," Lusa warned from behind.

"We need to get on that ledge." Toklo lifted his shoulders. "The firesnake slows down on corners."

"So?" Kallik gazed past Yakone.

"We can jump from the ledge onto its back," Toklo told her.

"No!" Kallik pulled away. Yakone slumped to the ground.

Toklo glanced back at the coyotes. "Would you rather be eaten by them?"

"We might be able to fight them!" Kallik growled. "We can't fight a firebeast, or snake, or whatever it is. It'll crush us."

"If you jump onto its back, it'll carry you like we carry Lusa." Toklo willed Kallik to understand that they had no choice. "We can protect ourselves from the coyotes. But we can't protect Yakone. Not forever! The coyotes will keep coming back until we can't fight them off anymore."

"He's right, Kallik." Lusa's voice wavered.

"But what if we jump and miss the firesnake's back?" Kallik's eyes were white-rimmed with terror.

"You *can't* miss." Toklo fought to stop himself trembling.

"I'll try it." Lusa's voice was barely a whisper.

Kallik dipped her head. "We'll all try." She ducked down and nosed Yakone to his paws. "Yakone!" she barked sharply. "You have to wake up!"

He blinked open his eyes and stared at her blearily.

Kallik glared at him. "Coyotes are chasing us. We have to jump onto a firesnake."

"Okay," Yakone mumbled thickly.

Lusa paced around them. "He thinks he's dreaming!"

"I don't care," Toklo growled. "As long as he does it."

Slowly, Yakone padded forward.

"That's it!" Kallik urged him on. "Keep going!"

"Lusa, find a way onto that ledge," Toklo ordered.

Lusa scrambled off the track and led them through scrubby bushes. She threaded her way up the hill, around boulders and over rocks. "Is Yakone okay?" she called over her shoulder.

"He's still walking." Toklo watched the white bear follow Kallik blindly up the slope. The coyotes padded after them.

At last, the stony slope leveled out and turned to rock beneath Toklo's paws. *We made it!* They were on the ledge. He hurried to the edge of the rock and looked over. The tracks shone many bearlengths below, but when the firesnake rumbled past, they'd be able to reach its back.

Toklo looked along the SilverPath. Smoke billowed in the distance. A screech split the air as a huge creature thundered toward them like an avalanche.

The firesnake!

"Get ready." Toklo turned to his friends. His pelt bushed as he saw the coyotes. They had reached the ledge and were lined up, teeth bared, just waiting for a moment to strike. "Quickly!" he called.

Kallik crossed the stone, nudging Yakone ahead of her.

"Lusa!" Toklo's heart lurched. The black bear seemed rooted to the rock. She was staring, frozen, at the coyotes.

"Don't look at them, Lusa!" Blood roared in Toklo's ears.

The coyotes lowered their heads and crept nearer.

"Lusa!" Toklo pounded past Kallik and grabbed Lusa's scruff in his teeth. "Come on!" His growl was muffled by her fur as he hauled her backward.

She came to life and struggled free. "I'm coming!"

"How do we get on?" Kallik stared over the edge as the firesnake thundered closer. "It's so tall!"

"Wait for a part of its back that is lower than the rest," Toklo ordered. "Then leap on as it passes."

Kallik swung her head from side to side, moaning. "I can't believe we're going to do this."

Lusa flattened her ears. "It's so loud!"

"Don't think about it, just do it!" Toklo urged.

Kallik looked at him. "What about you?"

"I'll be right behind you." The ledge trembled beneath his paws. The acrid tang of the firesnake billowed around his nose.

The coyotes crept closer. With an ear-piercing clatter, the head of the firesnake reached the ledge. Its long, silver body started to stream past, glinting as it rocked in the sun.

"There's a low back coming!" Lusa yelped.

Toklo didn't take his eyes from the coyotes. "Can you make the jump?"

"I think so!"

Lusa's pelt flashed at the corner of Toklo's vision. He heard a yelp, then a thump, and looked over his shoulder. Lusa had landed on a long, flat section in the firesnake's body. She scrambled to her paws. "Come on!"

Kallik shoved Yakone forward, and he hurled himself at the firesnake's back. Kallik flung herself after, landing beside Yakone a bearlength from Lusa.

"Come on, Toklo!" she bellowed.

Toklo leaped.

Pain shrilled through his pelt as teeth sank into his rump. He flailed wildly. A snarling coyote was dragging him backward. Bodies jostled against his flanks. Jaws snapped beside his ears.

Spirits, save me! Toklo tore free, blind with fear, and hurled himself at the firesnake's back. He slammed against it with a thump that knocked the breath from his body. His paws hung over the side, the wind dragging at them as the firesnake rocked beneath him.

"I've got you!"

Teeth clamped into Toklo's scruff. Splinters grazed his nose as Kallik hauled him up. Her warm, fishy smell washed his muzzle as he rolled onto the firesnake's back. Gasping, he lay limp and stared at the sky.

We made it!

Something thumped down beside him. A snarl sounded by his ear.

"Watch out!" Lusa wailed in terror.

Toklo scrambled to his paws. A coyote faced him, jaws dripping, eyes wild with rage. Toklo staggered as the firesnake swayed beneath him. The coyote leaped. It hit him with such force that he fell backward. A sharp wind snatched him and flung him aside as the coyote sank its teeth into his neck. Pain seared though his body and the SilverPath blurred as his head dangled over the edge. The coyote snarled at his throat.

"Help!" Toklo was fighting for every breath now. His vision began to fade.

White fur flashed above him. With a yelp, the coyote disappeared.

Toklo stared as Yakone loomed over him. As the white bear grabbed his scruff and hauled him to his paws, a hideous wail screeched below. Toklo glanced down and saw the SilverPath below turn red. Blood smattered the stones, and far behind, six coyotes raised their howls to the sky.

"Toklo!" Kallik and Lusa clustered around him.

Toklo staggered to his paws, weak with fear. The firesnake swayed beneath him. His rump stung like fire. Kallik gazed at him with wide, frightened eyes while Lusa pressed against him, trembling. Yakone sat down heavily. His injured paw was wet with fresh blood.

"We made it," Toklo breathed.

"I thought you were going to die!" Lusa's voice choked.

Toklo blinked at Yakone as the white bear caught his breath. "You saved me! You *all* saved me!" He stared at his friends as the forest slid past. They were on their way to the mountains, riding a firesnake, and heading home.

LOOK FOR

RETURN TO THE WILD

SEEKERS

BOOK 4:
FOREST OF WOLVES

Toklo

Toklo sat up, his head still spinning from the race back to the firesnake and from the thundering noise of its paws along the SilverPath. Lusa and Kallik seemed to have recovered, but Yakone lay limply on the heaps of pebbles, his eyes half-closed. His struggles to get back onto the firesnake had opened up his wound again; it was bleeding sluggishly and Kallik was hunched over it, giving it an anxious sniff.

After a moment she glanced up at Toklo. "Yakone is getting worse," she said quietly. "There's nothing I can do for him when there's no food or water, and no herbs to treat his wound."

"I know," Toklo began, "but—"

"Maybe we should have looked for something while we were hiding in the trees," Kallik went on, as if Toklo hadn't spoken.

"There wasn't time," Toklo protested. "If we'd tried to

hunt, the firesnake would have left without us. I know you're worried," he added softly, "but when we get to the mountains—to the Sky Ridge where I was born—everything will be fine. Trust me."

A spark of anger flashed in Kallik's eyes. "Oh yes, everything will be fine for *you*!" she exclaimed. "But what about me and Yakone? This isn't the right place for us, and you know it!"

Toklo bit back a furious response. He knew Kallik's outburst was just because she was so worried about Yakone. *I'm worried about Yakone, too,* he thought. *And I'm worried that Kallik is regretting staying with me and Lusa until we finish our journeys.*

As the sun rose higher in the sky, the day grew hotter. Toklo could see how uncomfortable Yakone and Kallik were. There wasn't a scrap of shade on the firesnake. At least Yakone's wound gradually stopped bleeding again, and he drifted into sleep.

Toklo crouched beside Lusa, facing forward, almost able to forget his own hunger and thirst as the firesnake drew closer and closer to the mountains. The light on the slopes began to fade as the sun slipped behind the topmost peaks. He drank in the view, feeling long-buried memories stirring in his mind.

I'm home.

The firesnake slowed down to navigate a tight curve in the SilverPath. As he peered through the half-light at the hills on either side, Toklo suddenly recognized where he was. Memories gushed over him like a flood, and he felt like he was staring down a dark tunnel to see a long-gone day lit up in bright sunshine.

This is where I came with Mother and Tobi, and we found the spilled grain!

Toklo remembered how proud he had been some days later when he found his way back to the grain. He pushed away the memory of the huge male bear who had driven them away from their find. *This is home, and that's all that matters.*

Toklo sprang to his paws. "Come on!" he yelped to his friends. "This is the place!"

His voice roused Yakone, who raised his head, grunting in confusion. Kallik heaved her shoulder under him to help him to stand. "Toklo says we're here," she said soothingly. "We have to get off."

While Yakone struggled up, gasping with pain as he put weight on his injured paw, Lusa leaped up and padded to the edge of the firesnake's back. Her berry-bright eyes were gleaming with anticipation. "We're really here?" she whispered.

"Yes," Toklo replied. His fur tingled as he gazed out at the familiar slopes and woodland. For the first time in many, many moons, he had returned to somewhere he had been before. The feeling was overwhelming. "Go on," he barked to Lusa. "Jump!"

The firesnake was still traveling slowly as it rounded the bend. Without hesitation Lusa launched herself through the hole in its side and into the air, and rolled as she hit the grassy slope beside the SilverPath, before bouncing back onto her paws.

"Are you okay?" Toklo called.

"Fine!"

Meanwhile, Kallik prodded Yakone over to the edge of the firesnake. "Just jump," she said. "I'll be right behind you."

Yakone gritted his teeth. "Okay." He fell rather than leaped off the firesnake, and landed on the ground with a thump. Toklo winced; that must have hurt.

Kallik paused briefly, then scrambled down, her hindpaws barely missing the pounding paws of the firesnake. Regaining her balance, she trotted back to where Yakone was struggling to his paws with Lusa's help.

"Hide!" Toklo called out from his position on the firesnake. "In the bushes over there!"

As he finished speaking, he bunched his muscles and pushed off into a massive leap. He staggered as he hit the ground and yipped with pain as he planted one paw on a low-growing thorn. "Seal rot!" he hissed.

Lusa had already vanished into the thicket that covered the slope not far from the SilverPath. Kallik and Yakone were close behind her. Toklo bounded after them, ignoring the stinging thorn in his pad, and dived into cover. He turned just in time to see the last segments of the firesnake vanishing around the bend. Its thunderous roar soon died away into the distance and the acrid smell faded, leaving the fresh green scents of the forest all around them.

Lusa took a deep breath and stood up, pushing her way through the branches into the open. "We made it," she said.

Toklo and the white bears followed her out of the thicket. Yakone was still limping badly, and his injured paw was oozing blood. His head was drooping, and his shoulders sagged with exhaustion.

"Why don't you rest?" Lusa suggested to him. "I'll look for some herbs to help your paw."

Yakone gave her a glance of gratitude and slumped to the ground again, but Toklo's pelt prickled with unease. "We shouldn't hang around for too long," he said, thinking of the aggressive male who had chased him and his family away from the grain. "There could be more brown bears here."

"Do you think they'd give us trouble?" Kallik asked.

"They might, if they thought we were trespassing on their territory," Toklo replied. "The best thing we can do is to be on our way quickly and find some forest that hasn't been claimed yet."

"Just a short rest, then," Lusa said, glancing over her shoulder at Toklo. "We'll move more quickly if Yakone isn't so tired." She was already sniffing around the bushes for the herbs she needed to help her injured friend.

Toklo grunted agreement, and kept watch while Lusa searched for herbs and Kallik tended to Yakone. Raising his snout to sniff the air, he picked up the lingering tang of the firesnake and the fresh scent of growing vegetation, but no scent of other bears. *For now,* he thought, his muscles tight and tense under his fur.

Lusa returned after a few moments with a mouthful of leaves. Toklo didn't recognize them; they certainly weren't the hornwort Lusa had used before.

"What are those?" he asked.

"I'm not sure," Lusa mumbled as she began chewing up the leaves. "But they smell good. They should help."

Toklo guessed she wasn't as confident as she sounded. *But there's no time to look for anything else,* he thought, working his claws impatiently in the grass. *We have to move. And those leaves can't do Yakone any harm. . . .*

Once Lusa had trickled the leaf juice into Yakone's wound, with Kallik watching worriedly, Toklo led the way up the slope, heading into denser woodland. The uneven ground dislodged the thorn in his paw, and though his pad still throbbed with pain, Toklo was relieved to be rid of it.

As they passed beneath the branches of the outlying trees, Lusa brightened up, gazing around with eager curiosity, but Yakone still seemed exhausted. It looked like it was taking all his strength just to put one paw in front of another. Kallik stayed close by his side, her anxiety wrapping around her like a dark cloud.

Every pawstep Toklo took deeper into the trees brought back more memories for him. The sensation of being pulled back into his old life was so strong that it almost overwhelmed him, and yet there were unexpected differences, too.

That lightning-blasted tree . . . he thought as they padded past the pale trunk and spiky, leafless branches. *Wasn't it by the river? Or was that a different tree?*

"I like it here." Lusa interrupted his thoughts with a happy sigh. "The forest feels safe, somehow, like it's going to look after us."

Toklo just grunted in reply. His memories weren't all good

ones, but he didn't want to say this to the others. And now that he was here, in the place that was so familiar to him, he felt the weight of responsibility for his friends even more. *It's my duty to help them, because this is my home.*

Thinking of his friends reminded him of the long path they had traveled together. The cub he had been, playing here in these woods with Tobi, would never have imagined that he would see and do so much in his lifetime. Toklo suddenly realized that he had never really believed he would make it home until now, when he walked beneath the trees that were familiar and at the same time unsettlingly strange.

"Toklo!" Kallik, who had been padding along beside Yakone, put on a spurt to catch up. "Do you really think we'll meet more brown bears in these woods?"

Toklo nodded. "There don't seem to be any others around right now, but sooner or later we will."

Lusa shivered. "I'm not sure I want to. Brown bears guard their territory even more fiercely than black or white bears."

Kallik glanced around uneasily. "I don't know how you two can possibly be comfortable under trees like this," she muttered. "Out on the ice, you can see for whole skylengths. But here . . . there could be a bear behind every bush, just waiting to leap out on us."

"Hardly. We'd scent them first," Toklo reminded her.

Kallik twitched her ears, refusing to be comforted. "And how can you fight in such tight spaces? You'd constantly be banging into trees, or getting tripped up by brambles."

"You just have to make sure the other bear is the one

banging into trees, or getting tripped," Lusa told her, giving Kallik a friendly nudge.

Kallik let out a snort, resolutely unamused, and dropped back to walk beside Yakone again. Her nervousness made Toklo even more careful to keep checking for signs of other bears as they plodded on through the forest. But he saw less evidence of them than he had expected: no scent, no scraps of discarded prey, no scratches on trees to mark the boundaries of territory.

That's good, he thought hopefully. Though he had spoken with optimism about finding part of the forest that no bear had claimed, he had never seriously believed that he would be able to establish a territory without fighting for it. Now he began to wonder if it might be possible after all.

But why *are there no other brown bears?* he asked himself after a while. *Did they all leave to find new territories, like I did? And if so, does that mean there's plenty of prey here? Or did they leave because there's a shortage of prey?*

DON'T MISS

DAWN OF THE CLANS

WARRIORS

BOOK 1: THE SUN TRAIL

Gray Wing toiled up the snow-covered slope toward a ridge that bit into the sky like a row of snaggly teeth. He set each paw down carefully, to avoid breaking through the frozen surface and sinking into the powdery drifts underneath. Light flakes were falling, dappling his dark gray pelt. He was so cold that he couldn't feel his pads anymore, and his belly yowled with hunger.

I can't remember the last time I felt warm or full-fed.

In the last sunny season he had still been a kit, playing with his littermate, Clear Sky, around the edge of the pool outside the cave. Now that seemed like a lifetime ago. Gray Wing only had the vaguest memories of green leaves on the stubby mountain trees, and the sunshine bathing the rocks.

Pausing to taste the air for prey, he gazed across the

snowbound mountains, peak after peak stretching away into the distance. The heavy gray sky overhead promised yet more snow to come.

But the air carried no scent of his quarry, and Gray Wing plodded on. Clear Sky appeared from behind an outcrop of rock, his pale gray fur barely visible against the snow. His jaws were empty, and as he spotted Gray Wing he shook his head.

"Not a sniff of prey anywhere!" he called. "Why don't we—"

A raucous cry from above cut off his words. A shadow flashed over Gray Wing. Looking up, he saw a hawk swoop low across the slope, its talons hooked and cruel.

As the hawk passed, Clear Sky leaped high into the air, his forepaws outstretched. His claws snagged the bird's feathers and he fell back, dragging it from the sky. It let out another harsh cry as it landed on the snow in a flurry of beating wings.

Gray Wing charged up the slope, his paws throwing up a fine spray of snow. Reaching his brother, he planted both forepaws on one thrashing wing. The hawk glared at him with hatred in its yellow eyes, and Gray Wing had to duck to avoid its slashing talons.

Clear Sky thrust his head forward and sank his teeth into the hawk's neck. It jerked once and went limp, its gaze growing instantly dull as blood seeped from its wound and stained the snow.

Panting, Gray Wing looked at his brother. "That was a great catch!" he exclaimed, warm triumph flooding through him.

Clear Sky shook his head. "But look how scrawny it is.

There's nothing in these mountains fit to eat, and won't be until the snow clears."

He crouched beside his prey, ready to take the first bite. Gray Wing settled next to him, his jaws flooding as he thought of sinking his teeth into the hawk.

But then he remembered the starving cats back in the cave, squabbling over scraps. "We should take this prey back to the others," he meowed. "They need it to give them strength for their hunting."

"We need strength too," Clear Sky mumbled, tearing away a mouthful of the hawk's flesh.

"We'll be fine." Gray Wing gave him a prod in the side. "We're the best hunters in the Tribe. Nothing escapes us when we hunt together. We can catch something else easier than the others can."

Clear Sky rolled his eyes as he swallowed the prey. "Why must you always be so unselfish?" he grumbled. "Okay, let's go."

Together the two cats dragged the hawk down the slope and over the boulders at the bottom of a narrow gully until they reached the pool where the waterfall roared. Though it wasn't heavy, the bird was awkward to manage. Its flopping wings and claws caught on every hidden rock and buried thornbush.

"We wouldn't have to do this if you'd let us eat it," Clear Sky muttered as he struggled to maneuver the hawk along the path that led behind the waterfall. "I hope the others appreciate this."

Clear Sky grumbles, Gray Wing thought, *but he knows this is the right thing to do.*

Yowls of surprise greeted the brothers when they returned to the cave. Several cats ran to meet them, gathering around to gaze at the prey.

"It's *huge*!" Turtle Tail exclaimed, her green eyes shining as she bounded up to Gray Wing. "I can't believe you brought it back for us."

Gray Wing dipped his head, feeling slightly embarrassed at her enthusiasm. "It won't feed every cat," he mewed.

Shattered Ice, a gray-and-white tom, shouldered his way to the front of the crowd. "Which cats are going out to hunt?" he asked. "They should be the first ones to eat."

Murmurs came from among the assembled cats, broken by a shrill wail: "But I'm *hungry*! Why can't I have some? I could go out and hunt."

Gray Wing recognized the voice as being his younger brother, Jagged Peak's. Their mother, Quiet Rain, padded up and gently nudged her kit back toward the sleeping hollows. "You're too young to hunt," she murmured. "And if the older cats don't eat, there'll be no prey for any cat."

"Not fair!" Jagged Peak muttered as his mother guided him away.

Meanwhile the hunters, including Shattered Ice and Turtle Tail, lined up beside the body of the hawk. Each of them took one mouthful, then stepped back for the next cat to take their turn. By the time they had finished, and filed out along the path behind the waterfall, there was very little meat left.

Clear Sky, watching beside Gray Wing, let out an irritated snort. "I still wish *we* could have eaten it."

Privately Gray Wing agreed with him, but he knew there was no point in complaining. *There isn't enough food. Every cat is weak, hungry—just clinging on until the sun comes back.*

DOGS WILL RULE THE WILD IN

SURVIVORS

BOOK 1: THE EMPTY CITY

Lucky startled awake, fear prickling in his bones and fur. He leaped to his feet, growling.

For an instant he'd thought he was tiny once more, safe in his Pup Pack and protected, but the comforting dream had already vanished. The air shivered with menace, tingling Lucky's skin. If only he could see what was coming, he could face it down—but the monster was invisible, scentless. He whined in terror. This was no sleep-time story: This fear was *real.*

The urge to run was almost unbearable; but he could only scrabble, snarl, and scratch in panic. There was nowhere to go: The wire of his cage hemmed him in on every side. His muzzle hurt when he tried to shove it through the gaps; when he backed away, snarling, the same wire bit into his haunches.

Others were close . . . familiar bodies, familiar scents. Those dogs were enclosed in this terrible place just as he was. Lucky raised his head and barked, over and over, high and desperate, but it was clear no dog could help him. His voice was drowned out by the chorus of frantic calls.

They were all *trapped*.

Dark panic overwhelmed him. His claws scrabbled at the earth floor, even though he knew it was hopeless.

He could smell the female swift-dog in the next cage, a friendly, comforting scent, overlaid now with the bitter tang of danger and fear. Yipping, he pressed closer to her, feeling the shivers in her muscles—but the wire still separated them.

"Sweet? Sweet, something's on its way. Something bad!"

"Yes, I feel it! What's happening?"

The longpaws—where were they? The longpaws held them captive in this Trap House but they had always seemed to care about the dogs. They brought food and water, they laid bedding, cleared the mess . . .

Surely the longpaws would come for them now.

The others barked and howled as one, and Lucky raised his voice with theirs.

Longpaws! Longpaws, it's COMING. . . .

Something shifted beneath him, making his cage tremble. In a sudden, terrible silence, Lucky crouched, frozen with horror.

Then, around and above him, chaos erupted.

The unseen monster was here . . . and its paws were right on the Trap House.

Lucky was flung back against the wire as the world heaved and tilted. For agonizing moments he didn't know which way was up or down. The monster tumbled him around, deafening him with the racket of falling rock and shattering clear-stone. His vision went dark as clouds of filth blinded him. The screaming, yelping howls of terrified dogs seemed to fill his skull. A great chunk of wall crashed off the wire in front of his nose, and Lucky leaped back. Was it the Earth-Dog, trying to take him?

Then, just as suddenly as the monster had come, it disappeared. One more wall crashed down in a cloud of choking dust. Torn wire screeched as a high cage toppled, then plummeted to the earth.

There was only silence and a dank metal scent.

Blood! thought Lucky. *Death . . .*

Panic stirred inside his belly again. He was lying on his side, the wire cage crumpled against him, and he thrashed his strong legs, trying to right himself. The cage rattled and rocked, but he couldn't get up. *No!* he thought. *I'm trapped!*

"Lucky! Lucky, are you all right?"

"Sweet? Where are you?"

Her long face pushed at his through the mangled wire. "My cage door—it broke when it fell! I thought I was dead. Lucky, I'm free—but you—"

"Help me, Sweet!"

The other faint whimpers had stopped. Did that mean the other dogs were . . . ? No. Lucky could not let himself think about that. He howled just to break the silence.

"I think I can pull the cage out a bit," said Sweet. "Your door's loose, too. We might be able to get it open." Seizing the wire with her teeth, she tugged.

Lucky fought to keep himself calm. All he wanted to do was fling himself against the cage until it broke. His hind legs kicked out wildly and he craned his head around, snapping at the wire. Sweet was gradually pulling the cage forward, stopping occasionally to scrabble at fallen stones with her paws.

"There. It's looser now. Wait while I—"

But Lucky could wait no longer. The cage door was torn at the upper corner, and he twisted until he could bite and claw at it. He worked his paw into the gap and pulled, hard.

The wire gave with a screech, just as Lucky felt a piercing stab in his paw pad—but the door now hung at an awkward angle. Wriggling and squirming, he pulled himself free and stood upright at last.

His tail was tight between his legs as tremors bolted through his skin and muscles. He and Sweet stared at the carnage and chaos around them. There were broken cages—and broken bodies. A small, smooth-coated dog lay on the ground nearby, lifeless, eyes dull. Beneath the last wall that had fallen, nothing stirred, but a limp paw poked out from between stones. The scent of death was already spreading through the Trap House air.